Hearth Song

Center Point
Large Print

Also by Lois Greiman and available from
Center Point Large Print:

Home Fires
Finally Home
Hearth Stone

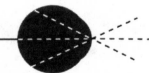

**This Large Print Book carries the
Seal of Approval of N.A.V.H.**

Hearth Song

Lois Greiman

CENTER POINT LARGE PRINT
THORNDIKE, MAINE

This Center Point Large Print edition
is published in the year 2016 by arrangement with
Kensington Publishing Corp.

The text of this Large Print edition is unabridged.
In other aspects, this book may vary
from the original edition.
Printed in the United States of America
on permanent paper.
Set in 16-point Times New Roman type.

ISBN: 978-1-68324-105-8

Library of Congress Cataloging-in-Publication Data

Names: Greiman, Lois, author.
Title: Hearth song / Lois Greiman.
Description: Center Point Large Print edition. | Thorndike, Maine :
Center Point Large Print, 2016.
Identifiers: LCCN 2016024200 | ISBN 9781683241058
   (hardcover : alk. paper)
Subjects: LCSH: Mothers and daughters—Fiction. | Large type books. |
GSAFD: Love stories.
Classification: LCC PS3557.R4369 H427 2016 | DDC 813/.6—dc23
LC record available at https://lccn.loc.gov/2016024200

To Kyah Rose Daun,
my favorite little tandem rider

It is strictly believed and understood by the Sioux that a child is the greatest gift from Wakan Tanka.

—Robert Higheagle,
early twentieth-century Teton Sioux

Chapter 1

Bravura Lambert rushed through the crowd. Cow ponies, spectators, and contestants flowed past like rushing waves.

"Oh!" she said, and smacked into an oncoming cowboy. Their eyes met. His were deep and dark, as gray as a rolling thunderhead, as intense as a bucking bull. His hair was tousled, his grin crooked. He wore his Stetson at a rakish angle, his chaps low on narrow hips. In his capable right hand he held a coiled lariat . . . every cowgirl's dream . . . or he would be . . . in about twenty years. As of now he had not yet reached the ripe old age of six.

"Excuse me," Bravura said and, hugging her own five-year-old to her chest, hurried past.

When Hunter Redhawk had invited her to attend the Little Britches Rodeo, she hadn't quite envisioned *this*. Somehow she had failed to realize that kids barely out of diapers would be racing amped-up Thoroughbreds and . . .

"Coming out of chute number three is our very own Maverick Lawson." The announcer bellowed the words from the crow's nest overhead as a shaggy legged beast exploded from a narrow metal stall. Bravura suppressed a shudder as the animal fishtailed and corkscrewed, tossing his diminutive rider into the mud like so much dirty laundry.

"Aww, that'll be a no time for young Maverick. But let's give him a hand, folks. He was all-around runner-up last year and will be riding a bull named Final Round later in the program."

Squeezing Lily protectively against her chest, Bravura shimmied through the crowd.

It was like a scene from a bygone century . . . one where dust and mud existed together with symbiotic ease. Where a good horse was as revered as a tidy 401K.

"Woooow!" Lily breathed and clung tightly to Foo Foo, the much-abused plush animal Gamps had given her years before. It might have, at one point, resembled a bunny. "That's amazing." The words whistled like a spring zephyr through the gap in her incisors.

Bravura could hardly disagree with the senti-ment, but shifted her gaze over the mob, searching for Hunter's aluminum trailer.

Another truncated cowboy lurched past in spurs and run-down boots. Ahead of him, his teenage sister swatted aside the loop with which he tried to rope her, never pausing the conversation she shared with her freckle-faced companion. Cowboy hats swung from stampede strings hooked over scathed saddle horns as their horses followed dutifully in their wake.

"Ooooh," Lily crooned and watched, mesmerized

as the geldings ambled past, muscular haunches brushing the dangling toes of her moccasins. These days, it frequently took no more than the *word* "horse" to send her into bouts of equine euphoria. "Look at that one, Mama. It's a Tobiano."

"Is it?" Vura asked, and scanned the crowd for a glimpse of Hunter. At six foot, four inches of Hunkpapa Indian, he wouldn't be easy to miss. Or so she had assumed. But dozens of trailers packed the grassy knoll that surrounded the arena. She searched more frantically. They were more than a half hour late, which, by motherhood standards, was hardly late at all . . . but still . . .

"That's its color pattern," Lily added. "They can be black and white or brown and white or palomino and white . . . or anything."

"I see." Vura didn't really understand the workings of the Indian Relay Race in which Hunter would be competing, but she did know that if they missed the event, she would remain unforgiven for the next hundred years in her daughter's adoring eyes. Hunter Redhawk's status was only slightly beneath that of the equine species and somewhat above the geese that waddled with snooty impunity across their newly purchased farm. Vura shuddered; whatever genius had decided to domesticate the haughty goose should be armed with nothing but a flyswatter and forced to spend a day in their abrasive company.

"The other one's a . . ." Lily scrunched her little face in concentration and peered past Bravura's left ear. "I think it's black. But maybe it's really a bay. Blacks aren't supposed to fade. But it's not even . . ." She paused. "What month is it, Mama?" Lily's unique personality . . . Vura refused to call it a syndrome no matter what the "experts" said, made it possible for her to cite a thousand details about topics of particular interest while leaving holes the size of moon craters in more commonly understood subjects.

"It's April, honey."

Lily bobbled her head, spun caramel hair brushing her mother's like a wayward halo. "So it's not even summer yet, right?"

"Right." Where the devil was Hunter? Or Sydney? True, Bravura's half sister was hardly of behemoth proportions, but she generally stood out in a crowd of homespun South Dakotans like a Thoroughbred in a pony ring. But . . .

Her thoughts spun to a halt as a horse breezed past, knocking her off balance. She staggered, clutching Lily to her chest, trying to stay upright. But the mud sucked at her boots and she was falling.

"Careful!" Strong hands grabbed her from behind before she hit the ground. She tottered, found her equilibrium, and straightened shakily. "You okay?" The voice was little more than a rumble of worry.

"Yeah. Yeah. I think so." Bravura smoothed an unsteady hand down Lily's runaway hair. But her baby seemed, as usual, unimpressed by such inconsequentialities as near-death experiences.

"Look, Mama! It's a red dun!" she exclaimed and pointed gleefully over Bravura's shoulder at the animal that had nearly plowed them under. Atop the mare's broad back, its miniscule rider seemed as oblivious to the drama as Lily. "See the stripes on its legs and . . ." She blinked, round eyes widening happily. "Hi, Tonka."

Vura's heart clutched in her chest. She turned suspiciously in her savior's arms, scowl already tugging at her eyebrows.

Tonkiaishawien Redhawk, hands still bracketing her body as if prepared to catch her again should she topple over like a drowsy toddler, raised dark brows and flirtatious lips. "You must be more cautious, Bravura Lambert."

She backed away, but bad luck had her tripping again. His hands jerked out, catching her a second time.

"Unless you were *hoping* to be saved by some handsome Sioux brave."

"What are you doing here?" She didn't like to be unfriendly, but Tonkiaishawien had made it his mission to irritate her since the moment they'd met nearly a year before. And he had accomplished that mission stunningly. Everything about him annoyed her: his unquenchable arrogance, his rugged elegance. Even the precise rhythm of his earthy dialect, so appealing in other Native men, was exasperating.

His chiseled Indian features remained as they were, but his eyes, bright with mischief, shone like dark jasper. "I am about to win a relay race. And what of you, Bravura?"

His long, artist's fingers felt warm and capable against her wrist. Irritation mixed with less acceptable emotions. They swirled like toxins in Vura's gut. "Of course you are," she said, and stepped firmly out of his grasp. "Where's Hunt?" Setting her daughter's feet on a relatively dry patch of earth, she straightened to her full height. Five feet, four inches of sturdy Midwestern woman.

Tonk nodded solemnly. A frolicsome breeze teased his hair, brushing the pair of beaded feathers across his cedar-hewn jaw. "I humbly accept your heartfelt gratitude for saving you from certain injury," he said.

"Well, I *am* grateful you didn't break my arms," she said, and knew beyond a shadow of a doubt that she was being ridiculous. Bravura Lambert was about as fragile as rebar, but there was something about Tonkiaishawien Redhawk's flirtatious likability that tended to get her dander up.

Men should be sober and dependable and hardworking like her father, or Hunter or . . . Or her husband, she thought hurriedly, and stifled a belated sliver of guilt. It wasn't as though she had forgotten about Dane . . . it was just that he'd been gone so long.

Tonk's lips, full and bold and despicably mesmerizing, shifted into a canted grin. "Had I known you were such a delicate flower, I would have worn my doe-skin gloves."

"Had I known you were such a pain in the—"

"Lily!" Hunter rasped and burst through the crowd to swing the girl against his bear-like chest.

"Hunk!" Lily crooned and wrapped her arms around his neck in an embrace that suggested utmost happiness and a fair amount of hero worship. "Where's Windwalker?"

"Are you all right?" He pushed her away a little, dark brows lowered over troubled eyes.

"Ai, they are both well and good, brother." Tonk said the words with dramatic flair. "You may thank me later for saving them from certain death."

Hunter ignored him completely. It was a talent Bravura had hoped to acquire. So far, no such luck. "You're sure you're not hurt?" he asked, and ran a broad hand down Lily's purple-clad arm.

"It was a dun horse," she said.

"What?"

"The mare that almost runned us over. She was a red dun," Lily said. "It's like a buckskin but more chestnutty."

Vura refrained from sighing. Lily Belle Lambert was as smart as a firecracker and Bravura adored her with every fiber in her being, but just once it might be nice if the child could switch mental tracks without having to be pried off the rail with a wrecking bar.

Hunter, on the other hand, seemed to consider her obsessions nothing out of the ordinary. "The horse that bumped into you? It was a dun?"

"Yeah." She nodded an affirmation. "And sooo pretty."

Hunter lifted his gaze, scanning the mob of humans and horses. "Was it the one ridden by the kid in the blue shirt?"

Lily shifted her ever-bright gaze toward the object of his inquiry and sighed. "Oooh. Isn't she beautiful? Sometimes red duns are called clay-banks. And sometimes they're called fox duns. But they has to have dorset . . . doral . . . dor—"

"Dorsal stripes," Hunter supplied and, running a protective hand down her back, set her on her feet before straightening to his imposing height. "Keep an eye on them," he ordered, and after catching his brother's gaze in an intimidating glare, strode into the mêlée toward the miniature cowboy on the dun.

"What's he doing?" Lily asked, and grasped Vura's hand.

"I think he's going to reprimand the boy."

"But he was just ridin'," Lily said.

Vura squeezed her fingers. "He should be more careful, Lily Belle."

16

"As should you," Tonk said, and Vura felt the muscles tighten across her shoulders.

"I was looking for Hunter. He's usually so easy to spot," Vura said, and managed, with some effort, to squeeze a little sigh into her voice. Womanly wiles, Dane had once said, were as foreign to her as Istanbul. "Being he's so tall and . . . you know . . . manly."

A tic jerked in Tonk's lean cheek. "Perhaps if you worried more about your daughter and less about my brother's . . . manliness, you wouldn't endanger Lily's life."

A little trill of misbegotten joy shimmied up Bravura's spine. It was impossible to say why irritating Tonkiaishawien thrilled her to the bone, but it did. She sighed as if it was beyond her shaky self-control to forgo fantasizing about Tonk's big brother, but the truth was considerably more mundane; even if Sydney Wellesley, her newly discovered half sister, hadn't tagged Hunter for her own, Vura would never think of him with anything but brotherly appreciation. He was a friend, a protector, and the best man she knew next to her father. And Dane! she reminded herself fiercely. Dane Lambert was a wonderful man. Everybody liked him. It wasn't his fault that he couldn't get a job closer to home. Times were hard, and the shale oil industry was booming in North Dakota. Lots of families had been broken up when the men left for the fracking fields.

17

"What would your husband say if he knew you were ogling another?" Tonk said the words as if he could read her mind. Which he couldn't! Vura was positive his mystic Indian act was just that. Still, guilt rushed in like a feverish wind. She forced a smile.

"How nice of you to worry about my handsome husband." She flipped her hair behind her shoulder as she had seen girls do since pubescence; it never felt quite right when she did it, more like an agitated goose with a neck issue. "Believe me, though, he's not the least bit jealous." And that was God's honest truth. She gazed toward the nearby arena, where a towheaded boy of twelve seemed intent on sustaining whiplash from a shaggy chestnut that strongly resembled a hirsute tornado.

"Then he is even more of a moron than I thought."

"What?" she asked, and snapped her attention back to Tonk.

"I said"—he lifted a single brow as if startled by her reaction—"he must be even more of a man than I thought."

She scowled.

He watched her, eyes as steady as river agates. "Still, I wonder why he is gone so long."

Anger mixed with a couple other volatile emotions. "I'm sorry, I thought it was generally understood that some men have real jobs." Tonk was an artist. She refrained from curling a lip at the idea.

"And is it not his job to care for his wife?"

She canted her head at him. "I'm sorry. What century did you say you were from?"

A muscle bounced in his jaw. "There are some truths that transcend time."

"Tonk!" someone called.

They turned in unison. The woman who greeted him had big hair and big boobs, both of which were currently displayed above the lacy edge of her cherry-red tank top. Impressive, Vura thought, as the temperature in Hope Springs, South Dakota, had yet to reach a long-awaited sixty degrees.

Sashaying toward them, she gripped Tonk's arm with brimming enthusiasm, held her Bud Light with equal fervor. "Tonkiaishawien . . ." Her voice, Vura thought, strongly resembled that of a female mouse made famous by Walt Disney, and even from that distance, she smelled vaguely fruity. Up close she must have resembled a peach grove. "How long has it been?"

"Sherri Unger." He smiled into her eyes . . . or thereabouts. "I thought you'd gone off to the oil fields."

"I did, but I'm back. Staying at the inn for a couple of days, in case you're interested," she said, and gave his arm a playful thwack. Her tittering laughter made her boobs bobble, and

Vura, for some mysterious reason, wanted to gag her with a sock. "But hey, I heard you was riding today."

"You heard right."

"Well, I guess it's my lucky day, then. You gonna execute your signature salute after you win?"

"If you'll demonstrate your usual display of appreciation," he said.

She giggled, glancing at him through lashes long as palm fronds. "Tonky, you're so bad."

Vura felt her hackles rise and her brows lower. But she kept her thoughts to herself. It was no skin off her nose if certain women liked to act like inebriated field mice. Taking Lily's hand in a steely grip, she pivoted away.

But Tonk yanked her to a halt.

If Vura hadn't been clutching Lily's fingers in her own, there was a distinct possibility she would have belted him. And what the devil was that about? As it was, she wheeled around, not entirely controlling the growl that curled her lips.

But Tonk merely raised his brows and nodded toward the palomino that was breezing past like a golden bullet.

"If you have a death wish, Bravura, perhaps someone else should watch Lily for the day," he suggested.

Like Mother Teresa there? she wondered, and couldn't help but snap her gaze to the blond bundle of brains who giggled behind him. Still, she was nothing but decorous as she tugged her arm free.

He released her slowly, fingers sliding against her hand for an instant.

She stifled a shiver.

He scowled and gritted his teeth. Silence echoed between them.

"You must be more careful," he said finally and, straightening carefully, backed away a half a foot. "Horses can be dangerous."

"Don't I know it?" Sherri said from behind. "I swear, every time I see Tonky ride, I think I'm going to pass right out."

No time like the present, Vura thought, and erred, again, on the side of silent diplomacy.

"Relay's gotta be like"—Sherri shook her bleached head—"the most dangerous sport in the whole world."

"Is it?" Bravura scowled.

"You needn't fret," Tonk said.

"What?" She glanced at him.

"I sense your worry."

She caught his gaze. "Well, of course I'm worried."

Something sparked in his river-agate eyes. She stifled a smile and only half-wondered why she was so mean.

"It would kill me if Hunter got hurt," she said.

His jaw bunched. His brows lowered. "Come, Sherri," he said and, taking the woman's elbow, steered her into the crowd.

21

Chapter 2

"This is insane." Beside Vura, Sydney Wellesley looked as pale as a January blizzard. Inside the rodeo arena, the bucking stock was taking a sabbatical as all eyes turned toward the sandy, oval track beyond the rodeo grounds.

Horses, pitchforks, and the myriad accoutrements of the traveling equestrian ringed the trailers hooked to every conceivable vehicle.

Nothing but a single, twisted wire pinned to metal T-posts stood as a barrier between the audience and the competitors. Five divisions had been chalked onto the sand. Inside each ten-by-twenty-foot square two horses were being held. Hunter Redhawk restrained an unruly gray. She shook her head and kicked out behind, but he soothed her, his expression impassive, voice quiet. Hunter Redhawk was an equine magician. Still, Sydney was right to worry. Madness reigned on that oval track, and Hunter's impressive size was no match for the thousand-pound animals that milled around him like sharks in unfriendly waters. He could easily get injured. Yet, Vura's gaze strayed to the left, where, behind the starting line, five men were mounted on war-painted ponies. They drew the eye like an emblazoned target.

Vura couldn't help it if one of those men was

Tonkiaishawien Redhawk. He sat tall and relaxed on a long-legged bay. Feathers fluttered against the gelding's dark forelock and quivered in his black, windswept tail. He reared, but Tonk seemed entirely unconcerned by the animal's restive energy. Instead, he simply leaned toward the animal's crest, one hand clutching on the reins, the other quiet on the bay's burnished neck.

Red paint had been streaked across his high-boned cheeks. Yellow dotted his bowed nose. But it was his torso that drew Vura's gaze. Of course he would be the one who chose to ride bare-chested, Vura scoffed silently, and ignored the muscle that flexed, hard as a fist above his leather breeches.

Sydney gripped Bravura's upper arm with fingers like talons.

"Take it easy, Syd," Vura soothed, but just then a shot was fired. Five horses charged toward the starting line. Sand sprayed into the air, hooves churned, but Tonk's mount was still rearing. Then, seeing his comrades spurting away, he twisted like a hooked trout and leapt forward. The crowd roared.

Beside Vura, Sydney screamed like a banshee. "Come on, Tonk! Come on!"

And he did. In three strides he and the bay were devouring the distance. In eight he was passing the fourth horse, then the third, then, straining, struggled past the second.

"Give him his head, Tonk! Give him his head!" Sydney shrieked. Lily added her breathy encouragement, but a leggy chestnut held the lead. Nostrils flaring, Tonk's bay challenged the forerunner, but as they rounded the last bend, a scrappy buckskin bumped his shoulder. The bay staggered and hit his knees. Onlookers gasped. Someone screamed. Tonk slipped but clung, one knee clasped over the animal's spine. The other horses raced past, but the bay was game. Leaping to his feet, he charged on. Tonk was still fighting to regain his balance as the others skidded to a halt in the chalked squares. Riders leapt from their mounts and dashed toward the horses held for the next lap. Throwing themselves onto the animals' bare backs, they galloped away just as Tonk was skidding up to his pinto. The bay reared again but Tonk was already flinging himself to the ground. One bounce and he was magically astride the paint. There was a flurry of hooves and leather and hair. The course was short and fast. There was a breathy gasp as the riders changed horses for the final lap and then Tonk was again challenging the leader. The horses fought like warriors. Eyes rimmed with white, manes flying like banners, they screamed toward the finish line. Bent low over his mount's straining neck, Tonk yelled encouragement and endearments. His hair melded with his mare's wild mane, black against white. No longer two separate entities, they strained

24

together, and the gray, game to the bone, dug for her final reserves and dashed past the frontrunner.

The crowd went crazy, screaming, chanting, cheering. Somewhere near the crow's nest, Indian drums beat a pounding rhythm.

Sydney yanked Vura in for a rib-cracking hug. "We won! We won, Vura. Four thousand dollars for the mustangs. Four thousand for the wild—"

The gasps that rippled through the crowd made her stop and turn back toward the track. Vura did the same. Even now Tonk was rising to his feet on the gray's bare back. Steadying his stance, he pushed himself to his full height as the mare danced a high-stepping gallop. With his free hand, Tonk motioned for applause and the crowd reciprocated. Seasoned cowboys, accomplished equestrians, and admiring laymen roared in approval, honoring his athleticism, loving his antics, cheering his boldness, but suddenly a plastic bag blew onto the track, and the gray, flush with the thrill of victory, reared onto her hind legs like a geyser.

Tonk dropped to the mare's back and grappled for her mane, but she was already falling, toppling over backward. She struck the ground and twisted wildly. Then, scrambling to her feet, she galloped away. But Tonk remained as he was, lean body sprawled in the sand, legs flung wide, eyes closed to a world gone quiet with dread.

Hunter was already sprinting toward his fallen

brother. Sydney slipped beneath the twisted wire and rushed onto the track.

Others were hurrying forward . . . cowboys, handlers, spectators, but Vura remained absolutely motionless, eyes straining, breath locked in her chest.

"He's not breathing!" The words hissed through the mob. "Anyone know CPR?"

"I do!" A curvy woman of thirty-something years pushed through the crowd and slipped beneath the wire. Racing across the sand, she dropped down beside Tonk's prone body. Red hair flying, she pumped his chest, closed his nose and breathed into his mouth. Pumped, breathed, pumped until suddenly Tonk's arms came around her and pulled her down. It took a moment for the crowd to realize he was kissing her. There was a second of hushed uncertainty. Then laughter and cheers roared through the masses as he rolled atop her to continue the caress.

As for Hunter Redhawk, he stood glaring at his brother's muddied back for a total of three seconds before hauling him up by the waistband of his leather breeches.

Tonk grinned, threw his face toward the sky, and raised hard-muscled arms in wild victory.

The crowd laughed and whistled as he assisted his rescuer in rising. She giggled, looking proud, if a little stunned, as she staggered toward the fence.

Riley, Tonk's cousin and best horse mugger, shook his head and trotted off to catch the gray.

On the sidelines, Vura closed her eyes and felt herself wilt.

"Are you okay, Mama?" Lily brought her back to the moment in a snap.

"Yes." She squeezed her daughter's tiny hand and forced a smile. "Of course I am, honey."

"He's okay, you know," Lily assured her. "He's not bad hurt."

"I know, baby," Vura said, and watched as the man in question strode toward them.

"Then how come you looked so scared?"

Vura pulled her gaze from the victor. "I'm not scared, sweetheart."

The quizzical brows dipped a little, questioning. "You don't gotta be mad, neither. I'm sure he only kissed that lady cuz he was so grateful."

Vura ground her teeth into a smile. "I'm sure you're right," she said, and shot a killing stare at the approaching Tonkiaishawien.

He stopped in his tracks not five feet away, expression cautious. "How did you like the race, Bravura Lambert?"

Vura did her best to formulate a response that included neither spitting nor curses, both of which, supposedly, would be a bad influence on her impressionable daughter.

Tonk raised one dark brow in foolish curiosity. It took all her dubious self-control to keep from wiping it off his face with the shovel that rested against a nearby trailer. But when he took a step closer, she found that her fingers had, quite magically, curled around the handle of a pitchfork.

A grin tilted his lips. She tightened her grip.

"Goldenrod . . ." Hunter's voice snapped her from her dark fantasy.

Lily turned toward her hero, eyes alight. "Hunk!"

He lifted her into his arms before shifting his gaze to Tonk. "The horses are asking for you, little brother."

Lily gave him a scolding glance from the corner of kaleidoscope eyes. "Horses can't talk, Hunk."

"What?" He settled her more firmly against his chest. "Why do you think this?"

She lowered her brows in an expression too old for her face. And he sighed. "I suppose I shouldn't say what I heard about *you,* then."

Her gumdrop lips pursed, her eyes squinted suspiciously, but she couldn't resist asking. "What'd they say?"

He shrugged, a simple lift of heavy shoulders. "Just that they like it best when you ride since you weigh no more than a dewdrop."

"What did they say about Tonk?"

He shot his brother a sidelong glance rife with frustration. "That, little snapdragon, cannot be repeated in polite company."

"Mama says I'm not very polite sometimes," Lily said.

"Well, that would depend who you're compared to, I suppose," Hunt said, and shifted his dark gaze back to Tonk.

Lily giggled. "Can I talk to them now?"

"The horses?"

"Uh-huh."

"That's up to your mother."

"Now's fine," Vura said and, releasing the pitchfork with an effort, turned to follow her daughter.

But Tonk stopped her with a hand to her arm. "I would ask one more minute of your time."

She turned toward him, already missing the fork.

"Please?" he added.

She pursed her lips and waited.

"I have been wishing to speak with you."

She waited a heartbeat, lifted a hand. "Then speak."

"Your daughter"—he shifted his feet, making her wonder for the first time in their acquaintance if he was uncertain—"Lily . . ."

"I know who my daughter is, Tonk."

Amber chips glowed in the burnt-umber depths of his eyes as he shifted his gaze away and back. "She has the gift of the old ones."

Vura stared at him. He was ridiculous, she reminded herself. Melodramatic, flashy, and foolish. Yet she felt the hair rise at the back of her neck. "What are you talking about?"

He scowled as if vexed by her naïveté. "She has a way with the wild beasts."

"Wild beasts . . ." She scoffed and refused to think about how their stupid geese, so boisterously opinionated when she herself was near, seemed to consider Lily one of their own. Even Milly, currently brooding a clutch of mottled eggs, tolerated her. "Like you?"

Mischief sparked in his eyes, making Vura curse herself for giving him the opportunity to think of himself in such an outrageously masculine fashion.

"I could be tamed," he said, and something about the way he watched her made her face flush. She set her teeth and reminded herself that he was only baiting her. Even if she was free, which she most decidedly was *not,* she wasn't his type. The big-boobed blonde was his type. And it was entirely possible that Vura and Sherri didn't share so much as the same number of chromosomes.

"Well . . ." she said, and glanced toward the track where Riley Old Horn was riding the gray and leading the pinto. "I'll inform the Ringling Brothers at the first opportunity, but right now I'd better—"

"I am concerned for her education."

"Concerned for her . . ." She scoffed again. It was becoming a habit. "What are you talking about? Lily's been able to read for months. Her math skills—"

He held up a hand.

She considered biting it, but he was already placing it reverently against his chest. His *bare* chest. Why wasn't he wearing a shirt? He owned a shirt. She was sure of it. Not that his state of undress bothered her. Why would it? "I do not speak of book learning, but matters of the soul, of the heart."

She rolled her eyes and turned away, but he stopped her again.

"She is Native, is she not?" he asked.

"Part." She didn't know why it was a difficult fact to admit. Though she had never known her mother, she had always been aware of the Sioux blood on her maternal side. Had always been proud of that heritage. "What about it?"

"Xboxes and iPods will not complete a child of nature."

"Oh, for heaven's sake," she said, and dropped her head back as if able to endure no more. "Will you give up the proud Indian act and spit it out so I can get back to—"

"I wish to tutor her."

She blinked once. "What?"

He looked peeved now, though for the life of her she couldn't have guessed why. "I wish to teach her of the old ways," he added.

She wouldn't have been more surprised if he had spontaneously morphed into a bumblebee. Less maybe. Surely the womanizing Tonkiaishawien

31

had no time for small turbo-charged children.

But his expression was absolutely somber. "She is a child of the wild and needs someone to teach her the ways of The People. How they revered their old, valued their young. How they retrieved their wounded in battle, honored the earth, spoke across the hills with no more than a puff of smoke." He scowled, voice softening. "Someone should teach her. Perhaps someone like me."

"She *has* someone like you. Kind of." She curled her lip. "She has Hunt." Though, in some ways, the two brothers could hardly be more different and still share a species.

"Hunt," he said, and shook his head as if such ridiculousness was laughable.

"What about him?"

"My brother is a good man," he admitted. "But he has embraced the ways of the white world."

"What are you talking about?"

"Look how he makes his living."

"By saving mustangs?" Sydney had established a wild horse sanctuary more than six months ago. Hunter had been instrumental in its success.

But Tonk shook his head as if saddened by her naïveté. "Surely you are not so deluded as to believe a profit can be made by saving the wild things."

"They seem to be doing all right."

He breathed a laugh. "That is because my

brother made his fortune in the Wasichu's world long before . . ."

"Long before what?"

He shook his head, stoic persona firmly back in place. "It matters not. The point is this . . ." He glanced away, gritted his teeth, and turned back, head held high. "Young ones should have a man in their lives."

"Oh, for . . ." She resisted rolling her eyes this time, but only because it was giving her a headache. "She has a man in her—"

"A man who isn't my brother," he snapped.

She raised a brow at him. "I was thinking of my husband."

"This husband of yours . . . how is it that I have never met him?"

Her face warmed immediately . . . which was ridiculous. She didn't have to explain Dane's absence to anyone. She was proud of the fact that he was ambitious enough to join the ranks in the oil fields. "Why would you?"

"I have met your father, your aunt, your sister. I have even met Blue."

She scowled. Honest to God, she hated that goose.

"And your point?" she asked.

"Why have I not met your husband?"

"He works out of state. You know that."

"As an indentured servant?"

She gritted her teeth. Native humor . . . so funny.

"He does not get a single day off to visit his family?"

She straightened her back. If she had a high horse, now would be the time to climb aboard. "I'm sorry if his work ethic offends you."

Anger or something like it flashed in his eyes.

"Listen . . ." she said, and spread her hands before her like a shield. The nail on her left index finger was chipped, perhaps proving there was nothing new under heaven. "I'd love to chat about Dane's occupation, since you are clearly fascinated, but I have work to do, too."

"It is wrong to leave her handicapped."

She tried to ignore the insult, but Lily was her world, and who was he to find fault? Just a transient interloper who brought her daughter gifts now and then . . . a pink chunk of rose quartz, a hand-carved stick horse. "What's that supposed to mean?"

"Horses," he said, catching her gaze and holding it hostage. "They are yet the soul of our people."

She longed to scoff, but the equine species *did* seem to have an indefinable something that brought Lily fully alive. Even Styx, the stupid stick horse, fascinated her no end.

"I get her out to Gray Horse as often as I can," she said, but guilt was already creeping in. Gray Horse Sanctuary was Sydney's brainchild . . . part working ranch, part mustang rescue, all intensive labor funded by love and unreasonable amounts of optimism. Bravura herself had put in a thousand man-hours and each one had been worth the effort just to watch the herd gallop against the backdrop of sun-dappled bluffs. But three months ago, she had purchased her own little acreage. A little acreage that needed as much TLC as an abandoned puppy. A little acreage that was a good half-hour drive from the sanctuary. Then there was Saw Horse, Inc. Newly formed construction companies, it turned out, put even puppies to shame in the needy department.

"Does she dream of them?" he asked.

"Of who?"

"Does she imagine being at the head of the herd, racing with the mustangs?"

"No, she . . ." Vura began, but how many times had Lily awakened with some wild horse tale as fresh as morning on her mind? "Not always."

The glimmer of his smile was all-knowing. "She deserves to have more time with the horse."

Anger bloomed again. "Maybe this is a surprise to you, Tonka Truck, but sometimes women have to work. Sometimes women are good for more than"—she waved wildly toward the oval track where he had lain unconscious just minutes before—"than kissing some idiot man back to life."

The silence following her outburst seemed rife with tension, surprise, and more than a little bit of amusement.

His grin cranked up another half an inch. "I am not in love with her, Bravura Lambert."

She remained in stunned silence for a good six seconds before cackling at the sky. The sound echoed off the nearby trailers like lightning on rim rock. "In love with her! In love with her? Why would I care if . . . I'm not . . ." She huffed something between a laugh and a growl. "I've got to get to work."

"That is something else about which I wished to speak to you."

She raised a brow at him. "Still need a definition of the word?"

"Just because I am not miserable does not mean I do not work."

She huffed a laugh, hoping she sounded dismissive. He crafted pottery, did some painting, dabbled with beadwork. Pretty pieces, sure, but not essential . . . not like building homes or constructing businesses.

On the other hand, he had shaped the horsehair vase that graced the entrance of Sydney's sanctuary. It was neither overlarge nor particularly ornate, but there was something about its earthy beauty that stirred a yearning near her heart. The fact that his beaded jewelry seemed to adorn every overfed bosom between the mountains and the Mississippi elicited other emotions entirely.

"Listen . . ." She gritted her teeth and set those

emotions coolly aside. "You're an artist . . . kind of . . . I get that. I just—"

"Kind of?"

The growl in his voice made her heart smile a little. But she simply lifted a disregarding shoulder and continued as if his irritation wasn't the most satisfying thing she had experienced all day.

"It's just that some of us need real jobs."

"Real—" He stopped himself, grinding his teeth to do so before drawing a breath that made his chest expand and his nostrils flare. In a moment he seemed to be back in control, although he did clench his fists once before exhaling slowly and softening his voice. "I cannot pay more than seven hundred a month."

She stared at him, allowing ample time for explanations. He said nothing. Clearly he had lost his mind along with his train of thought. *"What?"*

"Very well . . ." He nodded stiffly. "Eight hundred."

She blinked at him.

"Fine then," he snapped. "A thousand. But my horses can use your barn as well as the pastures."

"You want to"—she shook her head, breathed a laugh, and ventured a guess—"you want to keep your horses on my property?"

"A Native child such as the wild Lily, should not be bereft of sunlight on a horse's mane in the small hours of the day."

She stared at him in silence for a second, then, "I actually think you might be crazy."

"Is it madness to believe that the hills should be grazed as the Great Spirit intended? Or that the young should feel the beauty of them in their souls?"

She wanted quite desperately to argue, but where to begin? She settled for practicality. "My place barely has a single acre fenced."

"Very well," he said, and shook his head as if loath to do so. "I will construct the fences myself if you insist."

She stared at him. He returned her gaze, hard and sharp and cocky as a strutting rooster. Her mind spun. A thousand dollars a month would buy a lot of . . . well . . . a lot of everything. In fact, with that kind of money she could maybe afford a specialist for Lily. On the other hand, Tonkiaishawien Redhawk was as irritating as a toothache. Then again . . .

She clenched her jaw and interlaced her fingers. "Fifteen hundred," she said.

"Fifteen hundred dollars?"

"Yes."

"For twenty acres of leafy spurge and bull thistle?"

She canted her head in a take-it-or-leave-it gesture. "I believe there's a fair amount of cockleburs too."

He filled his nostrils. "Twelve."

She smiled. "Thirteen."

He narrowed his eyes. "Twelve fifty."

"Throw in a horsehair vase and you've got yourself a deal."

He raised a brow at her.

"Lily likes them," she said.

He watched her in silence for a breathless lifetime, and then he reached out his hand. His back was war-lance straight. And his hair, black as a crow's wing, blew softly in the wind, but it was his eyes that transfixed her. They gleamed with something. It looked like it might have been a challenge.

She slipped her palm against his earthy-artist fingers.

Electricity tickled through her, starting at her fingertips, sizzling up her arm, as warm as the sunrise, more intimate than a kiss. She caught her breath, knowing she should pull back, but his quiet-river eyes held her, somber, earnest, pulling her in, drawing her under.

"Vey?" The voice seemed to come from some distant source, some other world. "Vey! What's going on?"

Vura jerked her gaze up at the sound of her nickname. And there, not eight feet away, stood her husband.

Chapter 3

"Dane!"

Tonk watched Bravura's face pale, watched her eyes widen, and felt the tension ripen to the tips of her fingers.

"What . . ." She breathed heavily. "What are you doing here?"

The man she was addressing was bright-eyed and baby-faced. His fair hair, highlighted with streaks of honey and ash, could only be called "cute." Some might think him handsome, if they found Gerber faces appealing on grown-ass men. "I came to surprise you." He raised his brows a little, glanced at Tonk. "And I guess it's a good thing I did."

Tonkiaishawien took immediate offense at the implication . . . as if he was making time with Bravura. Tonkiaishawien Redhawk did not become involved with other men's wives . . . anymore.

Bravura snapped her hand from Tonk's embrace, pressed it against her thigh as if it had been burned.

"You didn't say you were coming home."

"That why you're here?" Dane asked. "To get a little play time in while I'm gone?"

Bravura's jaw dropped as did Tonk's brows.

"I believe you got the wrong idea, brother," he said.

Vura's husband took a stiff step toward Tonk. Their gazes clashed, blue on brown, and then Dane smiled. "I'm just yanking your chain," he said, and stretched his arm out to shake hands. "I'm Dane Lambert, Vey's old man. Looks like I put my money on the wrong team."

Tonk tilted his head, met his palm.

"I consider myself a pretty good judge of racehorses. But I guess I forgot to take the size of the jockey's balls into the equation. That was quite a ride."

Tonk merely stared. Mixed messages were darting at him like barn swallows.

"You must be Hunter Redhawk," Lambert continued and tightened his grip a little. His nails were clean, his palm as smooth as his pabulum complexion.

"No, honey . . ." Vura began, voice strained. "This is Tonk. You saw a picture of Hunter. Remember?"

"Oh yeah." He tilted his golden-boy head so that their gazes struck dead-on. "Hunt's a big guy, isn't he?"

Tonk ignored the dull jibe. He'd grown up with three brothers, all of whom could sharpen a better barb in his sleep; if he hadn't learned to deflect more deadly insults than that he would have died before puberty. Still, it gave him a little punch of pleasure to imagine jabbing a left-handed uppercut into the other guy's baby-soft jaw. What kind of man would leave his wife and daughter alone for months on end? Not that Bravura Lambert was helpless. Hardly that. She could knock a man flat with little more than a glance from her living-water eyes. And it wasn't as if she was irresistible to the male population. She was too tough, too *sturdy* to personify the ideal female form, at least by current society's questionable standards. And she had freckles. Scattered across her slightly tilted nose like confetti. What kind of grown woman had freckles? Then there was her hair, that wild mane of a thousand glistening hues that no artist would capture even if he could feel the burnished color of each living strand in his sleep. That hair that was rarely tamed by so much as a band of rubber. But when she laughed . . .

"I just . . ." She shook her head. "I can't believe you're here."

Dane relinquished Tonk's hand and swung his arm over his wife's shoulders. "Can't a man miss his honey anymore?"

"Of course, but I just . . ." She shook her head. "How did you even know where to find me?"

He winked at Tonk and kissed her cheek. "Didn't realize I was keeping such close tabs, did you?" he asked, and let his attention flicker, just for a second, past his wife's left shoulder.

In the distance, a big-haired blonde disappeared into the crowd. It almost looked like Sherri.

"Well . . ." Lambert turned. A dollop of smug pride shone in his powder-blue eyes. "It was good to meet you, chief." He turned away, taking Vura with him before twisting back to grin over his left shoulder. "Hey, you should drop by for dinner sometime. Vey makes a mean can of soup."

Tonk watched them leave.

"Was that Dane?"

He tightened his jaw but didn't glance over as Sydney Wellesley stepped up beside him. "Ai."

"I can't believe you got to meet him before I did."

"Quite an honor," he said.

"What?"

"Good race, ai?" he asked, tone carefully dry.

She scowled at the retreating couple before shifting her attention back to him. "Not bad."

"Not bad?" He raised one brow and glowered as Hunter laughed, approaching from behind with Lily perched on one ridiculously brawny arm.

"Be grateful, little brother," he rumbled. "This is high praise coming from the duchess."

Tonk snorted in response, though from the start Sydney Wellesley had looked like nothing so much as visiting royalty. "I think I would rather be insulted."

Sydney laughed. "The last thing you need, Tonkiaishawien, is to have your ego stroked."

Remnants of the just-past conversation washed through him. "There you are wrong," he said, and didn't glance after the woman who could tatter his self-esteem without breaking a sweat. "That is just what I need."

Sydney tilted her head at him, assessing. "Very well," she said, and narrowed her eyes as if in deep thought. Then, clasping her hands together, she tugged them to her chest and rounded her shoulders in euphoric glee. "Oh my gosh!" She squealed and hopped in place like a palsied bunny. "It's the Redhawk Warriors! Bambi. Roxy!" She glanced frantically from side to side as if flanked by her two best empty-headed buddies. "It's the Redhawk Warriors! Aren't they the dreamiest? Aren't they the hunkiest? I knew they'd win. I just knew it," she blathered and followed her performance with a chest-heaving sigh.

The men stared in immobilized silence. Even Lily, perched on Hunter's arm like a nesting songbird, was absolutely quiet.

"That was . . ." Tonk began and shook his head, trying to dislodge the scene from his memory. "Deeply disturbing."

"Did I do something wrong?" Sydney asked. Her tone was high-desert dry, her left brow elevated a scant fraction of an inch above the right. "Shall I try it again?"

"Absolutely not," Tonk said.

"You're scaring Lily," Hunt added, setting the

child carefully on the ground beside him. "And me."

"How about this then?" Sydney asked and, walking up to Tonk, kissed him lightly on the cheek. "That was amazing, Tonkiaishawien. Brilliant, and I thank you from the bottom of my heart."

The following silence challenged the first one.

"It was my idea," Hunter rumbled.

"And you"—Sydney turned to him with the light of adoration in her eyes before leaning in to caress his face—"*own* my heart."

"*He* got a kiss," Hunter said.

Her smile was knowing and sassy and a little vindictive when she moved in. Their lips met, locked, tasted, savored.

"Better?" she asked finally.

"Yeah," Hunter said, but his tone was a little scratchy.

If Tonk's emotions weren't still being stretched out of place like warm taffy, he would have laughed out loud at his big brother's obvious discomfort.

"I have but one question," he said instead. Sydney turned toward him, brows raised again. "What happened to the woman who could freeze a man's heart dead in his chest with one glance?"

She gave him a slanted grin. "She just watched the dreamy Redhawk Warriors win four thousand dollars for her rescued mustangs."

"If it just takes a little cash to generate that kind of affection, I'd be willing to write a check," Tonk said.

Hunter growled and Sydney laughed before glancing at Lily. "Come on, honey, let's get some cotton candy."

They left hand in hand, arms swinging between them.

"Don't be feeding my ponies that sugary crap," Tonk warned, but Sydney only laughed.

Funny, Tonk thought, watching them walk away. He'd be willing to bet that Sydney Wellesley had put in more hours of physical labor in the last twelve months than she had in the entirety of her life before that point. Yet when she had arrived, flush with her daddy's money, she'd been broken and bruised, as shattered as an antique doll. Sadness had enveloped her like a cloud. But in the months since her arrival, everything had changed. Now she was whole. Now she was happy. It didn't take a mystic to see that.

But perhaps it wasn't just that she had found purpose. Perhaps even her beloved mustangs weren't the entire reason for her newfound satisfaction. Which meant . . . He shook his head and finally acknowledged his brother's quizzical glance.

"If I didn't know better, I would actually think you had done something right by that woman."

"Miracles do happen," Hunter admitted and

Tonk snorted as he returned, ruminating, to his trailer.

Hunt was the reason for Sydney's contentment, he thought as he ran a dandy brush down his painted gelding's well-defined haunches. Hunt, the least charismatic man on the planet. He shook his head once in wordless wonder and reminded himself that he would not resent his brother's happiness. That would be childish and base, and while he often enjoyed being childish . . . and base, he didn't care to be in this situation.

Instead, he would be content with his art and his horses. Arrow sighed as Tonk stroked his neck with the brush's stiff bristles. It was enough to be able to watch beauty emerge like a fragile blossom in his hands. To pay homage to the Native way of life by caring for his animals and those in need. Of course, that was exactly what he had been trying to do when the baby-faced Lambert had come toddling along. He'd been trying to find a home for his horses when this all began. It was no good keeping them separated, stabling them at different locations. Best to have them all together so they could bond. The adrenaline rush of racing was terrifying enough when the horses were comfortable in each other's company. Keeping them scattered hither and yon helped nothing. Not his exercise program, not his time management, not his horses' emotional health. And if renting a pasture gave him some small time with little Lily, so much the better.

Satisfied with Arrow's well-being, he moved on to the bay and realized he'd be the first to admit he had no idea why Lily Lambert tugged at his soul. It wasn't as if he saw himself in her wild-urchin face. So her dad was absent for long periods of time. Tonk had considered himself lucky when his own father had been absent for even a short while. And Lily had Bravura. Her fierce loyalty, her obvious adoration, her foolish optimism. But sometimes, when he looked into the mother's eyes, he would swear he caught the shadow of encroaching panic behind the staunch, I-can-do-it-all attitude.

"Cousin . . ."

Tonk stilled his hand over the bay's lumbar vertebrae. There was a touch of soreness there. He would have to be mindful, he thought, and glanced up.

Riley Old Horn, Indian dark and cowboy lean, was eating M&M's while riding bareback on a dancing Sky Bird. Raising a blossoming teenager alone had given him the ability to multitask and troubleshoot all at once. Or so it seemed.

"Ry," Tonk said. They shared a smile. They'd shared much more since their earliest memories: purloined whiskey, secrets, and the driving need to ride anything on four legs.

"Keep this up and the championship is ours."

"Let us not count our chickens before they are hatched," Tonk advised.

Riley grinned. "Speaking of poultry . . . the boys are going to go cruisin' for chicks at the Branding Iron."

Tonk raised his brows in surprise. "You cruising, too?"

"'Fraid my ship has sailed," he said. "But Moll's staying with Abby. So I'll sit for a while. Maybe have a few drinks."

Desire burned like an open flame through Tonk, but the fulfillment of that desire had rarely brought contentment. And wasn't that what Bill W. and the Native way both espoused? "I believe I will stay with the horses."

"The horses are sick of the sight of you."

Tonk laughed. "But I am not sick of them. Go," he added. "Perhaps I will stop by after I get them settled for the night."

"You sure?"

"Enjoy the poultry."

Riley shook his head, slipped from Sky Bird's back, and handed over the reins. "Red meat only for me. See you later, cousin."

Not if his willpower held out, Tonk thought, and led the dancing gray to the hydrant for her post-race bath.

Chapter 4

"How do you like it, Vey?" Dane asked, and nodded toward a muscle car angled diagonally across two parking spots. The vehicle was as bright as the sun, as sleek as a bullet. Chrome gleamed like platinum on every fender.

Vura scowled at it, then glanced at him. "That's not yours."

"Ours," he corrected, and grinned. "It's ours, baby."

"But I thought . . ." She shook her head. For the past two years she'd barely been able to afford fuel for her own battered vehicle. And he hadn't helped out much. Sure, he made a decent income, he'd said, but expenses were over the moon in the boomtown of Williston, North Dakota.

She'd be a fool to mention that now, though . . . a fool to ruin his homecoming. Still, financial concerns gnawed her like a hound. "Can we afford that?"

He gave a half shrug, amped up that grin that had once shifted her teenage hormones into overdrive. "I needed to get to work somehow, honey."

"I know, but . . ." She stopped herself. *"Needed?* As in past tense?"

He drew a deep breath and caught her gaze. "I quit."

"You . . . What?"

He laughed. "You heard me, baby."

"You quit?" A dozen emotions stormed through her like tornadoes. "For good?"

His brows dipped a little. "I thought you'd be happy I was home."

"Yes. Of course." She paused, nerves jangling. How long had she hoped for his return? How long had she prayed that they would be a family again? "Of course I'm happy. But I thought you couldn't get a job around here. Wasn't that why you left in the first place?"

"Well, when a guy's woman starts her own carpentry company, maybe he don't need to work," he said. Perhaps there was a little bite to the comment. He'd never seemed entirely comfortable with the idea of her doing manual labor, but he bumped her with his elbow and grinned, taking the sting out of the words.

Still, she pulled away. "Dane, I'm barely paying the bills as it is. Saw Horse is just getting its feet on the ground. I can't—"

"I'm just kidding, honey," he said and, reaching out, tugged her between his knees as he settled his back against the driver's door of his sleek Dodge Viper. She could smell the beer on his breath. But she had always liked that scent. Her father had often enjoyed a Bud after work. More recently, they shared a brew and war stories from the construction zones. "But I missed you," he said and, sliding his hands down her arms, caught her gaze with his salt-taffy eye. "I thought you missed me, too."

"You know I did."

"Then who was that clown?" he asked, and jerked a nod at some unknown point to his right.

"What?"

"The guy who was looking at you like they had just discovered uranium in your pants."

She felt a flush start at her ears. "I don't know what you're talking about."

He slipped a hand onto the curve of her hip. "And you're all dressed up."

She forced a laugh. Maybe in high school she hadn't been so self-conscious about public displays of affection, but they made her itchy now. "I'm just wearing jeans."

"And if they were any tighter, it'd take a three-man crew to get you out of 'em."

The heat spread, aiming for her throat. "I just . . . Maybe I've put on a few pounds." She loved food. Always had. Always would.

"Well, if you have, they've all settled in the right places," he said, and nuzzled her neck. "I'm just wondering what happened to the overalls you used to be so adorable in."

She squirmed a little and tried to peer past his shoulder. This was her community, where she worked, where she raised her daughter. Then again . . . he *was* her husband. "I still have them."

"So are the jeans for the Indian chief?"

"I don't know what you're talking about." She'd always known she wasn't the kind of woman that men noticed. She couldn't manage an updo to save her soul. Why any right-thinking women would wear a miniskirt boggled her mind, and the mere idea of high heels set an ache in her lower back that could only be relieved by a peanut buster parfait and small fries from the Dairy Queen. Still, if the truth be told, maybe she had dressed with a little more care than usual this morning.

Guilt slipped in, melding uncomfortably with embarrassment.

"Tonka Toy," he said and, hooking his thumbs in her belt loops, bumped his crotch against hers. "Wasn't that his name?"

"Tonkiaishawien."

"Yeah, him," he said, and ground his groin gently into hers.

"He's just a friend. Not even a friend," she corrected. "The brother of a friend."

He shook his head. "You never did know when a man was interested in you. It took me six months before you so much as glanced my way."

"That's not true." The truth was, she had glanced plenty. She just hadn't thought he'd ever glance back. It might be a cliché as old as pigskins but quarterbacks could still achieve demigod status in Middle America.

"Until I kissed you," he said and, leaning in, nuzzled her ear. Surprised excitement sizzled sheepishly through her sleepy system. "Let's go home, baby."

"Home?" After the months of uncertainty, the lonely nights, the hours she had spent wondering what he was doing and with whom, the word sounded dreamlike coming from his lips. He hadn't really approved when she'd suggested purchasing a small acreage. The house was abysmal, the land unkempt, he had said. But that's what had made the price so reasonable. Low interest rates and Lily's need for space had convinced her she was doing the right thing. But in the end he hadn't spent more than a few days there. "To the farm?" she asked, though in these parts, twenty acres barely qualified as a lot.

"To the farm," he agreed and running his hand down her waist, kissed the corner of her mouth. "And the sooner the better."

"Okay." Her tone was breathier than she had intended, but Dane had always been able to make her believe she was the center of the universe when he put his mind to it. And if he could also make her feel like she was a noodle-headed middle schooler again, maybe that was because she loved him. "Just let me grab Lily and I'll be ready to go." She twisted away, but he drew her back with a hand on her arm.

"Lily?"

She laughed, searching his face. "Your daughter. You do remember her, don't you?"

He grinned, expression hopelessly charming, and pressed his body to hers again. "It's hard."

The blush spread into her hairline. An elderly couple was passing on her left. It took her a moment to recall that she had just tiled their bathroom floor two months before. Longer still to remember their names. "Hello, Frank. Sheila." Her cheeks felt hot. "Nice day, isn't it?"

"Beautiful," Sheila said.

"Very nice," Frank agreed, but they shifted uncomfortable glances to her husband and kept walking.

Dane's chuckle brought her back to the present. "Old farts should mind their own business."

"I have to work with these people," she said and felt, suddenly, more like a school*marm* than a school*kid*.

"All I said was that it was hard"—he grinned again—"to remember anything when you're wearing those jeans."

The flattery warmed her, but guilt was there, too, gumming up the works. How many times had she lied to her father to sneak out with Dane? Not that Dad had disapproved of him . . . exactly. "Lily'll be so excited," she said.

"I'm looking forward to seeing her, too," he said, and swept a thumb over her knuckles. "But we haven't had any time alone in months."

"Well . . ." She squirmed sideways a little. People were watching them. She'd always been proud to be seen with him, but things had changed. She wasn't fifteen anymore. At the end of a long day she generally felt closer to fifty. "She goes to bed early."

"That's what *I* was hoping to do," Dane said and, turning her hand in his, kissed her palm. "Remember when you used to sneak out of your old man's house to meet me? Nothing would have stopped you then."

She did remember, but the recollection always left a residue of guilt. Her father had trusted her. Foolishly, as it turned out. "We were just kids then."

"That's what I need now, honey. To feel like a kid again."

"But we're not, Dane. I've got a company . . ." She held his gaze. "Responsibilities."

"I've been working like a dog, too, Vey." His grin amped up again. "Now I want to do other doggie-type things."

"Quiet," she hissed and tried to pull away, but he tightened his grip on her hand.

"I meant we could maybe howl at the moon together." He swung her arm between them. "What did you think I was talking about?"

She rolled her eyes and tried to ignore the swift kick of arousal that snapped low in her gut. But Dane had always been an expert at making it possible to ignore everything but him.

"You know what they say, honey? You can't have a happy family if you don't have a happy marriage."

He had a point, of course. "Well, I guess . . ." He slipped his hand onto her hip, caressing softly. "Maybe Lil could stay at Gray Horse tonight."

"Gray Horse?" he asked, and glanced to the right.

"Gray Horse Sanctuary." She followed his gaze, saw no one she recognized and felt light-headed with relief. "Sydney's ranch. I renovated the house there. Built fences. Remember?"

He laughed and returned his attention to her. "I told you I can't remember much when you're in them jeans." He bumped his forehead against hers. "Or out of 'em."

She glanced sideways again and felt her breath stop in her throat. "What's she doing here?"

He kept his attention riveted on her. "What are you talking about?"

"Sherri. I think her name was Sherri," she said, and pulled her attention from the woman to Dane.

He glanced dismissively to the right, refocused on her. "So?"

"She was out West, too, I guess. In Williston."

"Well . . ." He chuckled. "The town's doubled in size in the last couple of years. I think there might be a few thousand other people I don't know, too."

"Why's she staring at us?"

"Probably because you're so dang sexy."

She opened her mouth for another question, but he spoke first.

"Hey!" He leaned back, eyes alight. "You're| not jealous, are you?"

"No. I just . . ."

"You are," he argued and tossing his head back, laughed out loud. "You're jealous."

"I'm not. I just—"

"Man, that turns me on."

She scowled. "You're sure you don't know her?"

"You think I'd lie?"

"No. Of course not."

He nodded, squeezed her hands. "Go on then," he said, and released her. "Go find a place for Lily."

"Don't you want to say hi at least?"

"Not without her gifts."

Something shifted in her chest, like the lightening of a burden. "You brought her gifts?"

"You didn't think I'd show up empty-handed, did you? But you'll just have to wait to see what they are." He grinned. "Hurry up now. Before I do something that'll embarrass you even more."

"Okay," she agreed and tugging free, turned away. She glanced back once, but he was already striding through the crowd with that signature swagger that had made a hundred schoolgirls sigh not so many years before. Or had a lifetime passed?

Dragging her mind back to the present, Vura searched for the Warriors' horse trailer and found it finally near the bucking chutes.

"Mama!" Lily was perched atop Tonk's broadbacked pinto when they saw each other. "Swift Arrow talked to me."

"Did he?"

She nodded, pointed chin bobbing rapid-fire as she pressed a palm to the gelding's winter-fuzzed shoulder. "He said he loves to run."

"Did he?"

"But he needs a little time to rest because his right hind leg is sore."

She glanced at Hunter, who shrugged. "He does seem a little off. But maybe if Tiger Lily brushes him, he'll feel better."

Lily stroked the gelding's parti-colored mane, eyes bright as moons. "Can I, Mama?"

Warmth flooded Vura like a spring tide. Strange, how just the sight of her daughter's impish face made the world right. Strange, how even though they spent the majority of their time together, it was nearly impossible to let her go. Still, she smiled and shifted her attention to Hunter. "As a matter of fact, I was wondering if maybe she could go back to Gray Horse with you."

"The Lily is always welcome with us." Though Hunter's words were absolutely gracious, and unquestionably sincere, surprise shone in his eyes.

"I wouldn't ask, but . . ." Off to her left, Tonk

was approaching with the gray mare. Her coat shone steel blue from her recent bath. "I just . . ." She winced, feeling guilty, though she could not, under threat of diets, have explained why. "I have some things I need to take care of."

"She can stay as long as you wish."

"Work-related . . ." she added and pulled her gaze from the man with the gray. Tonk's torso remained bare. Lean, dark-skinned muscle rippled above his leather breeches. She pursed her lips. Maybe Sydney's mustangs could spare enough of the winnings to buy him a new shirt. "Work-related things," she added and didn't bother to question why his state of undress concerned her.

Still, she could feel his gaze on her face and cleared her throat. "Is that all right with you, Lil?" she asked, and lifted her attention to her daughter's gamine features. A streak of mud highlighted her left cheek, but it would have been far more surprising if it had been clean.

"I get to stay with the horses?" she asked.

Hunter shrugged. "We humans are but a bothersome side note."

Vura shuffled her feet and kept her gaze from straying toward Tonk. "Would you mind keeping her overnight?"

"What's this?" Sydney asked, rounding the trailer to join them.

"The Lily will be staying with us for a time," Hunter said.

"Fantastic!" Sydney handed Lily a feather she'd retrieved from some unknown source. There had been a time when she'd seemed as cold as an arctic blast. But those days were long past, well before she had come to believe she could share a mother with someone as patently unsophisticated as Bravura Lambert. "We'll put her to work mucking stalls and scrubbing buckets."

"She's never going to want to come home," Vura joked and wondered with a peck of petty concern if it might be true.

"How long will she be with us?" Sydney asked.

"Well, I just . . . I have so much work to do." Her face felt as hot as a blowtorch. Tonk's attention felt even hotter, intensified by the lie. But she had no wish to tell her daughter that her father had returned. Not until they could spend time together. Could have a real family reunion. "It'd be great if I could pick her up in the morning."

"Oh man," Sydney said, and placed a hand on her fiancé's massive arm. "Hunt'll be in heaven."

Vura lifted her gaze to her daughter's. "Is that all right with you, Lily Belle?"

"Can I sleep in the barn with Arrow?" Her eyes were as round as agates.

Vura forced a laugh; she could count on one hand the number of times that she had left Lily overnight. "I'm going to leave that up to you guys," she said, glancing at Hunter before turning back to Lily. "You be good for them, okay?"

She nodded emphatically. "I'll scrub all the buckets twice."

"Well, give me a kiss first," Vura said.

Lily bent down, seeming blissfully impervious to the fact that she was perched five feet above the ground on an animal that could accelerate faster than a Ferrari.

Vura, on the other hand, couldn't quite seem to forget that the child could injure herself on a paper clip.

Chapter 5

Bravura opened the passenger door and slid onto the warm leather of her husband's newly purchased vehicle. The engine growled like a cheetah.

Dane waggled his brows at her. "Sweet ride, huh?"

"Yeah. Sweet." She cleared her throat, then tried and failed to curtail the next question. "What did it cost?" Connubial instincts suggested she enjoy the moment, go with the flow, but she was one mortgage payment from collecting ketchup packages from her local McDonald's. And though there was a hint of lingering cigarette smoke embedded in the plush ceiling fabric, the Viper still boasted that new car smell.

"I'm not going to lie to you; these babies don't

come cheap, but nothing's too good for my girl," Dane said, and backed across the grassy area that served as a parking lot.

As they turned onto Clay Street, Vura tried to find that carefree attitude they had once shared. But she was a mother now, a businesswoman, an employer and . . . dammit, how many times could she patch Lily's winter jacket before it fell apart like soggy shredded wheat? "How much?" she asked again.

"How much do I want you?" he asked, and shifted into third. The Viper fishtailed a little, spewing gravel as he slipped his hand onto her thigh. "Like crazy." His gaze was hot on her face. "Remember when I had old Jimmy? We got our money out of that thing, didn't we?" He slid his fingers along her thigh, smoothing them inward. Heat followed his fingertips. "And hey, the backseat in this thing is bigger than you'd think."

She resisted squirming, though honestly, she'd been living like a cloistered nun for most of her married life.

"Wanna try it out?" he asked, and traced his index finger over the center crease of her jeans.

She managed to shake her head. "It's just a few miles to the farm."

He shifted uncomfortably in the driver's seat. "I'm just glad the Vipe's insured against fire damage."

She gave him a look.

"Cuz I might spontaneously combust."

She shook her head at his theatrics and felt her troubles fall cautiously away. So what if he had purchased a new car? He was right, he had to get around. And it was good to have him back, to have him home. Leaning across the console between them, she slipped her hand onto his chest.

They careened onto Carver Road.

"Be careful," she warned, but he grinned as they roared up the final stretch toward home.

She was laughing as they squealed to a halt on the gravel outside their house, gasping as he pulled her into his arms and carried her toward the stairs that teetered down from a rickety porch.

"Mmm, you feel good," he said, and kissed her. Their lips met with a clash. Heat roared between them. He clattered up the steps, tripped near the top, and laughed at his own impatience. "Get the door, baby."

She fumbled to do so. The loose knob wobbled in her hand, but in a moment they were through. He let her feet slip to the floor and then he was kissing her full bore, fingers busy on her buttons. Cool air touched her skin, but in a moment it was replaced with his lips. He was already pushing her toward the floor.

"No. Dane. Not here." Desire roared through her, but this felt wrong. "The bedroom."

He swore in frustration, then hustled her backward. They laughed as they stumbled up the stairs, kicking off shoes, shedding clothes. By the time they reached the hallway, they were both panting. The backs of her knees hit the mattress. He peeled off her blouse, exhaled in reverent delight and cupped her breasts in both hands. "Man, I missed these."

"And me too, right?"

He lifted his face and smiled. "And you too," he said, and kissed her again, but this time the caress was warm and slow, full of the promise of forever.

"Are you really going to be home now?" She breathed the question.

"How could I leave you when you look like this?" he asked, and kissed his way down her neck.

"You left before."

"I'm home now, baby." He pulled her closer. "Let's make the most of it."

He was right, of course. He was so right, she thought, and kissed him with everything that was in her.

Desire and need and loneliness raged through her so hot and hungry she barely heard the sound that trickled up from downstairs. It took her a moment to recognize it as music, longer still to realize it was the ringtone that signaled a call from Hunter Redhawk.

"Oh." She pulled back a little, listening. "I've got to get that," she breathed, but Dane tightened his grip.

"What?" The word was little more than a panted gasp.

"The phone. I left it in my jacket."

"They'll call back," he said, and eased her toward the mattress, but she struggled against him.

"No." She wriggled out of his grasp and twisted around. "It's Hunt. There might be something wrong."

Seated on the mattress now, he scowled up at her, hands still on hers. "Baby, you've only been away from her a few minutes. We've been apart forever." His lips tilted up beguilingly, and he tugged gently on her fingers. "At least it seems that way."

He was right. Lily meant the world to her, but he was important too. The phone rang again, tearing her apart. "I'll be right back," she said and, pulling out of his grip, rushed downstairs.

"Hunt?" She breathed his name into the phone.

"Vura?" His voice sounded scratchy and distant.

"Is Lily all right?" She tried to smooth out her tone, but worry rippled through her.

There was a pause, a bit of garbled dialogue, then silence.

"Hunter?"

". . . will be well."

"What! What did you say?" She tightened her hand on the tiny phone. Worry turned to panic in the sharp beat of her heart. "What happened?"

"She . . . fault. I should not have allowed—"

Static filled the endless air between them.

"Is she okay? Hunt? Is Lily okay?"

"I do not . . . on our way . . . doctor . . ."

"Doctor?" Not again. Her head felt light. "What?"

". . . Custer Medical . . ."

"I'm on my way," she said, and headed for the door, phone still pressed to her ear. It took her a moment to realize she'd left her blouse upstairs. She spun toward the steps.

"I am . . ."

"Hunter! Hunt! Let me talk to her," Vura demanded, but the phone had gone dead.

"What's wrong?" Dane sat upright as she rushed into the bedroom.

"Lily's hurt!" She hit Redial as she searched for her hastily discarded clothes. "I've gotta go," she added and grabbed her bra from a sawhorse, her shirt from the floor.

"Hang on. Hang on!" Dane said. "You don't think I'm gonna let you go alone, do you?"

She hadn't even considered an alternative. "I just . . . I didn't . . ." She shook her head, mind reeling. "Thank you," she breathed and found his eyes with her own.

His fingers felt warm as they encompassed hers. "She's my daughter, too, Vey," he said, and kissed her lightly. "And you're my wife. Of course I'm going with you."

She nodded, realizing she didn't have to go it alone. Didn't have to be superwoman. Not anymore.

Chapter 6

"Let's go," Dane said and, grabbing his own shirt, tugged it on as they hurried toward the door.

Their feet tapped a frantic duet down the stairs. In a matter of moments the Viper's engine growled to life, and then they were flying up the driveway, gravel spraying in their wake.

"Where to?" Dane's expression was tense.

Still struggling with buttons, Vura steadied herself against the dashboard. "Custer Medical."

He nodded, no-nonsense. She had never loved him more. "What happened?"

"I'm not sure." Worry scoured her like a plague. It wasn't as though Lily was a stranger to the ER. She had sustained enough lacerations, abrasions, and contusions to open her own hospital wing, but at least Vura had been present for each emergency. "Just hurry. Please."

His face was grim as he glanced toward her. "I thought you could trust those people."

"I can. I do." But her mind was racing with doubts, clouded with guilt. She shouldn't have left Lily, should have been clearer about her daughter's propensity to find trouble, her heart-stopping ability to escape the house without so much as a whisper, her astounding need to climb on things that were not meant to be climbed. "Accidents happen."

He shook his head but kept silent as they careened around a corner. Still, it seemed like forever before they were pulling up beneath the emergency canopy. Vura was out and running before the Viper came to a complete stop, pushing through the door before another word was spoken.

"Lily Lambert." Her daughter's name felt desperate and raspy against her throat. "Where is she?"

"Excuse me?" The receptionist goddess behind the front desk looked peeved by Vura's very existence.

"A little girl, five years old, has she arrived yet?"

"Vura." Sydney appeared beside her suddenly.

Bravura turned, breath held, body stiff with panic as she shot her gaze down the hall and back. "Where's Lily?"

"Honey—"

"Where is she?" she snapped, and trying to forget her grandmother's last days here, twisted toward the hall that yawned like a dark maw into terror.

"Vura!" Sydney grabbed her arms, fingers tight, expression no-nonsense. "Lily's fine."

"What?" She yanked her gaze back to her sister's and tried to breathe, but her throat was tight with worry, raw with guilt. "What?"

"She had a little . . ." Sydney paused, expression

69

taut beneath troubled brows. "She had a little accident. But she's fine."

Vura scanned her face, searching for truth, for hope. "Then why is she here?"

Syd exhaled carefully. "Before you see her, I want you to remember that it looks worse than it is."

"Worse than what is? What happened?" she asked, and tried to jerk away, but Sydney snagged her back.

"Quit it!" she snapped.

Vura stilled.

Sydney inhaled slowly, exhaled audibly, reminding Vura with that one small motion that she had nearly died from a horse-related injury not so long before they had met. "Just breathe, honey. Breathe."

She did so, slowly, cautiously.

"It's not going to help if Lily sees you panicked."

Vura nodded, drew another shaky breath.

"There." Sydney inhaled with her. "Hunt's in the exam room with her."

Vura winced, finally remembering that in this little troop of walking wounded, Hunter was, perhaps, the most seriously injured. Not too long ago, he, too, had had a daughter. "How's he holding up?"

Sydney nodded, a tacit sign of approval. Funny, Vura had never quite realized she needed her sister's endorsement. "He'd walk through fire for her. You know that."

"I do." Vura let her shoulders relax a little, exhaled heavily. "I know. What room are they in?"

Worry echoed in Sydney's eyes. "I'll take you there."

They turned together.

"She's okay, Vura. She'll be all right. I promise. Her face is entirely unscathed. But . . ."

"But what?"

"There is some damage to her left ear."

Vura nodded, steeled herself.

"And there's quite a bit of blood."

"Blood?" The single word sounded faint to Vura's own ears, which was strange. She was no wilting violet. While other little girls had been wardrobing their Barbies, she had been building size-appropriate stables for her Breyer horses. And as teenage prom queens were primping in front of their full-length beveled mirrors, she'd been scooping up ground balls by the dozen. She'd been shortstop for the Black Diamond softball team for four consecutive years; she was no stranger to the emergency room. Still . . .

"But it's nothing life-threatening," Sydney added.

"Life-threatening!" The floor wobbled beneath her feet.

"She'll need a few stitches, though."

Her knees actually buckled.

"Don't!" Sydney's fingers clutched her arm again. "Don't lose it now. I'm not sure how much more Hunt can take."

"Hunter . . ." They were sisters . . . well, half sisters really, bound by the ties of blood. Still, Hunter Redhawk was the glue that held them together. "How's he doing?"

"He blames himself."

Vura winced. Guilt . . . so useless. So ubiquitous. "You're sure she's going to be okay."

"Absolutely."

"All right." She squared her shoulders, ready.

"Vey!"

Dane rushed through the door behind them. "What's going on?"

"She's going to be okay," Vura said.

"Thank God." He nodded, wrapped his arm around her shoulder, and thrust a hand toward Sydney. "You must be the long-lost sister."

"Yes." The upper-crust stiffness had returned so suddenly to Sydney's voice, it was difficult to remember the warmth that had imbued it only moments before.

He grinned a little. "You're almost as pretty as my Vey."

"Thank you. Lily's this way," Syd said, and led them down a hallway that echoed with worry. In a moment they were opening the door to a miniscule exam room.

A woman straightened and turned toward them,

trendy, horn-rimmed glasses reflecting the light. "Hello, Bravura." Behind her, Hunter looked as if he had been turned to stone, eyes glassy, features chiseled. Lily was entirely hidden.

"Dr. Shelby," Vura said, and stepped inside.

"It's nice to see you again."

"You too," Vura said, and in that moment the good doctor stepped aside.

That's when the floor lurched beneath Vura's feet. Lily's face, perpetually dirty, was all but covered in blood.

"Hi, Mama."

Vura steadied herself with one hand on the exam table and made her lips form the appropriate words.

"Hey, baby."

Lily grinned. Her teeth were pink.

Dane gasped. Lily's eyes went round as she raised them to her father's horrified face. "Papa?"

"She broke a tooth?" Dane snarled. "You people let her break her teeth?"

"No! No." Vura shook her head, keeping her voice even. "She lost that one weeks ago."

"Then what happened?"

The doctor scowled. "We're ascertaining that right now, Mr. . . . ."

"Lambert." He shifted his gaze to Hunter. An odd glint of territorialism shone in his eyes. "I'm the husband."

Dr. Shelby nodded. "I'm still examining her, Mr. Lambert, but I don't believe there has been significant damage to anything but the auricle of her right ear."

"Look," Lily said, and twisted sharply toward the wall. Her ear, that tiny innocent swirl, drooped toward her lobe like a sodden flag. "Hunk says I'm a warrior now."

Dane swore.

A muscle jumped in Hunter's cheek.

The doctor's brows dipped. "Perhaps it would be best if you waited outside, Mr. Lambert."

"Maybe *you*—" Dane began, but Sydney was already nudging him sternly back toward the hall. They were out of sight in a moment. The door closed quietly behind them.

The world seemed as silent as a tomb.

Vura drew a steadying breath. "Are you okay, baby?" she asked, and knelt beside Hunter's massive thigh.

Lily reached up to touch her ear, but Hunt curled a hand around her arm and tugged it gently back into her lap.

"Let it be, little warrior," he said.

She nodded, sighed, and turned her gaze back to Vura. "Black Angel's a good mama, Mama."

Vura's stomach roiled, though she could no longer see the ravaged ear. Reaching up, she placed a hand over Hunter's, effectively touching him and her daughter simultaneously. "What, honey?" she asked and, exhaling carefully, found Lily's eyes. Those perfect, undamaged eyes.

"That's why she bit me," Lily explained, school-marm voice firmly in place. "She was just trying to protect her baby."

Hunter clenched his jaw. Against Vura's arm, his thigh felt as hard as granite. "Brandon Coby stopped by with his mare." His voice was low and graveled. "She'd just dropped a foal a couple weeks ago." A tic jumped in his cheek. Self-condemnation shadowed his eyes. "I thought Lily was still filling the hay bags." He swallowed, mouth pursed. "Still inside the horse trailer. I should have . . ." He paused, fought for control. "I should have—"

"It's okay, Hunk," Lily said and, lifting one blood-smeared hand, laid the palm gently against his dark-skinned cheek. "It's just an ear. 'Sides, it doesn't hurt much."

Vura raised her gaze to the doctor.

"Fortunately, there aren't many nerve endings in that portion of the ear. And . . ." Dr. Shelby scowled a little, assessing her tiny patient. "She could be a little shocky."

Hunter's lips twitched. His eyes were unusually bright.

"Unfortunately, we don't have a cosmetic surgeon on staff. But I've had a good deal of experience since coming here." She smiled, not voicing the fact that a surprising amount of that experience had been practiced on Lily. "I've treated everything from blisters to gunshot wounds, so I could stitch it up myself. Or we can call in a specialist."

"How long before the surgeon could get here?" Vura said.

"It's impossible to say. At least an hour. More if other patients are waiting."

Vura nodded, winced. "And what about . . ." She paused. Now wasn't a good time to bring up finances, but in her experience, poverty was rarely convenient. "What about the cost difference?" Guilt flared up like a bitching ulcer. What kind of mother didn't have the necessary funds to treat her own child? "I'll do whatever's best for Lily, of course, and I have insurance," she rushed to add. "But my deductible's pretty—"

"I'm paying." The rumbled words were almost inaudible.

"No." Vura shifted her gaze back to Hunter. "You're not," she said, but when he turned toward her, she saw that one diamond-bright tear had escaped the dark barricade of his lashes.

"Listen, Hunt . . ." Her chest physically ached at the sight of his anguish. "This isn't—"

"Please." The tear traced a groove beside his full lips.

"All right," she said. "Okay."

Hunter nodded, cleared his throat, and lifted his gaze to the doctor's. "Can you contact the surgeon? See how long it would take him to get here?"

"Her," she corrected, and smiled. "I'll do that." In a moment she had left the room.

Vura forced a smile and rose to her feet.

Hunter stood up beside her. For one elongated moment, he held the child against his heart like a fragile blossom, but finally he handed her over.

Lily wrapped her spindly arms around Vura's neck, sending a shiver of gratitude skittering toward her heart. But she forced herself to meet Hunter's gaze.

"You don't have to pay," she said, but he shook his head.

"You are wrong," he said simply, and left.

The room went silent.

Lily sighed, distractedly twirling a finger in Vura's disheveled hair. "Do you think I'll have a scar, Mama?"

Careful not to jostle her battered daughter, Vura settled carefully into Hunter's just-abandoned chair.

A scar, she thought. They were lucky she still had an ear. "I don't know, honey. But try not to worry about it. I'm sure the doctors will do everything they can."

"I hopes I do," Lily said, and sighed. The sound whistled quietly through the gap in her incisors. "Cuz then for the rest of my whole entire life, everyone will know I'm a warrior."

Chapter 7

It took three hours for the surgeon to arrive. By then, Vura had said a hundred prayers, read *Buffalo Knees* a dozen times, and brightened her daughter's day considerably by telling her of Tonk's intention to bring his horses by. When they escaped to the lobby, forty-seven stitches had been sewn into Lily's battered ear.

Hunter rose to his feet, eyes haunted, big hands clenched.

Beside him, Sydney smiled. "I didn't even think it was possible," she said, and shook her head.

Lily blinked her marble-round eyes. It was late now and she wobbled a little as she squeezed Vura's index finger in one tight fist.

"But you're cuter than ever." Sydney narrowed her eyes as if trying to decipher the ways of the world. "If I had known that getting bit by a horse makes you prettier, I would have tried it years ago."

Lily wrinkled her garden-fairy nose. "I don't want to be pretty."

"Well, that's unfortunate," Sydney said.

"I wanna be tough," Lily said and, dropping her mother's hand, crossed the floor to Hunter. He lifted her in his arms as if she were as fragile as a dove's egg. "Like Hunk."

Hunter, Vura noticed, looked rather suspiciously as if he might burst into tears like a spanked toddler, but if Lily was aware of that fact, she didn't make mention. Perhaps the child was a bit more diplomatic than her mother.

Lily's face contorted. "Truth is . . ." The words were a whisper, meant for Hunter alone. "I was kinda scared."

His arms tightened around her, and his jaw clenched as she settled her earnest gaze on his.

"Can I still be a warrior, anyways?"

His lips trembled traitorously. Closing his eyes, he smoothed a broad hand down her runaway hair. "You are the mightiest warrior I have ever known, little one."

"Honest?"

He cleared his throat and refused to look at the women who watched too closely, could see too much. "We shall call you Brave Flower."

Her eyes widened even more. "Brave Flower," she lisped and smiled crookedly. "I like it." Sighing, she rested her head against his chest. His expression suggested he was being subjected to yet another form of diabolical torture.

Vura glanced at her sister, wondering how much he could take.

"He'll be all right," Sydney assured her and, slipping her arm around Vura's shoulders, turned her toward the exit.

"Are you sure?"

"He's tougher than he looks."

"Normally I wouldn't have even thought that was possible," Vura said, and Sydney chuckled.

"Hey . . ." Lily said, glancing up suddenly. "Where's Papa?"

It wasn't until that moment that Vura realized she had forgotten about Dane completely. Guilt sloshed messily with irritation.

"He, umm . . ." Sydney smiled, caught the girl's gaze with her own, and shrugged a little. "He had to go."

"He left?" Lily asked.

Hunter's brows dipped the slightest degree, but he said nothing.

"He had some very important things he had to do. But he was extremely worried about you."

"What important things?" Lily's voice was curious, entirely devoid of either irritation or guilt.

"I'm sure he'll tell you when you see him," Sydney said.

"Is he coming to the farm?" Lily brightened.

"Well, I'm certain he'll want to see you as soon as possible," Sydney told her and carefully tucked a wayward lock behind her undamaged ear. "He was very worried. But he looked exhausted. He'll probably be sawing logs by the time you get there."

"Sawing logs?" She narrowed her eyes. "In the dark?"

Sydney laughed. Hunter still looked as if he might not survive the ordeal, and Vura abolished the newest wash of emotion without trying to identify it. Lily would heal. Her little ear might always bear a scar, but her daughter would be fine. For that she'd be eternally grateful. "Thanks for staying," she said, and Hunt huffed an indiscernible growl.

Sydney was more articulate. "We're so sorry, Vura."

"Sorry enough to give us a ride back to the rodeo grounds?" Now that the crisis had passed, Vura felt as if the energy had been sucked out of her by a wet vac. Still, she doubted if she was as exhausted as Hunter, who looked as if he were fighting a legion of diabolical demons.

Slipping a hand through his arm, she gave him a little shoulder bump.

"We're driving you home," he said.

"Uh-uh." Vura shook her head. "We've taken up enough of your time already."

"We will drive you home," he repeated. "And deliver your truck later."

Outside, it had begun to rain, small, sharp drops that slanted in from the northwest and froze on contact. "You don't have to do that," she said, but Sydney disagreed.

"I think he actually does."

Vura tried to remain adamant, but she was too tired to argue. It was a tight fit inside Hunt's ancient pickup truck, but they managed to squeeze in, Sydney in the middle, Lily tucked like a precious blossom onto Vura's lap. It was a much slower trip home than it had been to the hospital. Time rolled lazily toward midnight.

"I'm sorry we kept you from your mustangs," Vura said, and smoothed a hand down her daughter's melted gold hair. The gesture was, she knew, entirely for her own benefit. Lily was already asleep, purple sutures dark against the delicate curl of her ear.

"Tonk did chores for us." Sydney slipped her knuckles over Lily's satin cheek.

"Chores!" Vura gasped but kept the tone quiet. "Shoot! I forgot about the birds." She snapped her guilty gaze to her daughter. Lily loved their motley flocks, but the child's eyes remained closed, downy lashes soft against flushed cheeks. "If the coyotes—"

"They're fine," Sydney said.

Vura steadied herself with a hand on the door as they took a careful turn onto the gravel.

"Tonk called a couple of times to check on Lily." Reaching out again, Sydney smoothed a wrinkle out of the child's lilac sweatshirt. "Said he'd already herded the chickens in for the night."

Vura dropped her head against the battered cushion behind her. "You can herd chickens?"

"Maybe it's an Indian thing." Sydney shrugged. "Or he might have had help."

Vura's hand joined her sister's on the dash. Her fingers looked surprisingly dark in comparison to Sydney's. "She didn't look like the poultry type."

"What?" Sydney turned toward her, surprised expression close in the darkness.

Vura immediately felt like an idiot. She didn't care if Tonk was given mouth-to-mouth by every busty skank in the state of South Dakota. "The redhead," she explained, and managed, quite admirably, she thought, to keep her tone as bland as oatmeal. "It was a good thing she was there."

The cab went absolutely quiet.

"To resuscitate him," Vura explained.

Hunt's brows had risen a half a hair. With another, the mannerism might have gone unnoticed. With Hunter Redhawk it was as loud as a shout.

"Okay," Sydney agreed. "But I was actually thinking about Mutt."

"Oh!" Vura tightened her grip on the dash and tried not to feel like an imbecile. How could she have forgotten about his dog? Mutt was, without a doubt, the ugliest canine to ever have lived. His coat, an indeterminate color to begin with, was as motley as an old rug. Half of his left ear was missing, and after a fight with an unfortunate adversary, it had been necessary to suture his right eye closed. Proving the old adage, she was sure, that it was wisest not to antagonize ugly enemies . . . they had nothing to lose.

The cab was silent again as their headlights

83

swept across her shabby yard. It was, Vura noticed, devoid of Dane's Viper. There was no reason in the world, she was certain, that that fact should make her angry at Tonk.

"Mutt. Sure. His dog. Well . . ." She cleared her throat as Hunt shifted into Park. "Thank him for me, will you?"

Hunter turned the key. The engine shuddered to a miserable death. "My brother or the dog?"

"What?"

"Do I thank Tonk or Mutt?"

"Both." Vura forced a quiet laugh and smoothed another hand down her daughter's hair, stealing a sliver of peace from the contact. "Well, I'm going to put her to bed. You don't have to come in." She eased open her door, but Hunter was already rounding the bumper of his truck.

"May I take her?" In the uncertain light, with the raindrops striking sharp and quick, his face looked as if it had been chiseled from ancient stone.

For a moment Vura found it almost impossible to loosen her grip, but his haunted expression convinced her to share. Turning, she settled her daughter carefully into the big man's outstretched arms. Lily sighed once and dropped her thistle-down head against his chest. His lips jerked under the onslaught, but he bore up and turned, foot-steps almost silent against the gravel, absolutely soundless on the hideous living room carpet.

"Upstairs?" he asked.

She nodded. "Put her . . ." She exhaled softly. Lily was fine. She knew that . . . and yet. "Put her in my bed, will you?"

He nodded once, dark eyes shining, and then he was gone, leaving her alone with her sister.

Sydney rubbed her hands together and glanced around the kitchen. "I've always admired this wallpaper." Oddly proportioned chickens perused them from every angle. Banties, Rhode Island Reds, Wyandottes, Orpingtons.

Vura raised a brow. "You ought to see the bathroom."

"Ducks?" Sydney guessed.

"Pigs."

"You're kidding."

"I wish. Want some coffee?"

"At ten o'clock at night?"

Vura shot her a glance. She had never known her sister to turn down caffeine.

"Make it quick," Sydney whispered.

Vura grinned as she reached for the coffeemaker that perpetually occupied her counter. "Don't tell me Hunt's trying to limit your intake again."

"He's such a bully," Sydney said, and Vura laughed. A bully he was not. A puppy maybe, or a teddy bear, possibly a wooly caterpillar. "You okay?"

"Yeah. Sure." Vura exhaled as she dumped water into the reservoir.

"I can't tell you how sorry I am."

"It's not your fault." She closed her eyes for a second as exhaustion washed over her in a fresh wave. "I just . . ." She shook her head and continued with the coffee preparations. "I shouldn't have—"

"No!" Sydney put a hand over her sister's. "Don't even start with the shouldn't-haves. You did everything right, honey. It was my fault."

Vura laughed and punched the appropriate button. "Maybe if we both share the blame, Hunt won't have to lift all of it."

Sydney glanced toward the stairs, where he had yet to reappear. "He's pretty strong."

It was the understatement of the decade. Still . . . "Can you convince him to forgive himself?"

"Probably not, but I'll try." Sydney glared at the unoffending coffeemaker. "We'll be so careful from now on. Like hawks. I promise."

Vura shook her head, settled her hips against the counter, and glanced out the window. So far she'd only managed to repair one of them. "Horses are dangerous."

"Yes." Sydney sighed. "I'm aware."

"Oh man!" Vura said, guilt and foolishness vying for room in her overtaxed emotional system. "I'm sorry. I didn't-t—" she began, but her sister waved away her worry.

"You know what?" She glanced out the same window, looking as if her thoughts were a thousand miles away. "I'm glad it happened."

"What?"

"Not this! Geez, not this," Sydney repeated, looking appalled. "*My* accident."

"The accident in which you broke your back and shattered your femur and lost your chance at a place on the Olympic team?"

"Yeah." Sydney grinned. The expression was a little shaky.

"The accident in which you nearly died?"

"That's the one."

"Tell me how that was such a boon," Vura said.

She smiled, a little sheepish, a little rueful. "I wouldn't have come here otherwise." She shrugged. "Wouldn't have seen this way of life. Wouldn't have found Courage."

Courage . . . the first mustang Sydney Wellesley had saved. But maybe that wasn't the courage she was talking about. It was hard to say. "Wouldn't have met you," she added.

"Or Hunter," Vura supposed and poured a cup of coffee. It didn't look quite right, but hers never did.

"Or Hunter," Sydney admitted and took the cup she offered.

A black and white rooster was stamped on the mug. A Dorking, Vura thought, and fervently wished she didn't know so much about poultry.

Sydney sampled her brew, then lifted her brows and lowered the cup.

"It's awful, isn't it?" Vura asked, and her sister

laughed. She did so easily these days. A complete transformation from the cool elitist who had arrived at the Lazy Windmill Guest Ranch just a few months before.

"Not awful . . ." she began, but Hunter appeared from the stairwell, expression somber.

"If you lie, she will only give you more."

Sydney wrinkled her nose, an expression that would never have crossed her regal features a year before. "I think you might have forgotten the coffee grounds."

"Seriously?"

"But you're an excellent carpenter, Bravura."

"And mother," Hunter added.

"Yeah. You're doing a fabulous job with Lily," Sydney added, and took another sip.

An additional dose of uncertainty zipped through Vura. She glanced toward the steps up which her daughter, the light of her life, had disappeared. "Are you sure?"

"I'm no expert on the subject." Sydney's mother had left her before her fourth birthday, and *she* had been the better of her two parents by far. "But I'm pretty confident."

"I *am* an expert," Hunter rumbled and taking the cup from his fiancée's hand, set it on the counter. By all accounts, *his* parents should have been canonized. The good, it turned out, *did* often die young. "And I'm absolutely sure."

"Thank you," Vura said, and in an effort to

refrain from blubbering like a prom queen, changed the subject. "Did, um . . ." She poured herself a cup of coffee. It did look pretty pale. "Dane didn't say where he was going, did he?"

"He was terribly worried," Sydney said.

"I know."

"I didn't realize until tonight how hard it is to sit and wait when someone's in surgery."

Yet Sydney had done just that, as had Hunter.

"I bet he's . . ." Sydney paused for a moment as if searching her imagination. "His parents live around here, right?"

"Up by Hill City." Setting her mug of non-coffee aside, Vura rinsed the glass Lily had used for breakfast. It seemed like a lifetime ago.

"Maybe he went there. He's been away from home a long time. He's probably checking in with them."

It was doubtful. His father barely spoke to him, and while that relationship annoyed Dane, his mother's simpering attentions seemed to bother him even more. He rarely visited them, always preferring more raucous company.

"I bet you're right," Vura agreed and stared dismally out her kitchen window at the darkness beyond. "I bet that's what he's doing."

Chapter 8

"Tonk!"

"There he is! The Indian of the hour."

"Tonkiaishawien!" The greetings rang loud, if a little unsteady as Tonk entered the Branding Iron Bar and Grill. It was an auspicious nomenclature considering its only concession to the glory of the Old West was one rusty horseshoe hanging kittywampus beside the window. In fact, the word *dive* might have been considered a euphemism, but Tonk had been in worse. Hell, who was he kidding? He'd had some of the best times he'd never remember in places considerably more crude. And tonight, he didn't want to be alone.

So he settled into a high-backed booth near the kitchen where the scents of burnt oil and ketchup were strong enough to make his stomach clench with something other than nerves. "Brothers," he said, and gave his companions a nod. Technically, only he and Riley shared blood. Though they were all remotely linked by Native genes.

They raised their glasses in unison. Four men, all a little glassy-eyed. In the bad old days, there would have been five, maybe even seven. Like Garth, Tonk had friends in low places. Just not as many as he used to. He sighed in silence and wished he liked country music. So much more acceptable than the alternative.

"Nice place," he said, and glanced around. The single, open room was crowded with cowboys, plowboys, and the occasional slumming suburbanite.

"Better than that hole in Mandan. Remember?" Jake Teton had shared a relay team with Tonk on more than one occasion. Now, Teton and his cousins ran an opposing trio of horses on an on-again, off-again basis. "Petey got drunk as a skunk and challenged that slick dude to a wrestling match. Then you jumped in. Remember?"

Tonk nodded, though in reality, he didn't remember much. Petey had not been the only one who had enjoyed one too many. Or, if he was going to be honest, an idea with which Bill W seemed outrageously enamored, *ten* too many.

Off to Tonk's left a trio of twenty-something girls were sharing laughs and secrets while eying the occupants of his booth. Their dark, glossy hair shone in the dingy overhead lights, and their smiles reflected interest. But they seemed painfully young, regrettably empty-headed, and Tonk had discovered, not so long ago, that he preferred the company of more mature-minded women. Women with a plan . . . maybe even a purpose. It had been the most depressing day of his life.

"You okay?" Monroe Jackson was one of

Tonk's holders and had a knack for keeping horses quiet in the box even when their comrades were galloping in at breakneck speeds. He wasn't much older than the girls who watched them, but he was a little more intuitive than the other guys. Or perhaps, more precisely, he was just a little less drunk.

"Ai." Tonk gave him a ghost of a smile and wished the girls were older. "I am well."

Riley Old Horn watched him in silence from beneath his battered cap. A corkscrewing bucking bull was emblazoned above its brim.

"Of course he's well!" Bill Pretty Weasel was short and broad with a crooked nose that spoke of one too many disagreements. His eyes had taken on that far-seeing wisdom that only Jim Beam and his unimpeachable ilk could impart. "He just won the jackpot."

"Ai." Jake's slow Native rhythm was accented with a belch.

"Hear, hear." Jackson raised his glass. Beer sloshed onto the table. The tantalizing scent of hops and hopelessness filled Tonk's nostrils like a tonic. But he tugged his sticky gaze from the uplifted mugs and nodded sagely.

"The Great Spirit smiled on us today."

"Yeah, and your ponies ran their tails off."

Tonk grinned, wished like hell he had a mug to raise. "And my ponies ran their tails off."

"Geez." Jackson shook his head. The motion

seemed a little erratic. He had cut his hair in Iroquois tradition. The single strip stood straight and tall down the center of his shaven head, only bobbling a little as he spoke. "I thought you were dead, Tonk."

"Not yet," he said, and curled his fingers into a fist beneath the table. At the far side of the bar, a couple was slow dancing to "Blue Skies." Their disjointed rhythm gave only a passing nod to Willie's rendition of Fitzgerald's hit from the twenties.

"That was some daredevil stunt," Jake said.

"Gotta give the people something to remember us by," Tonk said.

"I'll drink to that," Jackson said, and did so. The others joined in.

"Hey! Get a beer for the number-one relay rider in the country, will ya, honey?" Jake yelled, but Tonk shook his head, keeping his gaze off the beer that seemed as ubiquitous as rainwater suddenly. Ahead of him, a fair-haired fellow in a black cowboy shirt embroidered with yellow roses leaned across the table, exposing his partner's face for a moment.

Sherri Unger's penciled brows lifted as she recognized him. Her lips rose in a sly bow of feminine calculation.

Tonk nodded. She smiled and spoke to her partner, who didn't turn around, and in a moment his Western-cut yoke obliterated her face again.

"I just came for the company," Tonk said.

Jake glanced behind him, caught a glimpse of Sherri's carefully displayed cleavage, and laughed.

A leggy waitress arrived, shifting feet that suggested she'd been on them too long. "What can I get you?"

"Just a Coke."

She gave him a nod and returned to the kitchen, letting Tonk settle back against the worn oak behind him.

"A Coke!" Jake shook his head and drank. A dollop of foam stuck to the bristle on his upper lip. Who said Indians couldn't grow beards? Tonk's grandmother had sported a five o'clock shadow every day by noon. He remembered the old woman's rumpled face with fondness and trepidation. She had a backhand swing that would have made Serena Williams blush. She was also the first person to suggest he was not responsible for every misfortune that crossed his path, his parents' contempt included. It was a concept he was, at times, still struggling to accept.

But the mellow memory of his foster parents, Hunter Redhawk's biological antecedents, loosened the half hitch in his gut a little. They had saved him, braved his moods, eased his insecurities, nurtured his talents.

"Geez!" Jake said, and gave his head a wobbly shake. "If my ponies had run like yours, I'd buy a round for the house."

Tonk let his lips twist up a little. "If your ponies had run like mine, Jake Teton, you would have fallen on your ass."

Monroe Jackson chuckled in his beer. Pretty Weasel laughed out loud and slapped Teton on the back just to demonstrate there were no hard feelings. Across the room, a quartet of women flirting with their fourth decade sang "Save a Horse (Ride a Cowboy)" without the muffling comfort of a karaoke machine.

The bawdy lyrics soaked under Tonk's skin, easing his loneliness, dousing his tension. This was what he missed. Not the beer. Not the whiskey. Certainly not the hangovers. But this. This accepting camaraderie. This . . . Well, maybe he missed the beer some, he admitted, and felt his fingers quiver a little beneath the table.

"Tonk."

"Ai?" He pulled his attention from Monroe's brew to his face, realizing he had missed a few words of conversation.

"I said you wouldn't take twice that for Sky Bird. Right?"

Okay, so maybe he had missed more than a few. He glanced around the familiar faces, trying to catch up, to figure out what monetary worth they might put on the mare who would, and did, run her heart out for him.

"I *might* consider selling her for twice that . . . to someone I trust," he said, though, honestly, he still wasn't sure what number was being bandied about.

"Yeah?" Jake straightened, expression sober. Teton's team lacked a good anchor horse, and Sky Bird was one of the best.

Tonk tilted his head, paused a beat, and added, "Or three times that from you."

Teton huffed a snort, drank again.

Tonk watched him raise his mug, watched him drain his beer, so casual, as if it wasn't poison, as if he wasn't being consumed by it instead of vice versa. Oh yes, he had been consumed. There had been a time after his parents' car accident when he had been as self-destructive as a runaway train. Gambling, loan sharks, bar brawls. He had tried it all. And yet he survived. Life . . . it was a mystery.

"Here you go," the waitress said, and set a Coke beside Tonk's elbow. He'd washed off his war paint, had pulled on a chambray shirt and well-worn jeans in the dubious comfort of his horse trailer's tack compartment.

He glanced up now. "My thanks," he said, though he would rather be staked naked on a red-ant hill than drink this diluted sugar water. "What do I owe you?"

"I heard you were the big winner at the relay today."

She was pretty. Short hair, soft eyes, long limbs. But no dimples, no freckles, no dark halo of wild

96

wind hair that made a man's hands tremble to touch it. "The Great Spirit smiled on me."

She did too, just the slightest shift of her unvarnished lips. "Well, if the Spirit's happy with you, I guess this one's on the house," she said and, winking, turned toward the kitchen.

"Man," Pretty Weasel said, and watched her hips as she swung through the kitchen door and out of sight.

Teton blew out a breath. "How the hell do you do that?"

Tonk took a sip of his beverage. It was just as awful as he had anticipated. "Do what, brother?"

Pretty Weasel shook his head. The motion tilted him a little to the left. He was reaching full capacity. "I could be buck naked and dry as a cocklebur and she wouldn't even glance my way."

"I have seen you naked, brother," Tonk said and, grinning a little, forced himself to take another sip. "Believe this, she would glance."

"Then run screaming for the Hills," Jake said.

Jackson chuckled. Pretty Weasel grinned, sheepish and self-effacing. Some men were mean when drunk. Pretty Weasel was not.

Up ahead, Sherri rose abruptly. Her partner stood, too, speaking rapidly. His words weren't audible, but the tone was clear. Whiny with a touch of defensive.

"I didn't come back here . . ." Her words were

lost for a second. "I don't care if you inherit the entire state of Omaha."

He responded quietly.

She paused, scowling, perhaps rethinking geography. Women . . . Tonk thought . . . they weren't always brilliant. They weren't always gorgeous. Still, they drew him in a thousand indefinable ways. But perhaps it was their ability to forgive that appealed to him most.

Sherri's expression softened.

"He can't hold on forever, baby," Embroidered Roses said and, stepping around the table, slipped a hand down her tightly cinched waist. She turned away. The remainder of his dialogue was drowned in the ambient noise, but apparently whatever line he used worked magic because they left together, ducking through the crowd.

Tonk sighed to himself. So sad really, that he wouldn't be the one to take her home. But sadder still, heartbreakingly so, was that even if he was that lucky gentleman, it would not be enough. Not today. Not ever.

Somewhere in his mind a freckle-faced girl-next-door laughed with saloon girl gusto.

"You know what you need?" Pretty Weasel asked.

Yes, Tonk thought as a pair of capricious dimples flashed in his mind, but he wasn't going to get it.

Chapter 9

The aroma of fresh coffee was the first thing Vura noticed.

Her husband was the second.

"Dane!" She stopped short. He was standing, perfectly groomed and adorably coiffed, inside her disgusting kitchen. Flipping an egg, he grinned over his shoulder at her.

"I made you breakfast," he said.

"How did you . . ." She glanced at her entry, remembered he had a key to the door she tried really hard to remember to lock, and shook her head. "When did you get here?" He hadn't come to bed. And why was that? There had been a time when they couldn't keep their hands off each other. Not that she needed that. They'd grown up, matured. But it had been a long time. More than a year. Was she that unattractive?

He turned toward her, looking clean and close shaven. His turquoise shirt cast his eyes a deeper shade of blue. She felt crusty and exhausted by comparison.

"Listen, I'm sorry about last night," he said.

A whisper of aging doubt slipped between the chinks in her armor. "What about last night?"

"I shouldn't have left."

No, he shouldn't have, she thought, but didn't voice the words. "Where'd you go?"

He shook his head, expression apologetic. "I had to get out of there. Hospitals . . ." Twisting away a little, he switched off the burner. His hips were lean, his jeans designer. "They give me the willies. Ever since . . ." He paused, lifted the pan from the stove, and gave her that mischievous choirboy grin that could still set her heart aflutter. "Over easy, right?"

"Yeah." She understood his aversion to hospitals. He had only been six when his brother had died. Leukemia, hard fought and long mourned. The tragedy had left him an only child. Able to do no wrong in his mother's eyes . . . no right in his father's. Familial jealousy was not confined to siblings . . . at least according to Dane. "Thanks."

"Sit down." He motioned toward a chair. The cushion boasted a jaunty Rhode Island White. When she'd bought the house, the sellers had assured her she could keep the furniture. She had neglected to ask how much more she'd have to pay to have it removed. "Please."

She sat. He slid the eggs onto a plate, half-hiding the bold sunflower design that covered the surface. She'd inherited the dishes from her father, who had received them from a former admirer with incisors the size of kettle corn. Vura had always preferred the plates to the gifter.

The toaster popped. "White bread," Dane said.

"No nutrients whatsoever." He grinned as he opened the tub of margarine. "Every inch buttered." He slathered the toast generously, cut the pieces on the diagonal, and set them on the plate in front of her. "What do you think?"

"Looks great," she said, but her stomach felt a little jumpy. She didn't like controversy. True, she could spar with the best of them regarding shake shingles versus asphalt, but she needed peace in her home. "I just . . ." She shrugged.

"What?"

She looked up. "It would have been nice if you were there when Lily got out."

"You know I hate those places!" He took a deep breath, tightened a fist, and forced a smile. "After Jeremy died . . ." He winced, eyes as sad as a dirge.

"I'm sorry," she said.

"No." He sat down beside her, perching quickly on the edge of his seat. "*I'm* sorry. I want to be here for you, Vey. For Lily."

"I want you to be, too."

"Do you?" Grasping her hand, he tugged it against his chest. His fingers were always warm. He had laughingly said once that he had thought she'd married him for his body, but as it turned out she only coveted his body *heat*.

She stared at their intertwined fingers. "You know I do."

"Good." He grazed her knuckles with his thumb.

101

"Because I'm ready to pick up where we left off."

She inhaled softly. "I'd like to, but . . ." She paused, uncertain. Still, he seemed oblivious to her doubts. Turning her hand in his, he kissed her wrist, and despite her misgivings, warmth shimmered up her arm.

"Like to what?" he asked, and shifted closer. She could smell his aftershave, musty and a little overstrong. "Like to make love to me?"

She couldn't meet his eyes, and he chuckled. "Still as shy as a fawn about some things. So sexy." He kissed the corner of her mouth. She could feel the old weakness sift in, melting her resistance. "Come upstairs with me. I'll—"

"Mama?" The voice jolted her like an electric prod. She twisted toward the doorway. Lily stood there, hair tousled as she knuckled one eye.

"Baby." Heat diffused Vura's cheeks, though she knew she shouldn't feel guilty; Dane was her husband. Lily's father! "How are you feeling?"

The fuzzy, caramel-colored brows inched down a little. "It itches."

"I'm sorry." She held out her arms. Lily slipped into them, eyeing her father as she eased onto Vura's lap. "Papa's home," she said, and smiled at Dane over the top of their child's disheveled hair.

"I got my ear bit," Lily informed him.

Dane flashed a winning smile, and if a muscle ticked, almost hidden, in his jaw, who could blame him? They'd barely had two minutes alone

102

together. "I know, sweetie," he said. "I was there at the hospital, remember?"

For a little while anyway, Vura thought, and felt immediately ashamed of her uncharitable musings. He had every right to be uncomfortable in hospitals. Then again, there probably hadn't been a single soul in the entire complex who wouldn't rather have been elsewhere.

Lily reached for her damaged ear, but Vura caught her arm and kissed her fingers. She grinned, as charming as her father in a thousand tiny ways. "Hunk said I'm a warrior now."

"Hunk?" Dane asked.

"Hunter," Vura corrected and tucked her daughter's hand safely against her tummy. "Hunter Redhawk."

Lily bobbed a nod. "He's my friend. And the strongest man in the world. He carried me into the hospital and kept me safe until Mama got there."

"That's nice, sweetheart," Dane said, "but if he had kept you safe in the first place, you wouldn't have had to be there at all."

Lily's brows lowered in immediate defense. "It wasn't his fault."

Vura, too, had stiffened at Dane's accusation, but she forced herself to relax, to smile. "Papa made us some eggs," she said.

"Warriors work up an appetite, right?"

Lily blinked at him. "Whose are those?"

Dane raised a questioning brow at Vura, who

smiled and brushed hair away from her daughter's fairy-bright face.

"Lily likes to know which of the hens laid the eggs so she can thank them later."

Dane laughed. "Well, I'm not sure who laid them, but I fried them."

"Not long enough."

"What?"

Lily wrinkled her undersized nose. "They're kinda gooey."

"Lily," Vura reprimanded. "Thank your daddy."

She pursed her lips . . . a small display of rebellion followed by immediate capitulation. "Thank you, Papa."

"You're welcome. Say . . ." He rose to his feet. "I was thinking . . . maybe we could head out to Rapid City today. Do a little shopping, maybe take in a movie."

Tension crept back in, tinged with a touch of resentment. It was Monday morning. Vura had a three-man crew working on Mrs. Washburn's kitchen. The renovations had to be completed by Mother's Day. Some called the scrappy octogenarian feisty. Some called her cantankerous. But everybody agreed that Mrs. Washburn got what Mrs. Washburn wanted or every single occupant of Custer County would know why. And Saw Horse Construction couldn't afford a bad review so early after its inception. "I'm afraid I have to work today," Vura said. "But, hey . . ." She tightened her arms around Lily's waist and forced herself to sound upbeat as she shifted her gaze to Dane's. "Maybe Dad wouldn't mind if you took Lily today."

"What?" Father and daughter spoke in unison.

Vura glanced at Lily's face. The word *skeptical* would barely scratch the surface. She gave the tiny shoulder a playful nudge. "Dad usually takes Lily on Mondays, but maybe he'd be okay with you two spending the day together."

"Lily and I?"

"Yeah."

"Well . . . that'd be great," Dane said. "How about it, Lil? Just you and . . . Ohhhhh!" He tilted his head back as if wildly disappointed. "I almost forgot; I've got a job interview this morning."

"What?" Vura asked, and handed Lily a half slice of toast. "Already?"

"I wanted to get a jump on things," he said, and rose abruptly.

"Well . . . maybe she could go with you."

He laughed. "I don't think that would be very professional. Do you? In fact . . ." He pulled out his smartphone and glanced at the time. "I've gotta run. Enjoy the eggs. See you tonight. You too, Lily Belle," he said, and tweaked her nose.

In a minute he was gone. The kitchen went silent. Outside, Blue honked, heralding the sound of tires on gravel.

Lily scowled. "I'm sorry, Mama."

"Sorry?" Vura leaned sideways to study her daughter's expression. "For what?"

"That Papa doesn't like me."

Chapter 10

"What are you talking about?" Gripping Lily firmly, Vura turned her so they faced each other. Purple ponies danced across the nightgown that flowed over skinny thighs and brushed bare toes. "Your daddy *loves* you."

The tiny nose wrinkled again. Outside, a squad of geese added their deeply offended voices to Blue's as the sound of a diesel engine rumbled into the yard.

An impish grin replaced Lily's previous pout. "Pops!" she chirped and scrambling off Vura's lap, sped across the warped kitchen floor. The front door squawked as she hauled it open. "Pops is here!"

Even from the kitchen, Vura could see that her father was on his cell phone, but by the time he stepped from his pickup truck a moment later he had stashed it away. "Lily Bird!" he said and, squatting, opened his arms wide. Quinton Murrell might be as prized as husband material as he was as a carpenter, but his granddaughter was the center of his universe.

Vura stood in the doorway of her sadly dated house and felt the muscles in her gut relax at the sight of her two favorite people. Lily was already babbling like a proverbial brook by the time her father rose to his feet.

"I got bit," she chattered. "It hurt real bad Hunk said I was as tough as any chieftain ever. He called me Brave Flower. And Mama—"

"Wait! What?" Quinton raised his gaze to Vura and tightened his grip on Lily. She was perched on his arm like a spider monkey, bare legs dangling. "What's going on?"

Vura shook her head and opened the door wider. He was through in a moment, carrying his chattering cargo with him. "Lily had a little accident."

"An accident!" He skimmed his granddaughter's face, but in his doting estimation, her features were as perfect as a Rembrandt.

"My ear," Lily said and, turning her head, pointed at the offending member with one already grubby finger.

"Holy . . . spit!" His eyes widened, and his face, weathered from a thousand outdoor conditions, paled.

Despite everything, Vura grinned. "You're not going to pass out, are you, Dad?"

He didn't bother to rise to her ribbing. Or maybe he hadn't heard her. Quinton Murrell, tough guy and lady killer extraordinaire, had been known to shed tears when Lily sustained so much as a paper cut; the past five years had been extremely traumatic for him. "What happened?"

"A horse bit me." There was more than a little pride in the statement. "I had to get stitches. Forty-seven of 'em. But it's okay, cuz they're purple."

He clenched his teeth, probably holding back a hundred curses. Color was returning to his cheeks in a mad rush. "Was it the mustang?" The question was a little raspy.

"Courage?" Vura was surprised his mind had rushed in that direction. True, the horse had inadvertently caused Lily some trouble in the past. But since their hardly believable story had aired to the general public, the animal's image, drafted by Tonkiaishawien's admittedly gifted hand, had been reproduced on a thousand mugs, captured on a million T-shirts. Nevertheless, Lily was still the mare's number-one fan. "No. Courage is"— Vura waved a vague hand toward distant hills— "running free in the park somewhere, I think."

"It was a mama horse," Lily informed him sagely. "Courage isn't a mama. Not yet anyway. Ohhh . . ." She breathed a sigh, eyes wide, soft lips parted in awe. "But maybe she will be someday. Tonka says it takes mares almost a whole year to make a foal. But wouldn't that be wonderful? Wouldn't she make a great mama, Mama?"

"I'm sure she would, honey."

"Whose horse was it, then?" Quinton asked.

"It was a bay," Lily said.

Vura nodded at her daughter, spoke to her father. "Just some guy at the rodeo."

"A bay is a brown horse with a black mane and tail and black on its legs and ears."

"What was Lily doing with some random guy's horse?"

"The black on their legs are called points."

"I guess the mare was just passing by."

Lily nodded rapidly. "He was leading her by a pink rope and halter. Her baby was running loose." She scowled. "Why doesn't Courage have a baby, Mama?"

"I'm not sure," Vura admitted.

"Passing by!" Her father's tone was disgusted, as if nothing more dangerous than a cotton ball should exist in his granddaughter's world.

Vura shrugged.

Lily's scowl deepened. "Doc thinks Courage is only four years old. That sounds young. Cuz I'm already five. But that would be about . . ." She calculated madly, twisted expression showing her galloping thoughts. "Sixteen in people years. So she'd be old enough to have a foal, wouldn't she?"

"I think so." In fact, Vura had only been a couple years older than that when she had learned of her daughter's impending arrival.

"I bet my book would know for sure," Lily

said. *The Encyclopedia of Horses* had risen to biblical status in her mind recently.

"I'm sure it would," Vura agreed, seeing a light at the end of the ever-questioning tunnel. "Why don't you go check?"

"Okay," Lily said and, wriggling out of her grandfather's arms, trotted across the tilted floor toward the bedroom she shared with a hundred toy ponies and all things purple.

"So, what happened?" Quinton asked.

Vura exhaled and turned toward the counter. She wasn't going to cry just because her daddy was there. They had lost her mother in a car accident long before her earliest memory. Maybe that had forced their closeness. Still, even Quinton Murrell couldn't make everything right. She was pretty sure of that. "Do you want some coffee?"

"Did *you* make it?"

She gave him a jaundiced glance over her right shoulder. "Dane did."

"*What?* Dane's back?"

She shrugged and took a mug from the cupboard. It matched the plates. She kind of missed the lady with the kettle corn teeth. "Did I forget to tell you that?"

"Well, for crying in my beer!" It was only one of the many colorful phrases that had replaced more objectionable expletives since Lily's birth. There was nothing more comical than hearing the master carpenter growl, "Jumping jackrabbit" or "son of a bear cat!" when hammer met thumb. "Sit down," he said and, grasping her arm, tugged her toward the chair she had abandoned just minutes before. "Now . . ." He faced her. "Tell me, what the devil's going on?"

She stared dismally at the eggs that had long ago gone cold. The yolks blended almost seamlessly into the sunflower petals. Lily was right; they *were* gooey. "Everything?"

"Sounds like a lot." Rising, he poured them each a cup of coffee, then returned to sit in front of her again. "But I've got all day."

How many times, she wondered, had they sat like this together, her pouring her heart out, him listening, understanding, making things better just by being him? Even as a teenager, when she had told him she was pregnant, he had understood.

She felt tears well up.

"Hey." He slid a mug toward her. "What's wrong?"

"I'm a terrible mother."

"Did Dane tell you that?"

She blinked back tears, surprised by both the words and the emotion in his tone. Her father might not be Dane's biggest fan, but he had kept any negative opinions to himself . . . mostly.

"No. Of course not."

He exhaled and settled back in the chair a little, but his expression remained tense. "You're not a terrible mother," he said.

She felt her shoulders slump. "I know." Maybe. But Lily's ear . . . Lily's perfect ear . . . Her throat felt tight. Her heart hiccupped in her chest.

"In fact . . ." He gave her knee a nudge with his own. "You're a wonderful mother."

"You think so?" She sounded like a two-year-old.

"I know so."

"That's because you're the best father in the world." Now she was just getting sappy. She hated sappy almost as much as she hated geese. Why did geese exist?

"Yeah, well . . ." He smiled wryly, an expression that had made every divorcée between Sturgis and Sioux Falls as giddy as spring lambs. "I made my share of mistakes."

"At least you didn't let me get my ear bitten off."

"It was bitten *off!*" The sharpness of his tone made her wince. He gritted his teeth, shook his head. "Sorry. Just . . . start at the beginning, will you?"

"Okay." She nodded. "Once upon a time there was a beautiful princess."

He laughed. It was an old joke. Her mother, he said, had been a princess. He had been an ogre. And somehow, between them, they had spawned the perfect little hobgoblin.

"Lily and I went to watch Hunter's relay race yesterday," she said.

Quinton shook his head.

"Indian relay," she said. "I told you about it."

He scowled for a second then, "Oh . . . sure . . . three horses, four men with suicidal tendencies."

She shot a grin at him. "Yeah, anyway . . . his team was going to compete . . . kind of a halftime thing at the Little Britches Rodeo." She took a sip of coffee. Dane's was much better than hers, giving her confidence another hit. "Anyway . . ." She didn't, she realized, really know how to tell this story. So much had happened. The race, Tonk's concussion, Dane's arrival, Lily's injury. The entire day had been an emotional tornado. "Dane showed up."

"Out of the blue?"

She nodded.

"At the rodeo." He narrowed his eyes, shook his head once. "I thought he was in Williston."

She shrugged. "Me too."

"He didn't tell you he was coming?"

"No." She drank again and wished she wasn't so weirded out by that fact. He'd said he wanted to surprise her. What was wrong with that?

"How did he know you were going to be there?"

"I'm not sure. Maybe he talked to Glen or something. . . . Anyway, he showed up and wanted . . ." She paused, rapidly changing her phraseology. Her grandfather had once said that Dane generally got what he wanted and he always wanted something. Unlike Quinton, Gamps had never been averse to voicing negative opinions regarding her husband. "We thought it would be nice to spend a little time alone."

Something sparked in her father's eyes but was gone before she had a chance to identify it. "Sure."

"So I asked Hunt and Sydney if they could take care of Lily for a while." She tightened her fingers around the handle of her mug. Guilt again, as toxic as turpentine.

"Don't," he said.

She glanced up.

"Don't do that to yourself. You can't be with her twenty-four hours a day."

"*You* were."

"What are you talking about?"

"You were with *me* twenty-four hours a day."

A wave of nostalgia flittered across his face, but he scared it back with a scowl. "You know better than that."

She sighed, remembering. Her grandparents hadn't been saints. Well, her grandfather hadn't been, but Gamma probably should have been canonized. "How's Gamps doing?"

"I think he's actually enjoying the hospital."

She gave him a look and he smiled. "All those nurses to torment. Doctors to browbeat."

"I'm sorry I haven't gotten there more."

"I'll take Lily to see him today . . ." He took a sip of coffee. "If you ever get done telling me what happened."

"I don't even . . ." She shook her head again. "I don't have much to tell. Like I said, somebody came by Tonk's trailer with a mare and foal. They thought Lily was safely inside, filling hay bags. But you know how she is about horses."

"Crazy?"

"Crazy," she agreed. "She probably tried to carry the baby away or something and the mare took offense."

"Well . . ." His shoulders slumped. "I guess it could have been worse."

The understatement made her wince. "Hunt took her straight to the clinic. Sydney called me on the way."

"And you didn't tell me?"

The hurt in his voice ratcheted up the guilt. "I'm sorry, but I didn't even know what had happened until we got there and then . . ." She shook her head, remembering the panic.

He waved away her explanations. "So Dane went with you?"

"Yeah. He drove. Thank goodness. I would have probably wrapped my truck around a telephone pole or something."

"Where is he now?"

Tension crept in again. "He had a job interview."

"An interview? At seven in the morning?" The skepticism in his tone was more obvious than it used to be. She lowered her eyes, fiddled with the sunflower stamped on her mug.

"He's my husband, Dad."

"I know." For a second he tried to make it sound as if he had been implying nothing, but finally he glanced out the window and heaved a sigh. "I'm sorry. I didn't mean to . . . I'm glad he's back."

"Me too," she said, and wasn't entirely sure if she believed either one of them.

"Lily needs a dad," he added.

"I know."

"Otherwise she'll just be all girly."

She gave him a look.

"Like her mother," he said and nudged the handle of a ball-peen hammer that had somehow drifted onto the kitchen table.

She snorted.

"You haven't replaced Walt with this thing, have you?"

He was being ridiculous. Hammers were all well and good, but the DeWalt 18V nail gun was every girl's dream. "He's in my truck."

"Riding shotgun?"

"I let him canoodle with the drill driver on special occasions."

Quinton chuckled, but the sound was drowned in the honking of geese.

What now? she wondered and rose to peek out the kitchen window.

Tonkiaishawien Redhawk was just exiting his battered Jeep.

Vura ducked sideways, back flat against the

ugly wallpaper. Maybe Dad could say she wasn't home. Or maybe if she just didn't say anything, he'd go away. Or maybe . . .

"Hobgoblin?"

She snapped her gaze to her father. "Yeah?"

"Whatcha doing?"

"Nothin'."

Footsteps echoed on the stairs outside. The doorbell rang.

Her father's salt-and-pepper brows were lost somewhere beneath the brim of his ever-present baseball cap.

Three seconds ticked by, accented by the heavy beat of her heart against her ribs.

"You thinking of answering that?" Quinton asked.

She zipped her gaze to his. "Of course. Of course I am," she said and, peeling herself from the surprised-looking chickens, stalked regally to the door.

Chapter 11

"Tonk."

Tonkiaishawien stared at her. Bravura Lambert was dressed in a tattered T-shirt and oversized shorts. Lavender crescents shadowed tired eyes. Her hair was uncombed. It was as unsexy as a woman could get. He repeated that litany silently in his head and refused to think about what she had been doing prior to his arrival. It had nothing to do with him. He didn't mess with married women. It was against Bill W's lauded values. Against Native values. Against *his* values. But for reasons completely unfathomable, he remembered their embrace with heart-pounding clarity. Okay, truth was, it hadn't been an embrace at all. It was a handshake. Nothing but a handshake. So why did the memory of her skin against his make his knees wobble?

"Bravura." He gave her his best wise-chief nod.

The silence stretched between them like a bowline on a skittish mare.

She cleared her throat. Her cheeks were pink, her eyes snapped. Nothing sexy. Nothing at all. But why was she so scantily dressed? The thermometer hadn't topped sixty degrees in a coon's age.

"What are you doing here?" she asked.

"I do not wish to keep you from your husband." Thank God; he could still lie with foster-home panache.

Her body went very still for a fraction of a second, but then she shrugged. "Good," she said, and moved to close the door.

He caught it in one hand without thinking. Irritation was already circulating in his system like a hot shot of tequila. It was a good thing he wasn't attracted to her. A good thing he had, from the very beginning, intentionally annoyed the hell out of her so that she wouldn't be attracted to *him,* because she made him crazy.

"But we must talk," he added.

The tension again. She zipped her gaze toward the interior of the house, and he almost smiled. So she was thinking about how they had touched on the previous day. And it disturbed her. Though it had been nothing more scandalous than a handshake, the memory made her uncomfortable in her husband's presence.

Stepping outside, she closed the door behind her. They were very close. He could smell her scent. Rich coffee, fresh-cut wood, and maybe a hint of baby powder. Not the least bit sexy. "About what?"

He let the question lie fallow for a while. Her feet were bare. He hadn't noticed at first. Maybe that was because her legs were also bare, a truth that didn't bother him in the least. He was a shaman now. Kind of. Above such worldly considerations. Sometimes. But her toenails were painted a surprising shade of lilac. That wasn't sexy, either, just . . . unexpected, he told himself and resisted squirming like a schoolboy caught with a toad in his pocket. "I wished to discuss the agreement we came to yesterday."

She shuffled those bare feet. A tiny scar marred her left instep. He had no wish to kiss that scar. That would be weird. "I wanted to talk to you, too."

He straightened his back and waited.

She cleared her throat, seeming not the least disconcerted by the cold, though Tonk himself was wearing his beaded leather jacket and Justin Boots. But that didn't matter, either. So what if she was hot-blooded? It didn't mean a thing to him.

"I'm sorry . . ." Her lips, as full as fat ptarmigans, twitched a little. "But I won't be able to . . . I don't think you should keep your horses here, after all." Heat again, rising in her cheeks like embers.

Anger pushed through him, but he calmed himself. Remembering the twelve steps helped. Reminding himself that he had come to say the very same thing was even more beneficial; she was trouble, and he didn't need trouble. Didn't *want* trouble. But if the truth be known, if the awful facts were laid bare, it was *her* well-being, hers and Lily's, that had made him change his mind, that made him decide to keep his mounts elsewhere. He wasn't a jinx! It wasn't that. He didn't believe in such things. Not anymore. His parents' cruel words had been just that. Just cruelty. Still, mothers left; young girls drowned; parents, beloved beyond words, died far too young in automobile accidents. "We are in agreement then."

She raised a surprised brow.

She would be even more surprised if he kissed

her. If he backed her against the wall and . . . seriously, what was wrong with him? He didn't even like her. "Ai, we are in agreement," he repeated, as much to himself as to her. "Better to shun temptation than to battle it," he said and, leaving her with that shining wisdom, turned away.

"What!"

He kept walking.

But she wasn't finished. "What's that supposed to mean?"

He halted and turned to face her. Great Spirit, she looked like a high-bred filly ready to riot. "I did not intend to imply that you could not resist me."

She huffed a laugh and took a step toward him. "You . . ." She glanced back at the house and lowered her voice. "You think I find you tempting?"

She had no power over him. He had been restored to sanity as suggested by step two of Bill W's famous twelve-step program. Or he would be, once he came fully to his senses and excised her from his life. "I did not say as much."

"But that's what you meant."

He tilted his head the slightest degree. A wisp of wind caught the ends of his hair, brushing it against the beadwork of his jacket. He would be a liar if he said he did not enjoy the drama. "When you touched me yesterday, I assumed—"

She laughed out loud. "I didn't *touch* you."

He raised his brows.

"I mean . . . We shook hands. But it didn't . . . I didn't . . ." Huffing to a halt, she wiped her palm on her truly ugly shorts.

He watched her in silence for a second, letting the tension grow. "I did not find your touch offensive. That is not what I wish to imply, but you are a married woman, Bravura."

She stepped up close. Temper flared like a wild-fire in her eyes. "You didn't find it offensive?" The words were growled.

Something in his gut coiled up tight. Long ago Hunter had accused Tonk of loving to get people riled up. Which must explain this current conversation. It certainly wasn't her nearness that affected him. "But I do not think we should risk close proximity when—"

The door opened.

"Tonka!"

Tonk shifted his gaze sideways to find Lily perched in a man's powerful arms. It took him a moment to recognize Vura's father, longer still to realize there was only one unknown vehicle in the yard. His mind churned; that vehicle, he deduced, must belong to Quinton Murrell. Which meant her husband was gone at this small hour of the morning. He kept himself from scowling but couldn't curtail the thoughts: What kind of man would return to his wife after months of

122

absence, then disappear while the shadows were yet long? Curiouser and curiouser, he thought, and realized Murrell was watching him with a curiosity of his own.

Tonk refrained from shuffling his feet like a recalcitrant tike and nodded reverently to the child. "*Chitto Sihu.*"

Her grandfather narrowed his silver-blue eyes a little as if deep in thought. Then, "Brave Flower?"

Tonk glanced at him, more than a little surprised. "I did not realize you spoke the old tongues, sir."

Murrell shifted, settling a bright-eyed Lily a little higher against his ribs. Her legs, clad in purple tights bright enough to make you squint, clung like cockleburs. "I have a little Native blood, but it wasn't until I met Winona, Vura's mother, that I tried to learn something of the culture," he said, and shifted his gaze to his granddaughter. Devotion shone like an eternal flame in his eyes. The spark of respect that had been ignited at their first meeting bloomed a little brighter in Tonk's soul. Children were to be revered. It was the Native way. The fact that individuals failed did not mean that the culture as a whole did the same. Almost too late, he had learned that.

"I take it you heard about Lily's accident," Murrell deduced.

Tonk nodded before shifting his attention to

the child again. "Barbary regrets her actions and hopes you will forgive her impetuous ways, *Chitto Sihu*."

Lily's fingers tangled in her wild hair, then stilled momentarily. "You talked to the mama horse?"

"She spoke to me."

"What else did she say?"

"That in the future you should be more cautious when young ones are involved."

He wasn't certain, but he thought he saw Bravura roll her eyes in his periphery vision. Lily, however, didn't so much as blink.

"She bit my ear." There was only a hint of accusation in her tone. Children, he thought . . . miraculous.

He nodded solemnly. "My brother said you were as brave as a chieftain."

"I was."

He couldn't quite stop his smile, though it rather ruined the stoic Indian act he had been experimenting with for the past twenty-five years. "Already last night, the geese had heard of your injury and sent their condolences."

"You speak poultry?" Bravura asked. If she was trying to hide her cynicism, she sucked at it.

Tonk shifted his gaze to hers. "It is not speech so much as an exchange of thoughts."

"You exchange thoughts with poultry?"

He raised one brow, wondering if he looked

regal or ridiculous. "The Great Spirit blesses us all with thought, the humble and the haughty," he said, tacitly asking which of those she might be.

She gritted her teeth at him.

It wasn't until that moment that Tonk realized Quinton was watching them like another might follow a tennis match, brows raised, attention snapping from one opponent to the next.

"So you were here last night?" Murrell asked.

"He just came by to lock up the birds."

Tonk glanced at her. Did her explanation seem a bit hasty?

"That was nice of you," Murrell said.

Tonk shook his head and returned his gaze to the older man. "The coyote must eat, too. But he does not need to dine on the Lily's companions."

"Well . . ." Bravura's tone had gone strangely breezy. "It sure was great of you to stop by, Tonk, but don't let us keep you any—"

"I didn't mean to barge in," Murrell said. "Lily and I are going to take off."

"What?" Did her tone suggest panic? Full-on, all-out terror? "Already?"

Judging by her father's expression, he, too, was surprised by her horrified tone. "I want to get to the hospital early, then check on my crew."

"The hospital?" Tonk asked.

"Dad's ill," Murrell said. And there was pain there. Honest worry.

It would have been nice, comforting even, if

125

Tonk could believe he would have felt the same sorrow if his own father was sick, but he was not so deluded.

"Cancer." Murrell cleared his throat. "It's in his lungs," he said, and tightened his arm around his granddaughter a little, as if drawing comfort from the firefly brightness of her. "Don't ever smoke, Lily Belle."

"Okay," she agreed and absently circled her fingers in her hair again.

"Where is he convalescing?" Tonk asked.

"Rapid City Regional. It's a drive, but the local institutions . . ." He shrugged.

Tonk nodded, understanding. "Would you be offended if I stopped by to see him?"

He could feel Murrell's instant surprise almost as clearly as Bravura's disapproval, but he couldn't afford to let that sway him. Amends came in a variety of ways. There again the twelve steps and the Native way aligned.

Murrell spoke first. "Offended . . . no," he said, though his expression was quizzical. "Of course not." There was a moment of silence before he spoke again. "Are you a mystic, Tonk?"

Tonkiaishawien shifted his gaze momentarily to Vura. Her expression was a muddled mix of disapproval, panic, and confusion.

Their gazes held for a moment before Murrell spoke again. "Well . . . we'll leave you two alone," he said, and hurried down the rickety stairs.

"You don't need to do that," Bravura said, and scurried after them. "Tonk was just leaving."

Murrell only waved. But she continued toward his big Silverado.

"Dad . . . listen . . ." But he was already settling Lily into her car seat. "I wanted to talk to you about . . ." She froze for a second as if searching wildly for a topic that might delay him. "Mrs. Washburn's kitchen."

"Some other time." Slipping behind his steering wheel, he smiled with cherubic innocence and closed the door in her face.

They watched him leave the yard, tires practically squealing on the sparsely graveled drive.

It took several long seconds before Bravura turned back toward Tonk. Her eyes were slightly narrowed, her color high. She cleared her throat. "He probably was in a hurry to visit Gamps."

He watched her, the stoic Indian wondering what the devil was going on.

"Or Dane!" she said suddenly. "He probably wanted to talk to . . ." She cleared her throat. "He and my husband are great friends."

Well, crap on a cracker, Tonk thought, and almost reeled as an idea streamed into his brain. Could it be possible that Dane Lambert was such a twit, such an unmitigated disappointment, that even his father-in-law was happy to leave Bravura with another man?

Chapter 12

The silence stretched into eternity.

"So Mr. Lambert and Mr. Murrell are friends?" Tonk asked.

"Yes." She nodded erratically and turned back toward him. "Of course. Why wouldn't they be? They're practically . . ." She bounced one knee. "Well . . . you probably want to get going."

He watched her in silence. She glanced toward the road again, following the path of her father's escape like a lovelorn basset hound.

Close up, he could see that her eyes were not absolutely blue. Instead, they bore flecks of gold, chips of green, shadows of unlikely amber. How had he missed the amber? he wondered, but she waved a wild hand, ripping him back to the present.

"Thank you for . . . coming by. Lily will be disappointed that you won't be bringing your horses, but I'll explain."

"How?"

Irritation jumped in her jaw. "I'll say you got a better offer."

"I did not think you the sort to lie to your small daughter."

She narrowed her eyes, emitted a sound that strongly resembled a growl. "I have *never* . . ."

She paused. "I try very hard *never* to lie to Lily."

"Then why would you do so now?"

A hundred feral emotions were flaring in her wild-river eyes. "Tell me the truth, Tonkiaishawien. Why did you change your mind if not because you got an offer from a big-ches—"

She stopped herself. He raised his brows, breathless.

"Why did you change your mind?" she asked.

Was she jealous? Was that it? But no, that was crazy. She hated him. And that was fine. Better than fine. Best. Still . . .

"Well?" she asked.

Strange, he thought, how he wished now, almost desperately to lie himself, but lies, while simple and so very seductive, rarely improved one's circumstances in the long run. "I do not think a woman like you would understand the truth, Bravura."

"A woman like me!" She took one abbreviated step to the rear, rocking back on her heels as if struck. "What is that supposed to mean?"

He straightened, braced for the truth. "You do not need to make amends."

"What?" A little of the anger had seeped out of her tone. He almost missed it. Perhaps, if he were to be honest, she felt more accessible when she was mad. Not quite so very far above him.

"Only those with regrets must make amends," he said, and opened the door of his Jeep. Mutt pushed himself to a sitting position on the passenger seat, tattered ears pricked, right eye perpetually winking.

Vura tugged her fascinated gaze from the ugly animal with no small effort. "You think I don't have regrets?"

He watched her over the rusted edge of his 4door. "What I meant to say was you *should* not have regrets."

She blinked, then let her brows dip into a scowl. A wild-haired pixie with a grudge. "Are you serious?"

He scowled a little. Was there sorrow in her eyes? Pain? He wanted, quite suddenly, to reach out, to touch her skin, ease that pain. But he was nobody's fool. Sometimes. "Ai," he said instead and twisted to drop into his car.

"I let Lily's ear get ripped halfway off her head!" she snapped.

He paused, almost in his seat.

"I bought this place!" she continued and waved behind her at the pretty rolling property as if the sky was about to clatter down around her ears. "Which I can't afford. Can't fix up. Can't . . ." She huffed a laugh, sounding breathless. "I married a man who . . ." She stopped herself short, eyes widening as if appalled by her own thoughts, and changed track with the speed of a dashing thoroughbred. "I lied to Dad!" There was a finality to the words, as if she had come to the worst of her sins. He would have laughed out loud if she hadn't looked so devastated, so absolutely forlorn.

"Told him . . ." She took a deep breath and squared her shoulders, like a pugilist ready to take her best shot. "I told him I was staying overnight with Jamie Patterson."

He shook his head, befuddled.

"When I went to meet Dane," she said, and glanced toward the empty pastures. "He trusted me and I lied. Shamed him."

"Ah." He forced himself to keep a straight face, though the admission seemed almost sweet in its forlorn innocence. "And thus the guilt."

"Yeah." She blew out a breath and swept her gaze past the ancient stand of cottonwoods, over the bold red rock. Honest regret shone in her eyes. What kind of woman would mourn such a small sin for years on end? Pity stroked though him, brushed by admiration, shadowed by respect.

"But if you had not done so, there might be no Lily," he said.

"I know." Her voice was soft, distant, echoing thoughts she had probably considered a thousand times. "I know. And she's . . . she's everything. All things good. A miracle, really."

He nodded, listening, hearing the passion in her voice, seeing the truth in her eyes. What would it be like to own that kind of adoration, to feel that sort of allegiance? But he was being ridiculous.

He had experienced that comfort once . . . if not from his birth parents, from those who came after. He was one of the lucky few.

"But sometimes I wonder—" She stopped herself. The abrupt halt brought his attention fully back to her guileless eyes.

"What is it you wonder?" he asked. The Jeep's door stood as a kindly buffer between them, offering her space for absolution.

"She's autistic. High-functioning," she hurried to add. "Asperger's. Did you know that?"

He nodded. "My brother speaks of her often."

"Yeah, Hunt's . . ." Her shoulders slumped a little, as if she had somehow failed her child by admitting the truth. "Hunt's great with her."

He didn't bother to argue. His brother was accomplished at many things, but if the truth be told, Tonk didn't much relish hearing words of praise for another from this woman's wild strawberry lips.

She shifted her gaze away again. High above, a hawk circled, copper tail-feathers spread wide.

"Tell me . . ." he began, making her turn her attention back to him. He felt her gaze land on him gently. "Do you think the Asperger's is a product of your deception?"

She grinned a little. "It sounds even dumber when you say it out loud."

He chuckled, then exhaled quietly and sobered. The hawk circled closer. Bravery came in a thousand guises, but perhaps honesty was the most terrifying.

Silence pulsed between them like the beat of distant drums.

"My cousin was raped," he said finally. Releasing the words caused a physical ache in the center of his chest.

"What?"

He watched the far-seeing hills. "Jacquie Delorme." Pain echoed through him, gnawing like a cancer. "She liked to party. Not so much as me." He smiled. The expression hurt his face. "But she could hold her own." He tightened his fist and reminded himself to breathe. "Perhaps that's what I told myself. Perhaps that is why I left her alone in a place where she should not have been." He shrugged, spearing her with his eyes again, taking the blame, forcing the honesty. "Or perhaps I was too drunk to care."

"I'm sorry." The words were soft, almost inaudible in their earnestness, offering absolution he would not accept.

"Her daughter . . ." He gritted his teeth. "Ruby Ann. She was born with fetal alcohol syndrome."

Sorrow shone in her eyes. "Was she . . . Ruby . . . was she a result of the . . . of the rape?"

"Who is to say?" He tried to keep his tone light, but there was little hope of achieving such a feat. The thought of the child's lost-baby eyes would haunt him every day of his life, and it

133

was no less than he deserved. But he brought himself back to the present, to the burning, aching truth. "I did not mean to imply that there were other men during that time," he said. "She was only . . ." He cleared his throat. Off to the west, clouds were rolling in, scalloped edges brushed pink. "She was only sixteen when Ruby was born." He paused, telling himself to cease, demanding that he stop this horrid tale. There was no reason to revisit it. But he had never been good at taking orders. "Twenty-nine when she died."

Sadness burned in Bravura's eyes. "Jacquie or—"

"Ruby," he said, though he was certain there were days when his cousin wished it was she who had been taken. "Jacquie . . ." He shook his head, remembered. "She was beauty itself, and the boys . . ." He clenched his fists, fumbled on. "There were many of them. Some good. Some bad. Some jealous . . ."

She waited. He searched for strength, though honestly, he did not know why he would share such a tale with this woman.

"Joe Seagull . . . we called him Bird. He was an okay guy really. Just couldn't . . . couldn't get over the fact that my cousin had moved on. Thought maybe . . ." He pushed out a breath. "I do not know what he thought. Perhaps he simply wanted to spend some time with Ruby. Maybe he had become attached to her during his time with

Jacquie. Maybe. . . ." Dammit, he should have kept his mouth shut.

"What happened?"

"No one knows. Not even Joe, I think. He stopped by while Jacquie was gone. Ruby was thirteen, alone, and never very . . . not quite like other kids. They went to the reservoir, just to swim maybe. But he had brought beer and . . . hell . . ."

He laughed. It sounded awful, like something from a horror flick. "By the time I was that age, I could drink a six-pack before noon. She was found dead the next morning. Drowned." His throat hurt; his eyes burned. He turned them toward the hills, seeking solace.

"It's not your fault."

He knew that. Of course he knew that, and yet he did not, making him long for absolution. The kindness of her words scoured his heart. He raised his gaze to hers, as blue as the far-seeing sky.

"You couldn't have known," she said and, reaching out, settled a hand over the arm he had draped on top of his door. Her fingers were warm, igniting a small fire in his soul.

He steeled himself against that kindness. "Not when I was three sheets to the wind." He forced a smile. It felt painful in its gritty intensity, and for a moment they were frozen, locked in each other's gaze.

"Okay." She drew her hand away and forced a

laugh. "Point taken; I'm not the only one with regrets."

He filled his lungs and shrugged, hoping to look casual, perhaps almost achieving just that. "My father once said that where there is no regret, there is no life."

"Your dad sounds like a wise man."

"One of them was."

She raised her brows a little, and though Tonk warned himself against wandering deeper into the quagmire of truth, he spoke again.

"There are few who would call my birth father wise."

He had put more emphasis into that single statement than he had intended, but she pulled her gaze away and glanced toward the overgrown meadow nearby. Hidden in the age-old grasses, a pheasant called for a mate, ever hopeful.

"I guess I'm lucky," she said.

"This I knew when I first met your Lily."

Her eyes softened at the mention of her daughter.

"It was but confirmed when I met your father," he said.

"My life wasn't perfect, you know."

"Oh?"

She scrunched her face a little, as if searching for something with which to challenge the sadness of the story he should not have shared. "He used to tickle me until I'd pee in my pants."

The image of her as a child did something unwanted to his insides. "The man should be horsewhipped," he said, and she laughed, more naturally now.

"Gamps scolded me once for picking a crocus, said . . ." She paused, sighed. "There's too little wild left, and it should be revered, not plucked like a weed from the earth."

"There is great wisdom in your family, too," he said. "I am sorry he is sick."

"He'll be all right." She flickered her eyes to him and away. "I think he'll be all right. But maybe . . . Mrs. Washburn thought he should move into a nursing home."

"Difficult for a man who reveres the wild places."

"What else can we do?"

"Perhaps quality of life is more important to him than number of days."

"So what? You think he should just be allowed to drop dead in his vegetable garden? Keel over in his herb patch?"

He opened his mouth to state his opinion, but there had been those few moments of peace, so fragile they quivered.

"I think he is blessed to have a granddaughter who loves him with such fierce devotion."

"I . . . You . . ." She huffed a sigh, let her shoulders drop. "Maybe we could be friends," she said finally.

When she stood there with her soul as bare as her lilac toes? He doubted it, but he could hardly say as much. "Perhaps stranger things have happened."

She breathed a laugh, gaze drawn to the pastures again. "It might be nice to see horses grazing there."

He watched her, because he could, because he had little choice. Despite everything he had told himself, she drew him like that damned proverbial moth.

"You said you'd fix the fences, right?" she asked, and pinned him with her eyes. Again the moth.

"Ai."

"And you'll pay me."

This was a mistake, he thought, but could not seem to stop the words. "I will pay you."

She nodded, thinking. "You've got a deal then," she said, and turned away. But in a second she had stopped. Her eyes looked impish and ageless over the curve of her shoulder. Dark hair framed her face like a disheveled halo, and dimples flashed, as mesmerizing as fire in the darkness. "Am I going to regret this?"

"Almost definitely," he said, and she laughed as she headed toward the house.

Chapter 13

"There's something wrong." Mrs. Washburn, old as dirt and as opinionated as a cactus, stood in the center of her newly remodeled kitchen. Her arms were akimbo, her face screwed up with disapproval. Scowl as dark as an encroaching thunderstorm, she scrutinized the work Vura and her crew had sweat blood over for forty days and forty nights.

Behind the dissatisfied home owner, Maynard Grayson dropped his head in abject misery while Glen Eastman stifled an involuntary groan. Emil Johnston, better known as Hip for reasons long ago forgotten, looked as if he might very well burst into bloodcurdling curses; they had replaced the counter twice, moved the stationary chrome-backed stools repeatedly, and smoothed the flooring so not a single seam could be seen from any vantage point.

Of course, that didn't mean the room wasn't still as ugly as an open wound . . . at least to Vura's eye. Apparently, modern wasn't her thing. She wouldn't have guessed it would be Mrs. Washburn's, either, since she had been born during the dirty thirties when the harsh north-westerly winds were trying to blow South Dakota's top soil into Mexico. But, according to Mary Keterling, Mrs. Washburn's on-again, off-again best friend, Mrs. Washburn's youngest sister had called her sibling old-fashioned, thus fostering endless backbreaking labor and this festering eyesore.

Vura stifled a wince as she glanced around the room. Everything that wasn't white was red. And not a soft, inviting, "sit down and have a cup of coffee" red, but a blistering, angry red, a red that glared from the cabinets, dripped like blood from the hanging, overhead lights.

Vura had tried to coax her client into a more forgiving direction, but Mrs. Washburn, ever true to her convictions, no matter how misguided they might be, had stood firm. And really, it wasn't as if Vura was an expert on interior design. One glance at her sheep-infested bedroom would prove that. So she had acquiesced. Hence this . . . She refrained from shaking her head at the catastrophe Sawhorse, Inc. had wrought.

"But, Mrs. Washburn . . ." Vura tried to keep from whining, did her best to remain upbeat. Attitude was contagious, and she hated to see grown construction workers cry. Especially when they were of the caliber of her employees, talented men with golden hands who would work for Quinton Murrell's daughter out of nothing but a fierce sense of loyalty. "We did everything you asked."

"Hmmm . . ." The old woman shook her head

and rambled forward to run a gnarled hand over the flawless countertop and pet the ruby-red refrigerator. Opening it experimentally, she glanced inside.

"Is it the hardware?" Vura asked, and refused to share a frantic glance with her coworkers, who stood in a mute semicircle around her. The cupboard handles were as offensive as anything in the room. Made of glaring stainless steel, they were bookended with stylized roses and adorned every cabinet and drawer. Weird as they were, they matched the kill-me-now style to startling perfection, but she was desperately trying to think of something they could change that wouldn't require an additional hundred man-hours. Hip was beginning to pull at his hair like a fretful two-year-old, and truth be told, he didn't have that much to begin with. "Or maybe the—"

But suddenly Mrs. Washburn gasped. Pulling a wooden bowl of fruit out of the fridge, she turned with the decisiveness of a major general and thumped the thing atop the alabaster center island. She scowled, tilted her head, adjusted the bowl's angle, and . . . smiled. "There," she said, and clasped her hands together in girlish glee. "Perfect."

Vura blinked. Glen stiffened. Maynard was, quite obviously, holding his breath. And Hip, even older than their most opinionated client, wiped the back of his hand across his lips as if he was ready to do battle.

"Yes," Vura agreed tentatively, not entirely certain whether the elderly lady was being facetious. "Yes, you're right." Nobody blinked. "You're absolutely right. That made all the difference."

The kitchen was as silent as a tomb.

"Don't you agree?" Vura asked, and turned expectantly toward her men.

It took them a moment to snap out of their respective trances.

"Yeah!" Glen chirped.

"Definitely!" Maynard agreed.

"Kill me!" Hip rasped.

Vura gritted her teeth in the old man's direction, causing him to snarl an obliging smile. "You've always had good taste, Colley," he said, but the words were something of a growl.

"Better than some." She sniffed, then pulled her gaze from Hip to turn her attention back toward their masterpiece. "Bravura Lambert, you and your boys did a fine job."

"Thank you," Vura said.

"Although it took you long enough," she added.

Hip opened his mouth to retaliate, but Vura sent him a frantic look, begging for patience. He slid grouchily back into silence.

"We're sorry we couldn't get it done sooner," Vura said, and tried not to remember the fact that they had been forced to reorder the linoleum multiple times when their client had opted for a slightly different shade of pallid.

"Well . . ." Mrs. Washburn clapped twice, then glanced around with a critical eye. "I'll still have time to get things cleaned up before Mother's Day." If there was so much as a dust mote in the place, Vura had yet to find it. Mrs. Washburn's late husband had been known to hide in his toolshed after work so his wife wouldn't throw his clothes in the washing machine before he had stripped them off.

"Plenty of time," Maynard agreed.

"I wish my place was half so clean," Glen volleyed.

Mrs. Washburn smiled. "Well, I suppose you would like to get paid."

Please, Lord, Vura thought. "If it's not too much trouble," she said.

The old lady nodded as she pulled a handbag from an ugly nearby cupboard. The leather satchel was the approximate size of a pachyderm.

By the time they exited the house, Vura felt a little light-headed.

"Let me see it," Glen said.

Vura tilted the check toward her men.

"She actually paid us extra." Maynard's tone was awed, his ginger eyebrows arched in disbelief as he leaned close.

"I thought you said she was cheap," Glen said, and tapped an elbow into old Hip's arm.

"What was *that?*" Hip asked, and snapped his rheumy gaze toward the road that led to Main Street and Custer City's very own Drop On Inn.

"What?" Vura asked, terrified that some minor mishap would tilt them back into another fifty hours of labor.

"Oh . . ." The old man exhaled, noisily relieved. "Guess it's nothing. I thought I saw four horsemen coming down the drive. Couple of 'em had scythes."

It took a moment for Vura to laugh, longer for the others to groan. But in a moment they had forgotten the possibility of the apocalypse and were tossing their tools into metal boxes, then creaking open the doors of their respective vehicles.

"Hey!" Glen said, and set one foot inside his trusty Subaru. "Who's up for a beer?"

"Count me in," Maynard said.

Hip nodded.

"How about you, Vura?"

The question punched something low in her gut. It wasn't that she ever felt really out of place with the men. She'd known them all since before she could lift a screwdriver. But it hadn't been exactly seamless going from under-their-feet pest to over-their-head boss. Friendship she had always had. Respect was more difficult to come by. Maybe it *was* the twenty-first century, but out here in the far reaches of South Dakota, women were still encouraged to keep their houses clean and their mouths shut.

"You think I want to spend my time with a bunch of men who smell like sweat and sawdust?" she asked.

"Don't know why else you'd be in the business," Maynard quipped.

Vura laughed. "Meet you at Windy's?"

"Last one there's the designated driver," Maynard said and, winking, slipped behind the wheel of his amped-up Impala.

An hour later Vura had her steel-toed loggers propped up on the bar stool beside her.

"Them Carhartts?" Glen asked, and motioned to her clay-colored overalls with the rim of his beer bottle.

"Yeah." Vura took a sip of her Budweiser. "Want to borrow them?"

The other men chuckled with good-natured camaraderie. Glen was often ribbed about his diminutive size. If he hadn't had the capability to bench-press the lot of them, he might have taken offense.

As it was, he gave her a crafty look from the corner of his eye before shifting into a faraway stare. "Remember when she decided to wear her daddy's pants, Hip?"

The old man roused himself from some

shadowy half dream he'd been visiting. "The ones he'd left in the bathroom of the Graffs' new house?"

"It was about a hundred degrees in the shade," Glen said.

"And she decided her old man's overalls would be nice and roomy."

"So she kicked off her jeans."

Hip grinned.

Vura felt her cheeks heat up. This was exactly the kind of problem caused by knowing men since you were sporting Pampers and pabulum.

"Right there in the Graffs' unfinished bathroom."

Maynard, the only one who hadn't been present at that embarrassing moment, was listening with interest.

"Wasn't a bad idea," Hip said.

Glen nodded. "Until that Nettlebee kid . . ." He narrowed his eyes in thought, searching his memory banks. "What was his name?"

"Jim."

"That's right. She thought it was a swell idea until he decided to grab a smoke in that very same bathroom."

"You could have told him I was in there," Vura murmured.

"I could have," Glen agreed. His grin was wicked.

"So what you're telling me is you guys has

always been jerk-offs," Maynard said, and settled his beer on his only slightly rounded belly, bisecting the words, HOME IS WHERE THE PANTS AIN'T. Spring, summer, fall, and winter, he sported a short-sleeved T-shirt guaranteed to elicit chuckles or groans.

"Always," Vura agreed.

"Sweet Martha, I thought the whole damned house was going to come down with the ruckus that caused. You never heard such screeching."

Maynard shrugged. "Girls has been known to shriek some when you catch 'em in their skivvies."

"Girls . . ." Glen said, and shook his head. "It was Jimbo who raised the roof."

Vura gritted her teeth. Maynard chuckled. "Caught him unawares, I suppose."

"And in the left eye."

Maynard raised a brow.

"Hit him square in the eyeball. Poor kid couldn't see straight for a week."

"Same could happen to you," Vura muttered and took a delicate sip of her beer.

Glen laughed out loud. "I'm just sayin' . . ."

"Too much," Vura warned, though the warmth of their camaraderie had washed away the last vestige of her tension. "Unless you want me to regale our fellow workers here with tales about you and that nanny goat at Van Dake's."

Glen blushed bright magenta, and the stories began to fly in earnest.

. . .

"I'm not saying you ain't tough," Maynard said, directing the lip of his fourth brewski at Glen. "I'm just sayin' I don't think you can take ol' Hip there."

"Hip?" Glen asked, and glanced at the old man who was half-snoozing in his chair.

"I mean, I know he's older than sin, but even Mrs. Washburn didn't kill him."

"I thought she showed remarkable restraint," Vura admitted. The two eighty-somethings had shared more than a few heated "conversations" during the last few weeks.

"While we was remodeling?" Maynard asked. "Well, hell yeah, but I meant when they was an item."

Vura sat straight up. "What?" She grinned at the old man, who gave her a half-asleep glower. "You and Mrs. Washburn dated?"

"Them two was hotter than a biscuit back in the day."

"Was that day in the eighteen hundreds?" Glen asked.

Hip shifted his sleepy glance in the diminutive man's direction. "She was a pinup girl."

"A what?"

"What?" Vura echoed Maynard's surprise.

"During the war," Hip said. "They sent out pictures to inspire the boys on the front."

"No way!"

"You're kidding."

"She still inspires me . . . until she opens her mouth," Hip said, and almost brought the roof down.

By the time Vura finally thumped her second empty bottle onto the table a dozen half-true stories had been told and denied. "Well . . ." She pushed herself to her feet. "I gotta go."

"That's right." Maynard waggled his brows at her. "The boss's husband's back."

"Guess you better hurry then," Glen said. "So you can meet your boyfriend before your old man finds out."

She waved, left the bar on a waft of good karma, and drove to Rapid City. She had only had one beer for every three of her men's, but she was just as aware of her size as she was of her mortality and drove carefully to Regional Hospital.

Guilt settled in a little, displacing a fraction of the bonhomie caused by time with her employees. But despite his illness, Gamps would be the first to espouse the value of good work relationships. He had been employed full-time as a master plumber until his eightieth birthday. In fact, he still helped out if there was a need.

Pulling carefully into the parking lot, Vura killed the engine. Maybe the pavement tilted a little as she stepped onto it, but that could be just as much a result of too little food as too much beer, she thought, and decided she'd better fuel up soon.

The elevator ride to the third floor was a little daunting. Her head spun some, but by the time she reached room 375 she was back on her game.

It was when she opened the door and saw Tonkiaishawien bowed over her grandfather's body that things got a little crazy.

Chapter 14

"No!" Vura rasped, and streaking across the floor, grabbed Tonk's upraised arm. Their gazes clashed, steel on stone.

The world froze in petrified shock; then, "Bravura?" Her grandfather's voice sounded scratchy and weak from the bed beside her.

"Gamps!" she gasped, still holding Tonk's arm in a desperate grasp. "I won't let him hurt you!"

"What are you doing, girl?"

"What am I doing? What's *he* doing with that"—she jerked her gaze to his raised hand— "knife?" she said, but suddenly it didn't look so much like a blade as a smoldering bundle of weeds.

Tonk's brows rose the slightest degree. "Are you intoxicated?" he asked.

"Intoxicated! No, I'm not—" He'd spoken of quality of life rather than number of days as if he thought her grandfather's life might just as well end. Still, maybe she had been a little quick to jump to conclusions. One more glance at the weeds in his hand had them morphing into a braided bundle of sweetgrass. Its vanilla scent wafted kindly into the silent room. "I'm not," she repeated, but she wasn't entirely positive now.

"Vura . . ." Gamps said, "have you been drinking?" Her grandfather's words pulled her gaze to his pillow, forced her fingers to open, her arm to drop disgracefully to her side.

The old man's face looked parchment white, his lips nearly as pale. She winced, twisted fully toward him, and resisted wriggling like a teenager caught with a stink bomb. Her father's father had always been her champion, but champions came in a hundred varied forms and this one had never been an advocate of excessive coddling.

"I just . . ." She felt silly suddenly, and inordinately young, as if she had taken several shaky steps back into childhood. "I just had a couple of beers with the men."

"What men?" Despite his deteriorating health, Gamps's voice was as sharp as a hacksaw. She resisted closing her eyes at her own stupidity.

"My crew. We . . ." Her head spun a little, and she allowed herself to sink slowly onto the side of his bed. "We finished Mrs. Washburn's kitchen today. Thought we'd celebrate a little."

The old man scowled and nodded. The motion was weak. "That's right. Colley's kitchen."

Did he say the name with a modicum of

affection? she wondered. Could there be a shred of truth to old Hip's story of pinup girls and subsequent inspiration? "Yeah, Colleen Washburn." She smoothed out the blanket that rested over his ribby chest. "Have you known her a long time?"

"I'm a hundred years old," he huffed, but some of the gruffness had left his tone. "I've known everyone a long time."

"You're not a hundred," she said, and smiled at him, though he looked weaker than he had during her last visit. "Barely any older than Colley." It felt funny using such a girly nickname.

He harrumphed as if Mrs. Colleen Washburn, feisty octogenarian that she was, was as fresh as a spring blossom. "So you finished her big kitchen project?"

"Just a few hours ago."

"Was she pleased with the results?"

"She was," Vura said, and couldn't quite contain the surprise she still felt.

"Well then, I suppose you got cause to celebrate," Gamps said. "But remember, Bravura Marie, there's never a reason to overindulge."

And suddenly she felt even younger, like a toddler who had neglected to finish her greens. She squirmed a little. "I know, Gamps," she said, and felt his gaze scour her face.

"Good. Good." He patted her hand. "You've always been a fine girl, Bravura."

"Thank you," she said, and resisted the urge to

glance up to gauge Tonk's reaction. She would be an imbecile to care what he thought. And she wasn't imbecilic . . . usually. Never, in fact. Almost.

"But when I'm gone . . ." He tightened his grip on her hand, bony fingers digging like talons. "You've got to be strong . . . for that baby of yours, if not for yourself."

"Gamps . . ." She leaned toward him. "Don't talk like that."

"Like what?"

"Like you're going to . . ." Her throat tightened up. She cleared it with an effort. "Like you're going to be leaving us."

"Bravura—" His tone was a tired meld of frustration and tenderness. But she stopped him.

"We need you," she said, and fisted her hand beneath his. "Lily and I. We still have so much to learn." She forced a smile. It hurt her face. "I always use too much flux on the fittings. And you promised to teach me to weld."

Worry flickered through his ancient eyes, and then his gaze drifted sideways as if he were seeing things beyond her scope. His fingers felt cool and weightless against the back of her hand.

"Gamps?"

"She's proud of you, Bravura."

"What?" She turned her hand in his so as to grip his fingers. "Who?"

"Rosie." He said the name softly, then smiled

with a soft reverence that shook her soul. "Your grandmother's proud of you."

"That's nice," she said, though honest to God, he was scaring the living daylights out of her. Grandma Murrell had been gone since before Lily's birth. It had always been a throbbing source of pain to think how the most important woman in her life would have reacted to the news of her unwed pregnancy.

"Very proud," he said and, eyes clearing a little, squeezed her fingers. "So am I. Always have been. But I've earned some rest, haven't I, honey?"

"Rest?" She felt selfish suddenly and oddly disoriented. Was he talking about a catnap or was he, maybe, thinking about something much more final? She nodded, though now that she was here, she didn't want to leave. Didn't want to release his hand. "Of course. Of course you have. I just . . . I love you, that's all and I . . ." She resisted yet again glancing at Tonk. "I just kind of wanted your opinion on a job I'm bidding."

"Oh?" He had always taken an interest in her work, had always been inordinately proud of her abilities, though it was unconventional at best for a woman to be in her line of work. Now, however, barely a flash of curiosity shone in his faded eyes. "What job is that?"

She tried to stifle her fears. "Kenny Walters wants a cabin built on the river."

The old man shook his head weakly. "Kenny

154

always would spend a dollar if he had a dime."

Randall Murrell, on the other hand, could pinch a penny until it begged for mercy, but maybe that's what happened when you survived the Great Depression and skipped over a bunch of lesser ones like they were no more significant than a bump in the road.

"He wants it move-in ready by the Fourth of July." She grinned. "Wants copper piping throughout so you're not gonna have much time to lollygag about."

His gaze wandered away.

"Gamps?"

It seemed to take forever for his attention to filter back to her, and when it did, his expression was solemn. "She's waiting, Bravura."

"Who?" She actually glanced behind her, but the doorway was empty. "Who's waiting?"

He smiled, seemed to come back to her, patted her arm with his free hand. "You don't need an old man like me, honey. I want to go home."

"Home? Okay." She nodded, eager to help, to do. "We'll get you out of here as soon as we can. Find someone to help out. Mrs. Ketterling maybe. Or . . ." she began, but his eyes had fallen closed. "Gamps?" Her voice was little-girl desperate, but a woman spoke up before she could shake him awake.

"He needs to rest now."

Vura jumped at the words, turned her head,

blinked back tears. But there was no ghost behind her. Instead, Linda Binder had stepped into the room. She hadn't changed much since she had made her bid for Quinton Murrell's affections twelve years before. She smiled now, expression gentle.

"Come on, honey," she said and, stepping forward, placed a soft hand on her shoulder.

Vura rose to her feet.

"You doing okay?" The older woman slipped Tonk a tolerant smile before shifting her attention back to Vura.

She nodded, but truly she didn't know how she was doing and remembered her earlier buzz with nostalgic fondness. Sobriety sucked.

They stood beside the bed. Perhaps at one time there had been some friction between them. As a girl, Vura had been fiercely protective of her father. She wondered now if she'd been unfair. Somehow she had never considered the fact that he could have been lonely; in her mind he was invincible, a superhero with a miter box.

"He's a good man," Linda said, and smiled fondly at her patient's tranquil features.

Vura nodded again.

"Like your father."

Odd, so very odd, but despite all the years that had passed, Vura still bristled at the other woman's interest; Quinton Murrell was *hers,* she thought, and realized with some clarity that there was truly something wrong with her.

She cleared her throat. "Yes, thank you," she said. "He is. They both are," she rushed to add and forced herself to turn from the narrow bed. "How are you doing, Linda?"

"Well enough." She smiled a little. "I have a new grandbaby."

"Do you?" She flickered her gaze to Tonk, who watched them with amusement in his muddy-water eyes. She had to force away her scowl. "That's wonderful." They moved in tandem out of the room. "A boy or a girl?"

"A girl. Three months old. As cute as a duckling. I'd bore you with pictures"—she shifted her gaze to Tonk—"but you've got other things on your mind. Take it easy now," she said and, touching Vura's arm, made her way on crepe-soled feet to some distant room.

Silence echoed like death in the hall, but Vura could feel Tonk's attention on the back of her neck. The questions that bounced from his brain were as loud as a jackhammer.

"What?" she asked, and turned toward him.

One brow lifted; humor danced mischievously over his dark Native features. "I believe your father is old enough to fight his own battles."

"What's that supposed to mean?"

"She seems quite nice," he said, and fell silent, challenging her to argue.

"So?"

"So perhaps he did not need you to scare her off."

She scowled, disconcerted by how closely his words matched her thoughts of only moments before. "Yeah, well . . . what do you know about it?" Now she sounded like a confrontational nine-year-old. But she was on a roll. "And what were you doing in there anyway?" she asked and, pivoting just a little too sharply to make her equilibrium happy, stumbled toward the closest exit. Suddenly the air felt too close, the quiet too oppressive.

He turned with her. "Purifying the air."

She would have liked to scoff, but she had always been fascinated by Native traditions. "Oh," was about all she could manage.

"Our culture believes that smudging, burning the earth's sacred herbs, in the seven directions can bring healing and peace."

"That's . . ." She would have liked to tell him it was all rubbish, but even her currently atrocious mood wouldn't allow it. "That's kind of nice, actually."

They were silent for a while, no sound but the *ding* of the elevator, the crisp *click* of their boots on the sidewalk.

Up ahead, Vura's truck looked old and strangely lonely in the mostly forsaken lot. She fumbled in her overalls pocket when she reached the door and lifted the fob to click the locks.

"Well . . ." She considered an apology. But why try something so drastic? "Thank you."

He remained silent, insisting, as usual, on making things difficult.

She jittered a knee. "For"—she gritted her teeth, nodded toward the building—"what you were doing in there."

His gaze was steady on hers, rattling her nerves, eroding any lingering sense of peace.

"It was a nice thing to do." She glanced toward Fifth Street, remembering the coolness of her grandfather's hands, the distance in his eyes. Her throat closed up, locking back tears. "Well . . . I'd better get going before—"

"All will be well," Tonk said.

She snapped her gaze to his. Logic told her that he was just a man. But something in her longed to believe, just this once, that he somehow knew things she did not. "You think so?" She breathed the words.

"I know it," he said, and stood very still, watching her. "Your grandfather, he has lived a good life. You've no need to worry."

She glanced back toward Cathedral Street. Across the boulevard, the church looked more like a factory than a place of God. Vura stuffed her hands in the pockets of her Carhartts. Overhead, the wild geese were returning from warmer climes. She could hear the soft *whish* of their wings in the darkness. "He looked so pale. So . . . old . . . and I . . ." Her voice cracked, and though she tried to stop herself, she pushed her gaze hopefully back to Tonk's. "You really think he'll recover?"

She could sense his tension immediately. His brows dipped. Regret was sharp in his burnt-umber eyes. "I did not say that, Bravura."

Panic splashed up. "You said everything would be okay." She felt a little breathless suddenly. The day of her grandmother's funeral had been the worst day of her life. She didn't need a repeat performance to prove what family meant to her. "You said I have nothing to worry about."

"That is because he is at peace. Ready to leave this realm for another."

"Leave this . . ." She forced a laugh. "Well, it just so happens that that's *not* okay," she said, and slammed the palm of her hand against the driver's door of her unoffending vehicle. "It's not okay at all."

He nodded. "It's all right to be angry."

"I'm *not* angry! I just don't want to be lied to anymore!"

"Lied to . . ." He shook his head, but she was already jerking open her door. He caught her arm. "I have never lied to you, Bravura."

She froze, feeling the warmth of his fingers, the truth of his words. But she snatched her arm away and slid onto the cold comfort of the Chevy's cracked leather seats. "I've heard that before," she said and, slamming the door, roared away with Walt riding shotgun.

Chapter 15

"Vura," Dane said and, rising rapidly, shoved his cell phone into the pocket of his artfully distressed jeans. "I was just calling you."

"My phone didn't ring."

"Reception's terrible out here," he said, and shrugged. "Doesn't matter now." A smile replaced the smudge of irritation that had been on his face. It was one of the first attributes that had made her fall in love with him. That quick, nothing-can-touch-me grin.

"Is something wrong?" She kept her voice quiet. She was a firm believer in letting sleeping dogs lie, and Lily was as drowsy as a puppy in her arms.

"Can't a guy miss his wife anymore?" he asked. "Here." He kissed her cheek, then smiled at their daughter. "Let me take her."

Vura glanced at her daughter's perfect features, the downy lashes dropped over pristine cheeks, the clover-honey skin, the cotton-caramel hair. Unconscious now, breathing softly . . . quiet, as she only was in sleep. Sometimes Vura felt as if she could stare at her all day, just watch her breathe, in and out like a soft, warm breeze. A little unplanned miracle, that's what she was. But the little miracle was getting heavy. Getting bigger every day, so that Vura's muscles strained and her back ached just carrying her from the truck to the house. Still, it was difficult to let her go, to slip her into Dane's outstretched arms.

"You okay?" His gaze settled on hers, warm and supportive. Strange how such a simple thing touched her. Emotions bubbled. Tears threatened, but she nodded, holding them back.

"Yeah. I'm fine. Thanks."

He nodded once, then turned toward the stairs. For a moment Vura was tempted to follow, to touch her only child one more time before being separated for the night, but she forced herself to wander into the kitchen. Dane deserved to have a moment with his daughter. Besides, she hadn't eaten since noon, when she had still been worried about Mrs. Washburn's reaction to what Hip called the kitchen that hell barfed up. Even so, she didn't feel particularly hungry. Which was odd. Dad had said on more than one occasion that she could eat more than some horses and all boys. But maybe it was the memory of that god-awful kitchen that was putting her off. Still, food was a necessity, she reminded herself and opened her antiquated fridge.

She was still scanning the dismal contents when Dane shuffled in on stocking feet.

She turned toward him, momentarily forgetting her quest for sustenance. "Is she okay?"

"Who? Lily?" He tossed a thumb over his

shoulder and grinned, disarming as a kitten. "Didn't you just see her a minute ago?"

"Yeah. I know. But . . ." She felt silly. "Sometimes she wakes up . . ." She shook her head. Foolish took a sharp turn toward idiotic. "Did you put her in her own bed?"

He lifted his brows at her. "I thought it might be a little crowded with the three of us in our double." They had always planned on getting a king-sized mattress, but finances had been questionable from the get-go, then he had to leave for Williston and there didn't seem to be much point. He slipped his arms around her. "Don't you think?"

"Yeah." For reasons unknown, she wasn't quite sure where to look. "It's just that . . . sometimes she gets scared, and with you gone so much, I've gotten in the habit of letting her sleep with me."

Hip to hip, he leaned back and rocked her gently. "You know I wouldn't have left if I'd had a choice, baby."

"I know," she said, and felt a niggle of guilt for the times she *hadn't* known. That she had doubted . . . his motives, his loyalty . . . and sometimes . . . when the nights seemed to drag on forever . . . his intentions of ever returning.

"There just weren't any jobs around here."

She nodded and tried to understand. He had needed to prove himself, he'd said . . . as a husband, a provider. The fact that she could make a decent income while he struggled to get a job had gone mostly unspoken between them. That hadn't been his fault, either. It had always been so easy for her. Quinton Murrell was a demigod in the world of carpentry. Claiming kinship was like a magical key to every unfinished basement, every DIY gone wrong. That had been hard on Dane's ego. Perhaps there had been a time when Vura thought he should be able to put that behind him, for her . . . for Lily. In fact, she wasn't entirely sure she didn't feel the same way now.

"What?" he asked.

She glanced up and he tilted a grin at her.

"I know something's going through that adorable little head of yours. What are you thinking?"

She shrugged, paused, and loosed the thought. "It's just that I'm not sure if anything has changed."

"What do you mean?"

"It's not like the economy is booming here in the Hills. How are you going to get a job now if you couldn't before?"

He held her gaze with his. Adoration switched on in his eyes, melding with a yearning as soft as candle wax.

The expression melted something inside her, making her tongue thick and her limbs feel heavy. He'd always had that power in his arsenal when he wanted to use it.

"Dane—" she began, but he gently kissed her

neck between the edge of her collar and the curve of her jaw.

"Williston's no place for a family man, Vey. There are men there who'd just as soon slit your throat as . . ." He shook his head. Something flashed through his eyes. It almost looked like fear, but in a moment it was gone, replaced by overt admiration again. "Truth is, I couldn't stand being away from you any longer."

"I missed you, too, but what about—"

"Work?" he finished for her and chuckled softly as he leaned back, gazing at the ceiling and pressing his hips more firmly to hers. "I had no idea when I met that cute little pigtailed girl in shop class that she would be so obsessed with making a buck." He dropped his gaze back to hers with a grin.

"I'm not obsessed with it. I just want to be able to pay the bills. Maybe get the washing machine fixed. Buy a furnace that'll actually start in the fall."

He kissed her ear with slow intent and smiled into her eyes. "I'll take care of the washing machine."

She shook her head, though it was getting more difficult to think by the moment. "We might need a new one."

"Then we'll buy a new one."

She stifled a moan when he kissed the hollow of her throat and tilted her head back the slightest degree. "With what?" The question was little more than a rasp of pleasure.

"I believe legal tender is the generally accepted method."

"Money doesn't grow on trees, you know," she said, and felt stupid just for spilling the words.

But he laughed. "Geez, you sound as crotchety as my old man."

Her thoughts, slippery as eels, slid back to her grandfather, so frail beneath the unrelenting white of the hospital sheets. She straightened, pushed back a little. "Sometimes crotchety old men make a lot of sense."

"Not as much sense as the good-natured young. Like you and me." He squeezed her. "Life's short, baby. Let's live a little. Have some fun."

"That sounds great," she admitted. "But what about the bills?"

He shook his head, still smiling. "I'll get a job. I'm already looking. You know that."

"But you looked before you left, right?"

"My adorable little doubter," he said, and kissed her nose. "Yeah, I looked, but this time I'll take whatever's available. Short-order cook, dog poop collector . . ." He bent his knees a little to lock his gaze with hers. Sincerity shone in the depths of his eyes, but desire was just as clear. "Anything." The whispered word was as reverent as a prayer. "If it means I can be with my girl."

It sounded so good. So right, but doubt had

burrowed deep into her bones during the months of their separation. "Girls," she corrected softly.

His brows dipped a little, but in a second his lips twisted into a grin again. "You think I could forget about my Lily Pad?"

She didn't answer.

"Is that what you think?" His tone had sharpened a little.

"No. Of course not. It's just that . . ." She shrugged. It was odd, standing there in her Carhartts, slowly simmering with long-repressed desire, a blushing debutant in canvas overalls. "You've been gone so long."

He kissed her, softly, slowly. The caress fired up a half-dozen forgotten emotions, a cauldron of bubbling hormones.

"Well, I'm not gone now, am I?" he asked. His voice was low and quiet. The words brushed softly against her lips, against her soul.

"No."

"No," he agreed and kissed her again.

"So where *have* you been?"

"You mean today?" He pulled her closer, rubbed himself gently against her. "Didn't I tell you? I went to talk to Kevin. See if he had any job openings."

"I thought that was this morning."

A shadow of displeasure crossed his boyish features. He had never liked being questioned about his whereabouts. But Vura felt itchy, foolish, oddly dissatisfied. There had been a time when she had ditched her overalls for sundresses and swirly skirts. Had ditched who she really was, too, maybe. All the while insisting that it was *her* idea. But over the past several months, she had found a shadow of her former self, that girl who had known she was different. Had known and been proud.

"Kev said Emerson might be hiring."

"Really?" She didn't try to disguise the hope in her tone. Emerson, Inc. was one of the area's biggest steel building manufacturers. They had a good reputation and solid standing in the community. A community as tightly knit as an all-wool sweater. "Are they?"

Dane shook his head and hooked his thumbs into the hammer loops of her overalls. "Not right now, but I helped them out a little while I was asking around. Fred . . . you remember Freddie Langton, don't you?" he asked, and nuzzled her neck.

"Angie's uncle?" she asked, and felt her system amp up a little more. They'd gone to school with Angela Langton. Small, cute, and ultra-feminine, she had worn clingy shirts and butt-hugging leggings to class every day during their senior year. The effects had not gone unappreciated. But tonight Dane was acting as if she herself was as delectable as any lip-licking centerfold. So maybe their time apart hadn't been wasted. Maybe it had been good for them.

"Angie's uncle. Yeah." He nodded. "He was already ancient when we were in middle school. Anyway, he was pouring cement so I helped out. Thought maybe if they saw a guy with a little juice left in him, they might consider hiring someone this side of a hundred."

Vura winced, felt herself pull away.

"Baby . . ." He tugged her back. "What's wrong?"

"Nothing," she said, but her grandfather's tired face appeared in her mind.

"Come on, honey." He turned her back toward him. "This is me you're talking to."

She breathed a sigh, closed her eyes. "I'm afraid Gamps isn't going to . . ." She couldn't quite force out the rest of the sentence. "I'm worried about him."

"About your grandfather? Why?"

"He's really sick." She swallowed, silently chiding herself. She had friends who had barely blinked at the passing of their grandfathers, but maybe they hadn't learned to caulk a sink from their Gamps, to shoot a twelve-gauge, to do a hand-stand. Maybe they hadn't learned every single verse of "Stand Up for Jesus" while snuggled between him and the woman he loved more than life. "Anyway . . ." She cleared her throat. "He's been in and out of the hospital all month."

"Oh no." He breathed the words. "No wonder you've been so upset."

"I thought I told you."

"Did you? Yeah." He nodded. "I guess you did. With everything that's been going on, it must have slipped my mind." Exhaling heavily, he dropped his forehead against hers. "I'm sorry, sweetheart." He smelled wonderful, and his hand, where it caressed her back, eased away a little knot of tension. "I'm such an insensitive clod sometimes."

"Yeah, you are," she said, and they both grinned, faces close, chasing away a dozen worries.

"But listen . . . Randall Murrell is a tough old bird. He'll probably outlive us all."

"You think so?"

"Remember when he broke his finger while putting that sink in for . . . who was it?"

"The Gilberts."

"Yeah." He chuckled. "Gil told him to get his ass to the hospital, but he didn't. Just bandaged it up with electrical tape and finished the job."

Vura grinned. "He can be a little stubborn."

Dane huffed a laugh. "Mules can be a little stubborn. Your grandfather can be downright ornery."

"I know. But that's the thing. I've barely ever seen him sneeze. He always seemed so . . . invincible, almost. But now . . ."

"He's really not doing well?"

"I don't think so. I mean . . . he was resting pretty comfortably, I guess." She sighed, remembering the scene she had left less than an hour before. "Tonk was there. I think that actually helped."

"Tonk?" His hand stilled on her back.

"You met him at the race. Remember?"

"The dude with the girly hair, right?"

"I wouldn't call it . . ." She paused and wondered why she was arguing. She had always favored neatly cropped men. Half the time she was tempted to chop off her own hair, but she'd learned early on in her coverall-wearing days that being mistaken for a boy wasn't all that appealing. "Anyway, he . . ." She pursed her lips and remembered to breathe. "He burned some sweetgrass."

"Why?"

"To purify the air. Help bring him peace, I guess."

"I meant, why was he there?" he asked, and released her with a scowl.

"Oh." She shrugged. "Just to see Gamps, I suppose."

His brows lowered a fraction of an inch. "They bosom buddies or something?"

She scowled. It was a fair question; who would take time to visit an old man he barely knew? "Maybe Tonk has some amends to make."

"Amends for what?"

"I get the feeling he just wants to help out. Do what he can. I think he's kind of a . . ." She felt foolish again. "Kind of a medicine man or something."

He snorted. "I get the feeling he's kind of a con man."

"What?"

"Think about it, Vey. Your grandpa's not exactly destitute, is he?"

She shrugged. "I guess he's got some savings."

"Some savings," he said, and laughed. "Vey, just because he's as tightfisted as a troll doesn't mean he's not rolling in dough. You think it's a coincidence that he's just about to gasp his last breath and suddenly this guy shows up from out of nowhere with a bundle of stinking weeds and a . . ."

He stopped. She stared at him, heart pounding a slow dirge in her chest.

"I didn't mean it like that, baby," he said.

She shook her head, numb, wounded.

He swore and tried to pull her close again, but she tugged out of his grip. "I don't know what's wrong with me, baby. That's not what I meant at all. I've always liked the old man."

She breathed a laugh.

"I did," he said. "I mean, I know he wasn't *my* biggest fan after I knocked up his little princess, but he was a good guy. I always said that."

She stared at him aghast. *"Was?"*

"*Is!* I meant *is*," he said, and blew out a hard breath. "I just keep messing everything up today. I guess I'm more tired than I realized."

Sadness burned her throat, stung her eyes.

"Come on, baby," he said and, reaching out, grasped her hand. "Let's go upstairs, forget about everything for a few minutes." He smiled, suggestive. "Or a few hours."

She blinked back the tears.

"Okay?" He tugged her a little closer.

"Sure," she said, but even as she said it, she found herself backing away. "I just have to lock up the birds first."

He rubbed his thumb over her knuckles. "Can't they fend for themselves for one night?"

Maybe she should agree, go upstairs, forget about everything. Maybe a good wife would do just that, but the faces of her grandfather, her daughter, her father all blended together, spinning her into a miasma of should-haves and musts and what-ifs. "It's been kind of a . . ." She cleared her throat. "Kind of a tough week. If we lost a chicken, Lily would be heartbroken."

"Well . . ." Dane abruptly dropped her hand. "We wouldn't want to upset Lily."

"No, we wouldn't," she said, and twisted to turn away, but he caught her arm.

"Vey."

She snapped her gaze back to his.

"Jeez, you've always been a pistol when you're mad."

"I'm not mad, I'm just—"

"What?" he asked, and raised his brows at her.

"Tired."

"Yeah? That why your eyes are spitting at me like a wildcat's?"

"Listen, Dane . . ." She let her shoulders slump. "I don't have the energy to fight tonight."

"Good. Then you go on upstairs and—"

"I can't leave the chickens to—"

"Annnd . . ." He grinned, pulling her close again. "I'll go take care of the poultry."

"You don't have to do that."

"I know," he said, and kissed her. "But you've been carrying the load long enough. It's time I do my part."

"Sometimes the hens roost outside and have to be gathered up."

"Then I'll gather them up."

"Once they're roosting, they don't move, so they're kind of hard to find unless you know—"

"Vey . . ."

She stopped talking, took a breath.

"Let's just assume I'm smarter than the chickens, okay?"

She forced herself to forego any further arguments, though it was difficult. "Okay."

He nodded and kissed her again. "Maybe you could . . ." He shrugged, tugged on one of the straps of her overalls. "Slip into something a little . . ." He smiled and slid his hand between the Carhartts' metal buttons that were fastened at her hip. His skin felt warm as it burrowed beneath her shirt. "Less comfortable." He massaged gently.

174

She felt her head fall back a half an inch.

"What'dya say?" The question was breathed like a prayer against her sensitized ear.

"Okay."

"It'll be better than okay," he said, and kissed her again. "That's a promise."

Chapter 16

Vura awoke slowly, emerging from her so-real dreams with slow reluctance. She'd been sur- rounded by moonlit waters. Waves caressed her naked skin like liquid silk, and his hands . . . those gentle, powerful hands, flowed over her body in concert with the steady beat of his heart against her back. The slow rhythm of his voice awakened half-forgotten desires and set her nerve endings buzzing. The horse beneath them stood contentedly, waves lapping at her withers, carrying her tail like a flag on the warm currents. Starlight shone like diamonds on her glistening neck, on the water, on the long midnight hair of the man whose bare thighs cradled hers from behind. The man with the Indian-deep voice and the artist's magical—

She opened her eyes with a snap and shoved the dream to the farthest reaches of her mind. Reality shifted to the forefront.

She felt a little chilly, a little itchy. It took her a

moment to realize why: Instead of her usual T-shirt and shorts, she had donned a lacy little number Dane had bought her years ago. Cut high at the hip and low at the chest, it had not, she realized, been created for comfort. Even now, one of the narrow ivory straps was cutting into her shoulder. She tugged at it groggily. Her hair was still sloshed across her face like a dark wave, casting the morning in sable shadows, but her daughter's chipper little voice wrenched her to full wakefulness.

"Whatcha wearing?"

"What?" Vura yanked her gaze to Lily and past, grappling with memories. Where was she? What had she done? And with whom? Dane! Where was he? It took her a moment to remind herself she had nothing to feel guilty about; Dane was her husband. It took longer still to realize she hadn't seen him since their poultry discussion the previous night. "I . . ." She tugged her attention from the empty doorway to her daughter.

"What's wrong, Mama?" Lily asked, and climbed laboriously onto the mattress, a tattered Foo Foo in tow.

"Nothing." Vura inched the blankets up to her chin. "Nothing's wrong, honey."

"Did you lose your Black Diamonds T-shirt?"

"No. I just . . ." She cleared her throat, feeling foolish and wishing she had gone with an affirmative. The loss of her softball team's shirt would at least give her an excuse for the silly garment she was now wearing. But if she had learned anything as the mother of an über-curious child, she knew that a lie would haunt her until the day she cried uncle. "I just thought it would be nice to wear something different for a change."

"Oh." Lily was kneeling on the bed, lining up a hundred questions in her disheveled little head. "Did your Pops buy that for you?"

Vura blinked. The idea of her father purchasing such an article of clothing made her cheeks burn. "Listen, honey, why don't you go get dressed, and I'll—"

"Pops likes white," she said, and bounced slightly, head bobbling. "His truck's white."

Vura pulled the covers a little tighter to her chin. The stupid negligee was half-lace, half-torture, all embarrassment. "I know, sweetheart. Now, why don't you—"

"And his going-to-church shirts . . . they're white."

Vura glanced out the open door and into the hall. Where the devil was Dane? Had she been so deeply asleep she hadn't even heard him come to bed? But if he had joined her, why was he already up? Dane Lambert was not known to be an early riser. Then again, he had been gone a long time. And people could change. Maybe he was already out looking for a job. She shifted her gaze to the window. The sun had barely made an

177

appearance, but construction work often began at dawn.

"And Yogi . . . he's practically white," Lily said, referring to her grandfather's dog. As close as they could guess, Yogi was a cross between a golden retriever and a Newfoundland. Or maybe a bear. Luckily, he favored the temperament of the retriever more than the grizzly. "His snowmobile's white."

"You're right, honey," Vura said, and realized, not to her surprise, that the potentially endless list of all things white was making her eye twitch.

" 'Course it's got blue stripes, but it's mostly white. And you know what? His hair's kinda—"

"Hey, Lily Belle . . ." Vura interrupted gently, but her daughter ignored her with the smooth disregard of all self-respecting five-year-olds.

She screwed up her tiny face. "What do you call a white that's not real white?"

"I'm not sure, but I bet the chickens would like to get out of their coop. Your—"

"Pops's chickens!" she exclaimed and stopped bouncing as if just discovering the answer to the world's most fascinating mysteries. "They're *all* white."

Vura refrained from hiding under the covers. "That's true. But . . . wait!" She cocked her head as if hearing some unknown noise from the driveway. "What's that sound?"

"I didn't hear nothing." Lily dropped distractedly to her knees. "Your bedsheets are white," she said, and tugged at them. Vura tugged back.

"Maybe it's your grandfather," she suggested.

Lily paused for a second, then widened her eyes. "Hey . . . Pops's eggs," she said, and began bouncing on her knees, almost ripping the blankets from Vura's white-knuckled grip. "How come his eggs are white and ours aren't?"

The flannel shirt Vura had worn on the previous day was lying over the arm of the nearby rocking chair. She could almost reach it from the bed.

"Is it cuz his chickens are white?" Lily asked and, abandoning the blankets, bounced in a circle.

"Maybe."

"I like the white eggs. But I like ours better. And the speckled ones . . ." She hopped closer. "They're my favorites. Did you know that horses aren't born white? Hardly never. That's what Tonka says. They're dark when they're little. Even the Lipizzaner. Their hair is white, but their skin is dark so they're called gray." She paused for a second. "Do you think we could get purple eggs if we had purple chickens?"

"I don't know," Vura said, and grasped hopelessly at a much-used straw. "Maybe you could look that up in your book."

"What book?"

"Any one that's downstairs."

Lily considered that a second, then shook her

179

head and bounced again. "Naw. I'd rather talk to you about white stuff."

God help her. "I'd like to talk to you, too, Lily Belle, but I promised your Pops that I'd—"

"What was that?" The girl froze, eyes wide. And now the faint squeak of a metal door eased into the room.

"I told you I thought someone was here," Vura said, though that wasn't quite true. But Lily was already scrambling off the bed, rushing toward the window.

Her gasp was something between a squeal and a hiss. "He's here," she rasped, and then she was gone, sprinting out the door and pattering down the uneven steps.

Vura huffed a relieved sigh. It was tempting to lie in bed a little longer, to be lazy just this once. But Lily was not the kind of child who would ever foster sloth. She had inherited her energy from Quinton Murrell. Which made Vura wonder what her father was doing here at this time in the morning. And where was Dane? Had she already turned him away with her god-awful snoring?

Unsettled now, she shoved the blankets back and swung her bare feet to the floor. But the nasty thoughts remained with her. Maybe it wasn't her snoring he had found revolting. Maybe it was the five pounds she had gained since Lily's conception. Rising, she turned to gaze at herself in the mirror above the old-fashioned dresser that had come with the house. Her hair was a mess, scrambled like dark cotton candy around her face, and her legs were never going to be mistaken for a supermodel's, but . . .

Something snagged her attention. She turned toward the window just in time to see Lily's bare feet fly through the air.

She froze, gaze riveted on the scene below. The scene in which Tonkiaishawien Redhawk was swinging her tiny, recently injured daughter onto a sixteen-hand horse.

"Do not forget to sit upright," Tonk said, and nodded as the tiny girl straightened like a soldier on Arrow's solid back.

"Are you really going to keep them with us?" Lily's tone was awed, her eyes round with new-morning wonder as she wrapped a restless hand in the gelding's parti-colored mane. If the kid was any cuter, it would defy every single law of nature.

"Is that acceptable to you, *Chitto Sihu*?" he asked.

She nodded emphatically.

"Then they shall remain here," he said. "If you will help me keep them safe."

"Me?" The single word was breathy with excitement.

"Ai," he said, "but you will have to learn to ride like a warrior."

"Okay," she said, and pulled her fingers carefully from the pinto's mane.

It was not a simple task to keep from smiling, but he had no wish to insult her solemn reverence. Even in the dawn's cautious light, he could see the purple sutures that marched like soldiers, battered but valiant, across her torn ear. "Do not be ashamed to hold on if you have a need," he said. "But remaining aboard requires more balance than strength."

"Balance?" Her feet were bare, her toes cute as kittens. She'd shoved a stuffed animal securely under one arm. It might have been a rat.

He nodded. "It is said that long ago the Great Spirit split us down the middle so we could be as one with the horse, but no one is strong enough to hold himself astride by strength alone."

She made a face, thinking it through. "Even Hunk?"

Holy crimony, she called his brother Hunk? No wonder the great hulking bear nearly burst into tears every time the kid's name was mentioned. Or . . . Tonk watched her wide eyes, her attentive expression. Maybe it was because she was the embodiment of all things Native, intelligence, curiosity, spirit.

"Even Hunk," he agreed and refrained, with some difficulty, from denigrating the brother he had always so shamelessly admired. "But if you learn to be one with the horse, you will have no

182

need to use your hands," he added and lifted his free arm level with his shoulder.

She blinked at him, held her breath for five heartbeats, then tentatively raised both her arms in tacit concert.

He gave her an affirming nod. "Very good, small flower."

She grinned, gap-toothed and charming. "Am I ones with the horse yet?"

"You are well on your way, but you may have to learn a bit more still," he said, grateful that the gelding felt no need to do more than graze as the tiny figure sat still as a stone atop him.

"More?"

"A bit."

"Like galloping?" she asked.

He did grin now, loving her daring. "Perhaps your mother would be happier if you walked first."

She nodded, seeming to see the sense in that. "Can we walk now?"

It was a beautiful morning. Not a whisper of a breeze disturbed the stillness. The infant sun was warm on his back, and the scent of spring grasses tickled his nostrils with hope. Lavender clouds bubbled up over the long sweep of western hills, suggesting an afternoon of rain, but for now there was no better time to commune with the horse.

Nodding solemnly, he drew Arrow's muzzle

from his impromptu breakfast. "If you are sure your mother won't mind."

"Mama likes horses."

"Does she?" He could imagine Bravura Lambert astride and unfettered on one of his steeds, but he pushed the thought aside. "Very well then," he said and, grasping the end of the cotton lead in his left hand, shooed the pinto to the end of the line.

Arrow ambled off, then circled lazily.

Lily's arms dipped at the movement, but in a second she had raised them to shoulder height again.

Tonk nodded his approval. "Lean forward just a bit."

"Over the withers?"

He raised his brows, impressed by her vocabulary. "If you lean back too far over his loins, you will topple off his hindquarters if he moves unexpectedly."

"I don't want to do that," she said, face solemn.

"No," he agreed, "you do not."

"I already got my ear bit."

"Mothers can be aggressive if they believe their young are threatened."

"Lily!" Vura gasped and sprang like a tiger from the house behind them.

Chapter 17

It seemed to Tonk that a dozen things happened at once. Bravura Lambert shot like a missile onto her porch, Lily gasped, and Arrow, trusty steed that he was, skittered just a little to the right.

And suddenly the child was falling, slipping from his horse's back like a hapless Humpty Dumpty.

Terror ripped through him. He was leaping forward before the reality of the situation ever really touched his consciousness. Leaping forward, lifting his arms, and capturing the child against his chest like a carelessly lobbed football.

It wasn't a pretty catch. She was folded against him like an ungainly accordion, arms and legs scrambled, eyes wide with fear, but she never touched the ground, never broke so much as a fingernail.

Still, Tonk felt a little shaky.

"Are you all right?" His tone sounded breathy to his own ears.

She blinked into his face, amber hair a veil over her wild pixie face. "I'm sorry."

"Sorry," he breathed and felt his overtaxed heart bump back to life.

"I musta been leaning too far back," she said. "You said not to, and then when Arrow shied . . ."

"Lily!" Bravura rasped and snatching her daughter from Tonk's arms, crushed her against her chest.

The motion tugged her plaid work shirt nearly off her left shoulder, exposing a swath of ivory lace over creamy mocha skin. The image was strangely erotic, disturbingly disorienting. But her snarled question yanked Tonk's attention back to her face.

"What the hell do you think you're doing?"

He tried to think of an appropriate response. Generally he had a half a dozen smart-aleck answers ready to spout at a moment's notice, but there was something about that faded flannel shirt juxtaposed against her Indian summer skin that brought all his ready remarks to a screeching halt.

"I . . . I . . ."

"She could have been . . ." Bravura stopped, smoothed a hand down her daughter's tangled hair, and hugged the child more tightly to her half-exposed chest. "She could have been killed."

"I was just—"

"Just *what?*" She snarled the word.

His foolishly suicidal gaze tried to slip back to her chest, but he kept it resolutely on her face. "Sorry," he said.

"You were just *sorry?*"

"Not *just* sorry," he said, and felt the pressure of keeping his eyes front and center begin to take a toll on his psyche. Self-control had never been his strong suit. Holy crap, hadn't he proven that a thousand half-remembered times? "*Extremely* sorry."

"You bet your sorry ass, you're sorry," she growled. "You're the sorriest—"

"Am I gonna have to tell Pops?" Lily asked.

The adults snapped their attention to the child, who scowled meaningfully at her mother.

"You know how he feels about filthy mouths," she added.

"Oh!" Vura's eyes went wide, as if she had entirely forgotten her daughter's presence. "I'm sorry, honey. I was just so . . . I was just so worried that I—"

"It's okay, Mama. I'm not hurt," Lily said, and wriggled a little. The movement displaced her mother's shirt a bit more.

Tonk felt sweat break out on his hairline. "I should have . . ." he began but Lily squirmed again, and suddenly he had no idea what he should have done or shouldn't have done or honestly what he was even talking about. He tightened his jaw.

"What's wrong with *you?*" Bravura demanded.

"Are you okay, Tonka?" Lily asked.

"Ai," he managed, though he feared he was being overly optimistic. "I am well."

Her mother scowled. "Listen, Lily, why don't you go let the chickens out and gather the eggs."

"Come with me."

"I'll be there in a minute, honey. I just want to speak to Tonk for a second."

"Why?"

"It's grown-up talk."

Lily scowled. "I don't want you scolding him."

Her mother's brows rose.

Lily skipped her gaze to Tonk's. "He's probably feeling bad already cuz I fell off. But it wasn't his fault. He said I should be sure to sit in the middle."

"Did he?"

Tonk would never understand how the woman could enunciate so clearly through gritted teeth, but Lily seemed neither impressed nor aware. Instead, she continued glibly on.

"Uh-huh. Straight as a warrior, he said. But I musta leaned too far cuz I'm just a *young* warrior."

"That must be it. Now trot on over to the chickens, honey. They'll want their breakfast."

Lily opened her mouth as if to argue, but Bravura raised a brow and the girl, being no fool, scooted off.

Tonk watched her go. "She is a fine—"

"What were you thinking?" she snarled, effectively drawing Tonk's attention back to her.

Dammit, the shirt was still askance, still showing an abundance of all-too-touchable skin.

He exhaled, trying to find his equilibrium, his glib tongue, or at least his sanity. "The child wished to learn to ride."

"Well, that *child* happens to be my daughter. *My* daughter. Do you understand what that means? That means you have no right to throw her up on any old animal that crosses her path," she said, and tossed a denigrating hand toward Arrow, who snorted derisively, then continued to graze.

Tonk narrowed his eyes, temper brewing slowly. "Do you want her to fear?"

"What?"

"She is brave and free and wise beyond her years. But if you gasp every time she skins a knee or bobbles off balance, you will weaken her spirit."

"So now you're going to tell me how to raise my daughter?"

He gritted his teeth. "If you need help, I will try to do so."

"Well, I don't need help." She growled the words.

He narrowed his eyes. "It must be a wonderful thing to be able to raise the child with no help whatsoever."

"I've got help. She was with others. Look how that turned out." Her chest heaved with anger. His temper simmered in response, but he took a careful breath and held it in check.

"That is why she must touch the horse today. So that she does not fear them."

"I would rather she was terrified every day of her life than to be injured again."

He straightened his back, appalled. "Do not say such a thing."

She huffed, but he continued.

"It is your job to keep her from fear, to make her strong."

"Listen, buddy, I think I know what my job is, and it has nothing to do with letting her tumble off a horse like fallen—"

"You are wrong," he said, and found he could do nothing but hold her gaze now. "The mustang is her power animal."

"What are you talking about?"

"Her spirit is connected to things of the wild. The wind, the coyote, but, I believe, it is entwined most strongly with the horse."

She exhaled a laugh. "That's the stupidest thing I've ever heard."

He shook his head. "She is not afraid, but you can change that if you so desire."

She narrowed her eyes and clenched her fists. It occurred to him that a wiser man might back away. He was not a wiser man.

"You think I *want* her to be afraid?" she demanded.

"I think she has the courage of our ancestors, but fear is infectious."

"I'd have to be an idiot not to be afraid when I see my daughter fall."

"We all fear something," he admitted. "But we must not be afraid to live."

Her eyes narrowed dangerously. "You think I'm afraid of life."

He exhaled, forced his hands into the back pockets of his jeans for safekeeping, and carefully shifted his attention toward the overgrown pastures. "Perhaps I should get started repairing—"

"You think I'm afraid of life?" Her voice had risen slightly.

He almost closed his eyes, almost shook his head in silent self-disgust. What the hell was he doing here with this woman who hated him? There were women who didn't detest him. Maybe a few who actually found him appealing, who didn't stew and sputter every time he came within spitting distance.

"I'm raising a daughter on my own," she growled, chest heaving. "Starting a business. Buying a farm . . ." She swept her hand sideways. The motion encompassed the house, the barn, the tilting chicken coop, but it was impossible to notice any of those. Two breasts would trump a hundred dilapidated buildings. But he focused hard on a concave roof and tried to remember how to formulate words. Articulate words if he was lucky.

"I know a guy in Hot Springs who specializes in restoring old—"

"And you think I'm afraid of life?" she snarled.

There was no way out. He was just too damned good at digging holes. He resisted sighing.

Resisted wincing. "Sometimes we live fast so we do not have to take time to think. I have done that, Bravura. Do not make the same mistake," he advised and turned away.

But she caught his arm in a talon-like grip. "You think you're so—" she began, but she stopped in her proverbial tracks as a canary yellow Dodge turned into the yard, driven, of course, by the husband of the woman who was currently half-dressed and holding him captive.

Chapter 18

It took a moment for a dozen wayward thoughts to tumble into Tonk's overheated brain: It was barely six in the morning. Dane Lambert was just arriving. Bravura was in a stunning but inexplicable state of undress. How did these facts align?

Something rumbled from her throat. It sounded a little like a growl. Had Tonk been free to do so, he would have taken a step to the rear, though he was almost inclined to believe he wasn't the cause of her ire. Or at least not the *only* cause. Why had her husband been absent? True, she was a spit-fire, but wasn't it just that kind of woman who intrigued, who accomplished, who fulfilled and created and inspired? What kind of man could walk away from that?

It took a moment for the answer to soak into his soul: his kind. His kind would walk away. His kind was exceptional at doing just that. Or at least he had been before being dragged kicking and cursing into an AA meeting, where Bill W's crazy ideas of forgiveness and redemption were consumed like magic Kool-Aid.

But he tried. God knew, he tried to walk that line . . . to improve himself so that maybe someday he'd be good enough for . . .

He let his gaze slip back to Bravura as the sunburst muscle car pulled to a halt beside them. She wasn't his type, of course. He preferred women who had more . . . He gritted his teeth, thinking hard. Or at least some . . . Still, any woman who could raise a daughter like Lily deserved a good deal. Kindness, for sure. Thoughtfulness, definitely. But more than that. She should have all good things. What she deserved was a man like his brother, someone who would stand behind her, beside her.

Seeing her now, however, he wondered if she needed anyone at all. Her head was high, her eyes flashed with spirit, and for a moment he couldn't seem to pull his gaze away.

But the slam of the Viper's door shattered his reverie.

Dane Lambert stepped out, brows raised. "What's going on?"

Bravura shrugged, seemed to realize at the last

moment that she was still gripping Tonk's arm like a milling vise, and slowly peeled her fingers away. "Tonkiaishawien brought his horses." She said the words crisply, almost like a challenge.

Tonk tensed. It wasn't the first time he would be on the knuckles end of an angry husband so he would take his lumps, but it did seem a little unfair that he was about to be decked by a man whose wife he hadn't even had the pleasure of seeing naked. Step eight, however, insisted that he be willing to make amends to those he had harmed, and since his alcohol-induced stupidity did not allow him to remember all those he had injured, he was just going to have to take it on the chin from someone whom he would kind of like to pop. He clenched his jaw, tempted to do so, but Dane grinned and reached out his right hand. "Good to see you again, Tonk." They shook, civil as democrats. "But I don't understand." He glanced from one to the other without so much as a single curse. And what the hell was that about? His wife was a scrap of plaid from being naked. If the situation was reversed, Tonk would swing an uppercut into the other man's jaw, coax his wife into the house, and spend the day doing something far more constructive than grinning like an ape. "You going for a ride?"

A muscle ticked in Bravura's cheek, but she managed to pry her jaws apart. "I said he could keep his horses here."

Tension bubbled around them like boiling tar, but if Dane noticed, he was a master of deception, Tonk thought, and wondered if he had just hit the nail dead on the head.

"If that's okay with you," Bravura added.

Another silence, stretched to the breaking point then gently released by Dane's easy shrug.

"Sure. I mean, we've got the space, right?"

Holy cats, what was wrong with this guy? Okay, maybe not every living, breathing woman in America was ready to throw her panties at Tonk's feet, but he had the blowing-in-the-wind hair, the invincible warrior-stance, the entire proud Native persona firmly in place. Surely, he was something of a threat to this idiot man's seemingly unimpeachable security.

"Right," Bravura said, and made the single word sound surprisingly like a curse.

"I will pay, of course," Tonk said into the odd abyss.

"Well, that's great then. It's a win-win." Lambert raised his brows a little. "But hey, honey . . ." He grinned at his wife. "Maybe you should button up a little before you catch a cold."

Bravura's scowl darkened. She lowered her gaze to her shirt. Then, hissing a thin gasp that might have been comical under less stimulating circumstances, clutched her shirt together at the chest.

Dane chuckled a little. "That's my Vey," he said

and, wrapping a companionable arm around his wife's shoulder, drew her up against his side like an adorable puppy. "Totally unaware when she's got something else on her mind. Once when we was kids, she raced Billy Clayton across the reservoir. Beat him, too. But maybe that was because she'd lost her bikini top. Didn't even realize she was half-undressed till she climbed out of the water. Remember that, honey?" he asked, and gave her a friendly little shake. "Hey, Tonk, you wanna join us for breakfast?"

"He can't!" The words seemed to spurt from Bravura's lips. Her cheeks were as red as an autumn apple.

Tonk raised one questioning brow. If things got any damn weirder, he could sell tickets.

"I mean, he's got to take care of his horses and . . ." She glanced away, looked like she wished she was anywhere else, and tightened her grip on her shirt. "We don't have any . . . bread . . . for toast."

"Well, shoot. If I had known that when I went out this morning. I could have picked some up."

Tonk watched Bravura's eyes shadow with doubt. Watched her clench her teeth as if biting back inquiries, and it wasn't as if he didn't know he should leave. It wasn't that he was unaware of the fact that he should allow them some privacy to hash out their differences. If this Dane Lambert was a red-blooded male, that hashing out wouldn't take long, not with Bravura all flushed and disheveled and breathtakingly stunning in that sweet-earth way that was hers and hers alone . . . And . . . dung on a donut, he had to get out of there.

But before he could take a single step toward sanity, she spoke.

"You left this morning?" she asked, and Tonk found himself immobilized again. Why the devil didn't she know when her husband had vacated the premises? But Dane smiled and tightened his arm companionably around her shoulder.

"You were sleeping so sound. I didn't want to wake you," he said and, grinning suggestively, winked at Tonk. "Not after last night."

Her cheeks burned hotter, but something flared even brighter in her eyes. What was it? Embarrassment? Rage? Tonk resisted taking a cautious step back. "Oh, well . . ." She cleared her throat, inhaled. "That was . . . considerate of you. Thanks."

He chuckled. "Don't thank me yet," he said and, releasing her, hurried to his car. "Not until you see . . ." He paused as he popped the trunk on the Viper, then pulled out a long flat box. PANASONIC was printed in bold letters on the top.

Bravura scowled at it. "What's that?"

"What's that?" Dane echoed and laughed as he jerked his gaze to Tonk's in chummy male bonding. "Leave it to Vey to be so caught up in her own little world she can't even recognize a fifty-four-inch, high-definition flat screen. Hey . . ." His grin amped up a little. "Give me a hand here, will you, buddy?"

It took a moment for Tonk to realize the man whose wife was standing next to him in a scrap of nothing, the man whose wife he was trying like hell not to ogle, was referring to him with convivial camaraderie. But he jerked himself out of his weirdness-induced trance and stepped forward to take one end of the ungainly box.

"It's a television," Dane explained and winked at Tonk as if they shared some secret only Y genes understood.

"But we . . ." Hands still fisting her shirt across her chest, Bravura scowled at the offending box. "We already have a television."

"Is that what that is?" Dane asked and, after folding back the sleeves of his fancy cowboy shirt, tossed his chin toward the house. "You okay backing up the steps with this thing, Tonk?"

"Ai."

"Great," Dane said, and turned back to his wife. "I thought that clunky black box was something left over from the Dark Ages or something."

"You left me to . . ." She tightened her jaw and shifted her line of interrogation. "You bought it this morning?" she asked, and Dane chuckled as Tonk rose carefully to the first step.

"Well, sure. I bought a few things for you in Williston, but a couple pairs of jeans and a new handsaw aren't going to cut it after all these months."

"You bought me a handsaw?"

He laughed at her hopeful tone.

Well, crapola, wasn't he a jolly elf? And did he usually laugh while considering where to bury the bodies of the men who gawped at his wife?

"I know you don't think you'll use it, baby. But you'll love it when you get used to it. Once we get hooked up, we'll be able to get a hundred stations. Grab the door for our guest, will you, sweet-heart?"

Bravura stepped past Tonk to swing open the door. It squealed like a crypt in a second-rate slasher flick.

Dane rambled on. "Westerns, soaps, the jewelry station."

"Jewelry station?" Bravura sounded dubious at best.

Dane grinned over the TV at Tonk. "I knew that would get her. The only kind of sparklers Vey is interested in are diamond-cut wafering blades . . . or whatever the hell they're called. But, hey"— he shifted his attention back to his wife—"you'll be able to get . . . what's that show you like so much? *This Old House*. It'll be like that Bob Vila guy is right there in our living room."

"That's . . . great," Bravura said, but if she was trying to sell that lie, she would have to do so to someone who didn't have brothers.

"Isn't it?" Lambert asked, and shuffled into the living room. "Let's just set it down in the corner there."

Tonk did as told. The living space was cluttered but cozy, occupied with piles of children's books, a plethora of toy horses, and wallpaper stamped with images of . . . cattle, maybe?

Bravura stared at the Panasonic as if it had just committed a felony.

"Come on, honey, tell me you like it," Lambert coaxed, and taking her into his arms, bumped his hips against her.

"It's . . . That was really nice of you."

"And I got some cool stuff for Lily, too. Wait till you see. You sure you don't want to join us for breakfast, Tonk?"

The question jarred Tonk from a hundred uncharitable thoughts. "No. Thank you. I will see to the horses and begin the fencing."

"Fencing?"

"It is part of my payment."

"Oh, well, great. I'll be out to help you later. After I convince my wife here that she's the luckiest woman on the planet." He winked again. It was as creepy as hell, and strangely, rather made Tonk want to sock him in the throat.

Bravura blushed, and he laughed. "It may take a while," he said, and set her free. "I'm going to get Lil's gifts in. Why don't you get dressed up, baby. We'll have ourselves a nice breakfast."

"Oh . . . okay," she said, and turned uncertainly toward the stairs.

Tonk scowled. Since when did Bravura Lambert feel uncertain of anything? he wondered, but it only took him a moment to remember it was none of his business. A little longer to pass the living room bovine, escape the kitchen poultry, and tap down the steps into clean, fresh air.

Lambert went with him. "So you're Hunter Redhawk's brother, right?"

"Ai."

"You live with them at the institute there?"

It took Tonk a second to follow his line of inquiry. "I occasionally help out at Gray Horse Sanctuary, but I do not live there."

Silence echoed around them. Perhaps this guy wasn't as foolish as he seemed, Tonk thought. Perhaps he had simply been waiting for his wife's absence before he jumped him like a wolf on a hapless deer.

But his tone remained convivial. "So, where you bunking?"

"I rent a place in Buffalo Gap."

"Yeah? I used to raise hell in the Gap before . . ." He tilted his head toward the house behind them. "Before the family come along. Whose place you renting?"

"Halvorson's."

"Honey Halvorson's?" Dane raised his brows. "You lucky dog."

"Do you know her?"

Dane laughed, expression nostalgic. "Everyone knows Honey. But, hey . . ." Reaching out, he shook Tonk's hand again. "Thanks for helping out."

"You are welcome," Tonk said, and turned away. He felt strangely disoriented, oddly off-kilter, and he didn't know why. Okay, maybe it was because he had just spent ten minutes in the company of a dime-store cowpoke and his mostly naked wife. But come on, it wasn't as if Bravura's attire had really been that scandalous. One could see more skin at the beach . . . if one had a beach. So maybe it was his self-enforced celibacy that made the situation so disorienting.

Retrieving the lead of the grazing Arrow, Tonk opened the crooked wooden gate that led to a tiny pasture and led the pinto inside, but his mind never stopped spinning. What the hell was going on here? What kind of guy didn't care that his wife was scantily clad while talking to another man? And why would that guy leave in the small hours of the morning when he had a woman like Bravura Lambert in his bed? Okay, she could be a bear cat when riled, and Tonk himself favored soft women, sweet women, women who didn't want to kill him at the drop of a hat. But Bravura was probably as cuddly as a bunny where her husband was concerned.

It was impossible to say why she started spitting

tacks when Tonk was near. But he had seen her with Lily, had felt the warmth, had heard the laughter. Not that he cared. Not that he was attracted to her. But other men might be. She wasn't, after all, physically repulsive. Reaching for Arrow's halter, he snugged up the cheek piece, ready to turn him loose.

But just then a few sheets of paper, blown from Lambert's Viper, tumbled past in the rising wind. Tonk managed to stomp on one . . . tuck it into the pocket of his jeans.

"Dumb ass," Tonk muttered and managed to snatch a receipt from a nearby buttonweed. "No respect for our mother." Arrow glanced at him from one suspicious eye. "What?" Tonk asked. The pinto shook his head a little. "He's a polluter," Tonk explained. Arrow blew a gust of air through wide nostrils. It sounded a little like a scoff. "Listen, I don't have anything against the cute little dime-store cowpoke."

That eye again.

"I don't," he said, and wondered dismally when he had become such an abysmal liar that he couldn't even fool a horse. He had spent a lifetime faking everything from interest to innocence. But old Bill W insisted that he change. He glanced toward the house into which the cowpoke had disappeared, and though Tonk did his best, he couldn't quite banish the image of Bravura in the other man's arms. Bending, he retrieved another scrap of paper that had come to a halt against a leaning post. He crumpled the narrow sheet in his fist and ground his teeth.

What the hell was he thinking? She was married. Married! And if he was trying to change, honestly attempting to improve, then he had to at least honor that sacred vow.

Letting his shoulders drop, he stared into the pinto's eyes. They were solemn and bright and unwavering.

"Fine! You're right. Again. Is that what you want to hear?" he asked and, pivoting on his heel, led the gelding back toward the trailer. "We shouldn't be here." He glanced toward the house, wondering, against his will, if they were, even now, tearing the clothes from each other's bodies. "We're leaving," he added and stepped into the trailer. "But don't act so damned smug, cuz you're going to be missing out on a butt load of grass."

The pinto snorted and followed him inside. Shod hooves rang solidly against the matted floorboards.

"And the other two . . ." He nodded toward the duo that remained in the trailer. "They're gonna blame *you*."

Arrow shoved his muzzle into the nearest hay bag, not caring a whit.

"Yeah, well . . ." He secured the gelding with the nearest clip. "You think it doesn't matter right now, but wait until Lark finds out." Two slots ahead, the gray mare pawed at the wall, making the trailer clang like the inside of the Liberty Bell. "See what I mean? She's going to make your life a living hell."

The gelding snorted, spewing out a spray of green goo before returning happily to his alfalfa.

"Some proud steed you are."

The front door of the house banged again. Lambert tapped down the stairs, cute hair bobbling.

Tonk gritted his teeth, coming up with a hundred reasons to dislike him, though Bill W suggested it best to leave judgment to a higher power. The idea stopped him cold. "We're leaving. Right now," he said, but just when he was about to step out of the trailer, Lambert turned to retrieve yet another item from his Viper.

With his back turned, the roses embroidered across the shirt's yoke were visible for the first time.

Tonk froze. He'd seen that shirt before. At the Branding Iron. On the man with Sherri.

He pressed his shoulders against the wall of the trailer and tried to catch his breath, his wits. It couldn't be him. It couldn't be. No man, no matter how irrational, would step out on a woman like Bravura with a chippy like Sherri Unger.

Certain that was true, Tonk reached for the door, but doubts struck him like boulders. What if he was wrong? What if Lambert was doing just that?

He physically winced at the thought. Bravura would be devastated, and Lily, that wild warrior child, would be wounded, left to wonder if she was somehow to blame, if it was her fault her father was a pile of dog—

He stopped himself, remembering to be fair, or, if that was too gargantuan a feat, at least to be honest; he didn't know if Lambert had been the whiny guy with Sherri at the bar. He didn't know, but maybe he would stay close, just in case.

Chapter 19

"Man, you look great," Dane said, and smiled as Vura entered the room. She felt funny in her curve-hugging sweater and blinged-out blue jeans, but it was the greasy feel of foundation on her skin that gave her the true out-of-body experience. Then there was the fact that she had stabbed herself in the eye with the mascara wand, making her blink like a blinded barn owl.

But Dane had asked her to get dressed up, and maybe temporary myopia was a small price to pay for a solid marriage. "Thank you," she said.

"For the compliment or for the big-as-a-barn Panasonic?"

"For both . . ." She glanced toward the living room, where he had set up the TV. Despite the fact that those particular walls had been papered with pictures of dairy cows and red barns, it was still the ugliest thing in the room, at least to her way of thinking. The fact that there was an even bigger box standing near the door made her feel a little queasy. "I guess."

"You guess." He laughed. "Listen, I know you're not crazy about electronics, but this little baby is 4K Ultra HD. You can catch a YouTube video while watching"—he shook his head— "*Game of Thrones.*"

"*Game of Thrones?*"

He chuckled. "Let's just say it's ultra-cool. You can surf the web without interrupting your viewing pleasure. So it'll be good for business."

"Will it?" she asked, and scowled at the slightly curved screen. It was difficult to understand how a TV the size of her porch could be more helpful than a Sawzall. Or a new router. Or really dynamite rolled steel scaffolding.

"Sure. You'll be able to stay in tune with the latest remodeling ideas." He stroked the black screen like another might fondle a puppy. "Or find out who's offering the best prices on"—he shrugged again—"Sheetrock. You'll love it."

Maybe it was her nonresponse that pulled him out of his lustful perusal of the television.

"But not as much as I love you," he said and, catching her arms, gazed into her eyes.

"Do you?" she asked, and hated herself for the quiver in her voice.

"Baby," he said, and grinned. "Didn't I just pay seventeen hundred dollars to prove it?"

Quiet. Be quiet, she told herself. Her husband liked to spend money on her. Millions of women would love that . . . wouldn't they? Maybe she should, too, but . . .

"That's what I'm talking about." She said the words softly. "We don't *have* seventeen hundred dollars, Dane. If you had been here for the past fourteen months, you'd have known that. I've been working like a slave just to make the mortgage payments."

His face tightened. "It wasn't my idea to buy this place."

"I know. I know it wasn't," she said, and tugged her arms free. "But Lily . . ." Tonk's opinion about her daughter's needs rushed to her mind, but she wasn't foolish enough to voice another man's opinions. Not yet anyway. "Lily needs room to run. It helps her relax. That's what the specialists say."

"We're paying for specialists now?" His brows, so genially high just moments ago, lowered into a pouty ridge. "I thought we didn't have any money."

"For TVs and designer jeans," she said, and swept an aggravated hand toward his pants. "For muscle cars and . . ." She shook her head, running out of steam.

"So what you're saying is, we don't have money for the things *I* want."

Frustration ripened toward anger. "We don't have money for the things we don't *need*."

"The things *you* don't want. I can't win with——" He stopped himself, exhaled, then, capturing her right hand, he ran his thumb over her palm. Calluses made little moguls down the center line. "Listen, I don't want to fight. And this"—he nodded toward the Panasonic that loomed like a gargoyle against the lumbering dairy cows— "this is just a onetime deal, honey. Just a few homecoming gifts." He pulled her back against him. "Surely you can forgive me for buying a couple of little gadgets for my girls." He grinned that grin that used to make her stomach pitch. "I forgive *you*."

Where was that girl who used to go loopy over his grin? That girl whose feet never touched the ground if he so much as glanced in her direction. That girl who was sure that wearing miniskirts and mascara was a small price to pay even if they chafed against the Bravura her father had raised. The Bravura who knew how to plaster a wall at age nine, could install . . .

Her thoughts ground to a halt.

"Forgive me?" She stiffened, though she told herself not to. "What are you talking about?"

He raised his brows a little.

Anger inched toward rage. "Forgive me for what?"

He shook his head. "Listen, baby, let's just——"

"Forgive me for *what?*"

"I've been gone a long time. I know that, honey."
He shrugged. "So you got lonely . . ."

"What?" Confusion mixed with the anger,
swirled with frustration, producing a heady
potion.

"And, hey"—he shrugged, disarming and
understanding and so handsome Angie Dotson,
head cheerleader, had once said he made her toes
curl—"I did, too. But we can put that all behind
us now that I'm home."

Her mind was whirling. "You don't think . . ."
She paused, barely able to force out the words.
"You don't think I was . . . unfaithful."

"No. Of course not," he said, but was there a
question in his tone. "It's just . . ." He nodded
toward the front door through which Tonk had
disappeared not thirty minutes earlier. "Just a
little flirtation maybe."

"A little flirtation. What does that mean?"

"Forget it, baby. I have. Let's just put it behind
us."

"Put *what* behind us?"

"The others. All that's important is us now."

"What *others?*" she demanded and jerked back
a pace.

A muscle ticked in his cheek. He exhaled
softly. "You tell me, Vey."

She stared at him, heart thumping murderously.
"There haven't been any *others*. Not for me,

anyway. I thought I could say the same about you. But when you're so casual about"—she made air quotes with four fingers—"a little flirtation, I wonder—"

"So you're not stringing him along? Really? Then the chief out there must be what? Your long-lost brother? Like that Hunter dude? Do you run around with your tits hanging out with him, too?"

If he had struck her, she wouldn't have been more surprised. Dane Lambert could be selfish. He could be childish and moody and undependable, but he was not cruel. Or if he was, he was, without exception, craftier about it. Unless he was drinking. He could get nasty when he'd been drinking. But it was a little too early for that. Wasn't it? Then again, where had he been all morning? And why hadn't she heard him leave? She shook her head as a dozen rampant questions stormed through her blistering mind. But at that second the front door slammed, and Lily pattered in from behind them.

"Mama!" Her voice, filled with excitement and wonder and little-girl breathlessness, broke Vura from her trance.

"Yes?" She tried to relax, tried to fix a smile on her face before allowing herself to turn. "What is it, honey?"

"The eggs are hatching!"

Vura exhaled, attempting to find that quiet

haven she harbored for her daughter. "The goose eggs?" she asked, then turned and gasped.

Blood was smeared like rhubarb jam across her daughter's left cheek.

"Lily!" She took one stumbling step forward and stopped. "What happened?"

"So much!" She was jittering with excitement. "Three of 'em musta hatched before I got there, and the fourth one is cracked. That means there's just six more left to—"

"No. Honey, what happened to your face?"

"Oh." Lily raised one grubby hand, but Vura caught her wrist before she touched the wound, though it was hard to tell how much was injury and how much was blood. "I musta cut it on a wire while sitting with the babies."

Of course. Milly, with a goose's diabolical planning, had positioned her nest directly beneath a barbed-wire fence. "Oh man," Vura sighed and settling onto her haunches, gripped her daughter's chin in uncertain fingers.

"Good God!" Dane's words were little more than a croak as he got a clear view of their daughter's face for the first time. Vura set her jaw but did her best to ignore him.

"Grab your giddy-up bag, Lily Belle. We're going to town."

The downy brows drew abruptly together. "What for?"

What for? Was she kidding? Vura wondered.

But of course she wasn't. When Lily was invested in something, she was totally immersed, all in. "We're going to visit Dr. Shelby."

"But I gots to be here when the rest of the goslings hatch."

"You can go see them again as soon as we get back." She was already herding her daughter toward the door, searching for her wallet, gathering her keys.

"But she didn't mean to hurt me," Lily wailed. "It's her job to protect her babies. You said so."

"Good God!" Dane said again.

Vura gritted her teeth and refrained from telling him to shut up. Grabbing Lily, she pulled the child to her chest.

"I don't wanna go!" She was screaming now, arms thrashing, legs kicking. "I don't wanna go. I gotta be here with the babies."

"Lily, be quiet!" Dane ordered.

She ignored him as only a five-year-old could. "What about the coyotes? What if the coyotes come while we're gone?" Her little face looked stricken. Tears popped from the corners of her eyes like raindrops.

Vura shot her desperate gaze to her husband. He shook his head, then glanced hopefully at the giant box beside the door.

"Hey, Lil . . ." Hurrying over, he hunched down beside it. "I got something for you."

She blinked as he opened the carton. Inside, a

scaled-down, adrenaline-red roadster was parked.

"It's a Dodge Viper. Just like Daddy's. Except for the color," he said. "As soon as I saw it, I knew I had to get it for my Lily Belle."

A tear had made its way to her chin, charting a brave course through the blood and the dirt.

"Look," he said, and honked its tinny horn. "It's an authentic replica."

She pursed her lips and perfected her scowl. "Can I use that?"

"Sure, baby," Dane said, and flitted a proud glance at Vura. "Sure you can. But I'll have to get the batteries installed first. If you're really good, when you get back, you can—"

"The box," she said, and zipped her hopeful gaze from him to Vura. "We could put Milly and the babies inside. They'd for sure be okay if we took them with us."

Vura felt her knees buckle. Yeah, she was tough. But that didn't mean she didn't want to faint dead away when her baby's face was covered in blood. Holy cats, didn't she have a right to faint? "That's a good idea, Lily, honey," she said. "But this is their home. Milly would be scared if we put her in there." Scared and hissy and probably mad enough to tear their faces right off their heads. Vura made her way toward the door. "I'm afraid they'll have to stay here. Listen, though . . ." she added before the kicking commenced again. "Papa will look after them

214

while we're gone." She glanced hopefully at Dane.

But Lily shook her head with violent intensity. "Milly doesn't know him. She only knows me. I *gotta* stay! We have to put them inside now that they're hatched. You said so," she insisted and bucked wildly.

"Lily!" Dane snapped and grabbed her arm with rough impatience. "Quit acting like a child!"

The world went quiet. She blinked, eyes as wide as moons. "But I *am* a child."

He glowered at her. She glowered back. "Then you can't have the Viper," he said. "They're just for big kids who know how to behave."

She set her tiny jaw and scowled. "Can I still have the box?" she asked, and Vura, not knowing whether to laugh or cry, headed for her truck.

Chapter 20

"I can't believe she didn't even wake up when I carried her in." Vura's father sat across the kitchen table he had crafted from a wind-felled oak. His plaid flannel sleeves were folded back from thick-veined wrists. He looked homey and wise and as comforting as homemade stew.

"A barbed-wire attack followed by forced tetanus boosters is probably exhausting. Not to mention the unholy fit she threw over leaving the goslings."

He shook his head and glared into his coffee mug. The pristine porcelain contrasted sharply with his sun-darkened fingers. "It wasn't anything serious, though, right?" he asked, and when he glanced up again, his eyes looked suspiciously bright; for reasons Vura would never fully understand, those tears seemed to set everything right.

"Even if it was, I wouldn't tell you." She took a sip of coffee, hiding her grin against the rim of the cup. "Cuz I'm fresh out of Kleenex and I can't stand to see a grown man cry."

"I don't know when you became such a smart a . . ." he began, then glanced toward the room where Lily slept. The day she was born, he had quit swearing. Cold turkey. Since then he'd been converting every conventional swear word into creative, if rather anticlimactic expletives. ". . . asterisk," he finished poorly.

Vura laughed out loud. Peace settled cautiously into her jittery belly. She managed a shrug. "Might have been the same time you became such a pansy."

"You watch your mouth, young lady," he said, and she laughed again, loving him wildly. He rose to his feet. Retrieving a shallow plastic container from the cupboard, he set it between them before settling in again. "She didn't need any more stitches?"

She shook her head and scowled at the Tupperware. "I guess it was just a scratch. But to look at her . . ." She exhaled carefully. "You would have thought she'd been in a fight with a lion. Or maybe I overreacted." She sighed. "Who's your cookie connection this time?"

"Well, who could blame you if you did? It's been a heck of a year," he said.

She nodded but wasn't ready to abandon her line of questioning. "The cookies," she said, and took a sugary confection from among its perfectly formed compadres. "Who are they from?"

"Maybe I made them myself," he said, still holding a grudge for the pansy comment.

"And maybe the sky is made of blue icing," she countered and took her first bite.

Quinton snorted and leaned back in his chair. "You're lucky you have that little girl in there or I might kick you out on your . . ." He gritted his teeth and glanced toward the bedroom again.

"Asterisk?" she guessed and grinned. But the cookie was drawing her attention. She narrowed her gaze and considered. "A little too sweet for Mrs. Vanderman," she said, and tried another sample. Somebody had to do it. "Too much molasses for Linda Harmson." She tasted carefully, like a connoisseur sampling a new cabernet. This had been a little game of theirs for as long as she could remember. Trying to catalog the women who trotted through Quinton Murrell's life had been a constantly entertaining, if rather fattening job. "I'm going with"—she polished off the first treat—"what's her name?"

He merely stared. If the truth be known, he might never have enjoyed the game as much as she did.

"You know . . ." Impatience had edged into her tone a little. "The giggler."

"I have no idea what you're talking about."

"Oh, come on." Picking up her second sample, she giggled manically, then hiccupped a burp onto the end.

He shook his head in obvious disgust.

"You're right. That wasn't quite it. Maybe it was more like . . ." She tried again, but somehow a chunk of cookie got lodged in her throat, making her cough spasmodically.

Rising, her father banged her on the back with enough force to dislodge the obstruction *and* illustrate his disgust.

She fought for breath, and he grinned a little.

"Serves you right," he said, and settled back into his chair. "For mocking your elders."

"Elders!" The single word came out a little raspy. Maybe she shouldn't be surprised that one of his lady friends was trying to kill her. She hadn't always been as genteelly understanding as she was now. "I was on track and field with her sister." She would have liked to mock him more, but it was still a little hard to breathe. She cleared her throat.

Quinton tapped a thumb against his cup, face thoughtful.

"Come on. You remember her," Vura urged. "She always wore those low-cut blouses that showed—"

"Roxanne."

"That's right." She crowed the words. "Roxanne . . . what was her last name?"

A muscle jumped in his jaw. "You didn't have to get married."

"What?" His somber tone stopped the cookie halfway to her mouth.

He exhaled softly, shifted uncomfortably in the chair he had crafted from the same tree as the table. Though it might look flawless to the average mortal, Quinton Murrell had a knack for finding flaws in his creations. Strange, she thought now, that he hadn't expected the same kind of perfection where she was concerned. Strange and never appreciated so much as right now.

"I worry sometimes"—he tilted his head a little, tightened his lips—"that you thought you had to get married for my sake."

Her gut tightened again. So many feral emotions storming through her.

"Maybe . . ." He took a deep breath. "Maybe I didn't react as well as I should have when I found out you were pregnant."

She put the cookie down, remembering the shame, the guilt, the gut-eating worry.

"No. You did everything right. It was me who was . . ." She glanced out the window. He had a pretty setting here. She had always liked it . . . their two little acres just on the edge of town. "I'm sorry if I was—" She winced.

"Sorry?" He glanced toward the room where Lily slept, pushed to his feet, and chuckled a little. "You think I cry like a baby for things I'm not crazy about?"

She smiled. "Still . . ."

"Still nothing!" He sounded belligerent and a little angry. "Lil's the best thing that happened since you were"—he shrugged, a single lift of capable shoulders. Their gazes met, a soft meld of gooey thoughts—"old enough to lift a circular saw."

She laughed, hoping it didn't sound as watery as it felt.

He settled against the slats of his chair. "How's he doing?"

She cleared her throat and fiddled with the second cookie. "Who? Dane?"

He nodded.

"Good. He's good. Just . . . looking for a job."

"Well, that's great."

"Yeah. He checked in with Emerson, Inc."

"Oh?" He took a sip of coffee. "When was that?"

"Yesterday morning. He said Fred was laying some cement, so he helped out for a while."

The room went quiet.

"What?" Vura asked, and felt tension crank up her spine.

"Nothing."

"What?" she repeated.

"Freddie didn't mention it. That's all."

Suspicion crept in again, sneaky as a gray goose. But she kept her tone steady. "You talked to him?"

"Yeah but, hey, he's busy as a one-legged . . . he's busy as can be. I'm sure it just slipped his mind."

She nodded.

"So, Dane's looking for construction work. That's great."

"Well, not specifically. He said he'd take anything he can get this time. To stay close to home."

"That's good," he said, but his upbeat tone sounded a little strained.

She turned her cookie. "You might as well just spit it out, Dad."

"Spit what out?"

"Whatever you're thinking."

He glanced toward the bedroom again, but his cell phone rang before he spoke. "Just a minute . . . Quinton Murrell," he said, then listened for a second and stiffened. "When? Okay. I'll be right there," he said, and caught his daughter's gaze with his. "It's Dad."

"Is he okay?"

"I don't know." His voice was strained, his expression solemn. "Mrs. Ketterling says he was just having some breakfast when . . ." He winced, shifted his gaze toward the window. "She says we'd better come right away."

Chapter 21

"Gamps." Vura tried to control her breathing, control her movements as she stepped into her grandfather's living room. Mrs. Ketterling, the woman they had hired to help since his transition back home, stood in the corner, watching, hands clasped, florid face rumpled with worry.

Little had changed since Gamma's death six years before. Every faded picture hung where it had at her passing. Each piece of furniture remained in place, just a little older, a little more tired. But Vura failed to notice the timelessness as she snapped her gaze to her father. Quinton Murrell caught her eyes for a moment before shifting his attention back to the old man's drawn features. "How you doing, Dad?"

Randall Murrell was stretched out on the couch. An afghan had been pulled diagonally across his body. The crocheted eyelets opened here and there, granting a view of his khaki pants, his darned socks. "Use it up, wear it out, make it

222

do or do without" had been his motto for years beyond memory.

His old eyes, as faded as the furniture, turned toward her. "Bravura," he said, but the tone was raspy, almost inaudible.

"Yeah, Gamps, it's me," she said, and settled carefully beside him on the floor. "How are you?"

The pale lips tightened, the coarse eyebrows beetled. "Stubborn."

She huffed a laugh and reached for his hand as a modicum of relief swooshed through her. "I know that."

"Doesn't mean *you* have to be."

"What?" His fingers felt cold and fleshless in hers. He took a shuddering breath. Air wheezed like a cold nor'westerly down his trachea. Vura shifted her attention to her father, but he said nothing.

"Sorry." The single word was clear enough from her grandfather's cracked lips, but she must have heard him wrong. In the twenty-four years of her life, she could count his apologies on one hand. Then again, what did he have to apologize for? He had doled out wisdom and life lessons just as steadily as his wife had offered cookies and kisses.

She shook her head. "What are you talking about? You don't have anything to be sorry for." She fiddled with the afghan. Gamma's favorite aunt had crafted it twenty years before Vura's birth. "Unless it's for scaring the living daylights out of me for no good reason." She cupped his fingers with her opposite hand. Why were they so cold? So deathly cold? "Is that it?" she asked.

"There you are," he breathed.

"Yeah, I'm . . ." She scowled, scared. "I'm right here, Gamps."

He smiled a little, but his gaze seemed to have drifted off to a point just beyond her left shoulder. "My girl."

Vura felt the lump grow in her throat. Felt her eyes sting and her throat tighten with emotion.

"Rosie." He said the name softly, as reverently as a prayer. "Not much longer."

"Rosie? No, Gamps . . ." She swallowed, tried to focus through the blur. "It's me. I'm—"

"Ahhh . . ." He sighed, shifted his gaze ever so slightly to meet hers again. "Our grand-daughter." He nodded, slowly, as if it took the greatest of efforts. "Bravura."

"Yeah. Yeah." She shot a glance at her father again. "I'm here, and Dad's here. We're going to take care of you."

"She did that," he murmured.

"What?"

"My Rosie," he said, and sighed softly. "Took care of me. Since the day we said our vows."

"I know, Gamps. I know."

"Didn't have no ring." It was a fact that he had regretted, but Rosalind Quinton Murrell had kept the twist of wire she'd worn on the dedicated finger of her left hand for more than a year. And when he had purchased a modest diamond, she had insisted with a strong woman's tenacity that he solder the seventeen-gauge onto the narrow gold band, melding the metals as surely as they melded their lives.

Vura waited in silence, knowing the story, loving the outcome.

"Couldn't afford one." That misty smile again. "Didn't matter. I was young, full of myself." A quiet chuckle rumbled through his narrow chest as if he laughed at something unheard, something he had shared with no one but the love of his life. But he sobered. "Never good enough for her."

"Gamps . . ."

"Never was," he repeated and tightened his hand on hers. "But she stood by me. Stood up for me. Even when our Dena was taken." His gaze wandered again. "My fault," he whispered. "And after . . ." He glanced out the window, over the gardens they had worked together for more than half a century. Rows of potatoes, patches of herbs, clusters of irises. "She stuck. Always stuck, though I was no good."

"That's ridiculous, Gamps. She loved you. Was crazy about you."

He nodded, silent for a long moment. "Comes down to that, I guess. Just that." He sighed. "Ain't no figuring it out." He caught her gaze with his.

"Was what we wanted for you, Bravura. All we ever wanted."

"I know."

He winced, jerked.

"What's wrong?" She leaned closer. "Listen, just hang on." Tires crunched on the gravel in the drive. Relief flooded her. "The ambulance is here. Just—" she began, but when the door opened and closed, no EMTs rushed into the room. Instead, Tonk stepped inside. Eyes solemn, he nodded to Quinton, brushed his gaze over Bravura, then knelt, solemn as a prayer, beside her.

"*Menewa*," he said.

Gamps's shoulders slumped just a little. "Tonkiaishawien."

Light glimmered in Tonk's eyes. Lifting his gaze, he smiled, as if seeing what Vura could not. "So she waits."

"Still loves me," Gamps said, and shook his head.

"Some men have all the luck," Tonk said.

"And some have miracles."

"Are you ready?"

"Yes."

Tonk placed his hand on the old man's forehead. "Then let the Great Spirit . . ."

"What are you doing?" Vura asked and, dropping her grandfather's hand, jerked to her feet.

Tonk breathed a sigh. "Dying is hard on the living."

"Dying! What are you talking about?" She

stabbed her gaze at her father, but he merely stood, brows low over troubled eyes. No help there. "He's not dying. He just . . ."

"We must learn to let go, Bravura," Tonk said. "He has lived well. Does he not deserve to die the same?"

"What the hell do you know about it?" she demanded and dropped to her knees again. "Gamps, I'm sorry. I don't know what he's doing here. But it's okay. The ambulance will come and—"

"My girl," he said and, reaching up, grasped her hand. "Such a fighter. Always . . ." He gasped, breath rattling, body jerking.

"Gamps! Dad! Help—" she said, but the old man came back to her slowly, grip tightening.

"You don't have to try so hard. Not so hard."

"Listen . . . don't worry about anything. Everything's going to be okay. You just—"

"Tonkiaishawien . . ." He shifted his far-seeing gaze back to Tonk.

"Ai?"

"Don't fail her," he said and, closing his eyes, let his fingers go lax.

"Gamps!" Vura sobbed his name, pulled his hand against her chest. "Gamps. Don't leave me."

"Bravura," Tonk said, and touched her arm, but she jerked away.

"Please. Dad!" She glanced over her shoulder, chest aching.

"Honey," he said, and crowded in behind her. "Let him go."

"Let him go? What are you even . . . ?" She huffed. "He can't die."

"I know, sweetheart, but—"

"But nothing. He promised to teach me to fly-fish, to shear sheep, to—"

"Hobgoblin," Quinton breathed and drew her up beside him. She had no choice but to release her grandfather's hand, to let it drop against his too-still chest. But the rage remained.

"What have you done?" She jerked toward Tonk, snarling. "You had no right."

"I am sorry."

"Sorry! You can't—" She shook her head, wild, afraid. "Help him. Please."

"There is nothing I can do. He is gone."

"He's not gone. He's right there. He's right—"

"Bravura!" Tonk's voice was sharp. "Your grandfather is dead."

She jerked as if slapped, ready to deny, to curse, to blast him and the world, but his expression was so solemn, so sad and reverent and final that there seemed nothing she could say. Nothing she could do but stagger across the echoing floor and into the light-falling rain.

Chapter 22

The funeral was held on a Tuesday.

It should have been raining. Why wasn't it raining? Vura wondered and realized she was angry at the sunshine that dazzled the eye. Mad at the crocus that dotted the pastures, incensed by the robins that hopped and warbled on the lawn outside Zimmerman's Funeral Home.

Dane, solemn and handsome in his suit coat and tie, had accompanied her and Lily inside before wandering off to speak to the mourners.

Near the front of the parlor, the casket, an oaken box with sprays of wheat etched at the corners, was open for viewing. Vura felt her throat clench and her stomach twist. She turned woodenly from the sight of it.

She had tried to remain strong for her daughter. But inside, she felt weak, weak and fragile and broken. Beside her, Lily threw Foo Foo into the air for the hundredth time. And for the hundredth time it flopped to the floor from which it was retrieved once again. She tugged at her mother's hand, tipping her slightly off balance as she scooped the ratty thing back into her arms.

"I'm so sorry for your loss." Mrs. Coleman was a handsome woman with a creased face, the requisite silver-blue hair and, if the stories were to be believed, a colorful past.

"Thank you." Vura had recited the words dozens of times by now, had hugged, consoled, and been consoled, but had still not approached the casket.

"He was a good man."

"Yes. He was," Vura said and, feeling Lily try to pry away, tightened her grip.

"Was he ill for long?" Mrs. Coleman asked.

"No," Vura said, and wondered now if she was wrong. Wondered if he had suffered more than she had known. More than she had allowed herself to believe. If that was the case, how many other things was she refusing to see? To admit. "Well, you're lucky then. My cousin, Mavis, you might remember her, she has a grandson about your age. She's suffered from Alzheimer's for the longest time. Doesn't even recognize—" Her voice droned on. Vura nodded, made the appropriate noises.

Beside her, Lily fidgeted. Perhaps Dane had been right. Maybe they should have left her at home. But they had been forced to find someone to rush to her father's house to care for Lily and it seemed wrong to leave her again. Besides, there was a closure here, a finality that Vura had thought would be important. Now, however, her nerves felt stretched to the breaking point.

"I want to see Grandpops," Lily interrupted Mrs. Coleman without preamble.

The elderly woman's dialogue came to an abrupt

halt, but she smiled. "Well, I'll be praying for you," she said, and shuffled off, blue hair piled up like an ice cream cone.

"I wanna see him," Lily repeated.

Vura turned to her daughter with a hundred misgivings, but she had explained death as best she could, had answered the dozens of questions and fielded as many concerns. And somewhere along the line she had assured Lily that she would be able to see her great-grandfather one last time. She regretted that promise with gut-wrenching dread now.

"Listen, honey . . ." She knelt, meeting the kaleidoscope eyes full-on. "How would you like to get some dessert with your daddy? I think the Purple Pie Place is open."

Lily's brows lowered belligerently. "I want to see Grandpops."

"I know you do, sweetheart." Vura's mind felt gray and worn, her muscles stripped by sadness. "We all do, but—"

"Where is he?"

She exhaled carefully and forced a smile. "His body is in that casket." She nodded toward the ornate coffin she had not yet gotten the nerve to approach. Lily turned to scowl at the thing. "But his spirit—"

"He's in a box?" Lily asked, and twisted in that direction, but Vura held her tight, turned her back.

"Listen, Lily—"

"Why's he in a box?" Her voice had risen in a potent mix of panic and anger.

Frustration spurted through Vura. She had explained the situation as best she could, but really, who had a handle on death? She scanned the room, looking for a savior, but her father was consoling his aunt and Dane was nowhere to be seen.

"I want to see him," Lily repeated.

"I don't think that's—"

"I want to see Grandpops!" The decibels were rising with her agitation.

"Listen, Lily—"

"I wanna see him." Her little body had tensed. "I wanna see him. I wanna see him!"

Vura's face felt hot, her body stiff, but she rose to her feet, grasped her daughter's hand, and took a faltering step toward the casket.

Lily paced along beside. Their footfalls sounded loud and hollow against the industrial-strength carpet as they made the long journey toward the front of the parlor.

Inside, stretched out on almond-colored velvet, Randall Murrell looked like nothing so much as a caricature of himself. His platinum hair was parted wrong, his waxy skin stretched tight over bones sharpened by death.

Vura stared, repulsed and shaken, but her daughter grasped the lip of the casket and rose to her toes for a better view.

"Lily!" Vura admonished and tried to lift her daughter against her chest, but she wouldn't release her hold. "Lily, let go."

"That's not Grandpops."

Embarrassment and sorrow flooded in, but she squatted, lowering her voice. "Yes, it is, honey. He just looks different."

Lily scowled, then, reaching inside, she touched the old man's hand. From the back of the parlor, someone inhaled a shocked breath, but Vura was entirely absorbed by her daughter now.

"Gamps is dead, Lily." Sorrow welled, scouring her throat, burning her eyes. "He's gone."

"Gone?" Lily shifted her wide-wonder gaze toward her mother.

"Yes."

"Ohhh . . ." Understanding seemed to dawn on her like morning light. "He went to see his Rosie."

"Yes." Vura cleared her throat. "Yeah, he's with Gamma now."

"So that's just his old skin?"

"What?"

"His old skin . . . like a rattlesnake. Tonka says rattlers slither out of the used-up stuff when they're ready for something new, something better. So Grandpops left his old skin behind so he could be with his Rosie again. Right?"

"I guess so."

"Well, that's okay then."

"What's going on?"

Vura glanced up. Dane stood behind them, brows low.

Vura shook her head, not sure where to begin.

"Here you go," Lily said and, stretching even farther onto her patent-leathered toes, reached into the casket to place her bunny between the old man's hands. "Take Foo Foo so you don't never forget me."

"Lily!" Dane rasped and pulled her from the casket. "You have to behave!"

She turned toward him, eyes wide with surprise. "I am behaving."

"Be quiet," he ordered.

She blinked, scowled. "Does Grandpops want me to be sad?"

Dane gritted his teeth. "He wants you to be—" he began, but Lily's gaze had already darted away.

"Hunk!" she chirped and squirming out of her father's grasp, raced across the floor toward Hunter Redhawk. The big man caught her in his arms, lifted her against his heart.

The sight of the two of them together shot a warm draft of hope through Vura's weary system.

"You've got to learn to control her."

She tugged her gaze from the pair. "Who? Lily?"

"You can't let her run around like a wild Indian when . . ." He glanced to the right as someone approached and shifted his features into a more congenial expression.

"Hey." Sydney Wellesley placed a gentle hand on Vura's arm. "How are you holding up?"

"Fine. I'm fine," she said, but Dane shook his head. All traces of negativity had disappeared, replaced by an expression of exasperated sympathy.

"She's exhausted," he said, and placed a comforting hand on Vura's waist. "Between the funeral and Lily and work . . ."

"I'm fine," Vura repeated and Dane smiled.

"You're a dynamo," he said, and rubbed her back. "We all know it, Vey. But you've got to ease up some."

"Would it help if we took Lily for a while?" Sydney asked.

"That's not necessary." Vura felt relief and dread mix like a toxin at the thought of being parted from her daughter again. "I'm going to—"

"Keel over if you don't relax," Dane said, and turned his winning smile back on Sydney. "I think it'd be great if you could take Lily Belle for a bit."

"It's a deal then," Sydney said, but Vura was already floundering, searching madly for arguments or excuses or thanks.

"I don't want to bother you again," she said, but Sydney was already shaking her head.

"Look at him," she said, and glanced toward her fiancé. Vura followed her line of vision.

Hunter Redhawk stood as still as a butte, every iota of attention directed at the child in his arms.

"Does it look like she's bothering him?"

Perhaps Vura would have argued, would have insisted that Lily stay with her, but there was such warmth in her sister's voice, such reverent adoration in Hunter's expression.

"Okay," she agreed.

"All right. We'll see you later then," Sydney said and, tugging her gaze from the pair, settled her attention back on her sister. "Call if you need anything."

Even the cemetery seemed to be in mourning, but the church basement, where they gathered later, was noisy with conversation. A young couple approached Vura, hand in hand. She was dressed in a modest skirt that reached midway to her shapely calves. He wore a conservative suit.

"You must be Randall's granddaughter." The man had basset hound eyes and a melodious voice.

"Yes." Vura reached out to shake hands.

"I'm Steven Hayward and this is my wife, Lyndsey." He waited a beat, but the names were unfamiliar. "From Eagle Butte."

Understanding dawned a bit belatedly. "Oh, hi," Vura said, and shook his wife's hand. "Thank you for coming."

"Eagle Butte?" Dane asked, and Vura turned a little to include him in the conversation.

"The Eagle Butte Kids' Ranch is a . . ." She

236

shook her head, not sure how to describe the organization she had heard about for as long as she could remember. "I guess you'd be better equipped to explain it," she said, and turned toward the couple again.

"We like to think of the ranch as a refuge," Lyndsey said.

Dane shook his head, smiled prettily. "For . . ."

"Kids who have lost their way."

"Lost their way?"

"Difficult kids, some people call them."

"Oh, well, we have one of those," Dane said, and grinned as he nodded toward Lily.

Vura felt her gut tighten, but Lyndsey was already speaking. "Is that little charmer your daughter?"

"That's our Lily Belle," Dane said and, dropping his arm, gripped Vura's hand in his. "But I was just kidding. We're crazy about her, aren't we, Vey?"

Vura pulled her gaze from her daughter's animated features. She was chattering like a mynah as Hunter carried her from the room. "My grandfather often talked about the time he spent at Eagle Butte."

"Your granddad was a lost kid?" Dane's tone was amused. The couple went silent. Dane grinned into the quiet. "Sorry. Randall Murrell always seemed like he didn't think he had any . . . like he didn't have any faults."

"Did he?" Lyndsey asked. "I guess we didn't see that side of him. For us he was nothing short of a gift from God."

"Did you see him a lot?" Dane asked.

"He usually stopped in a couple of times a year with gifts for the children."

"He brought Christmas presents?" His tone was nothing short of stunned.

"Sometimes," Lyndsey admitted. "But he came more often in the summer."

Why hadn't she known? Vura wondered.

"People tend to forget about those in need once the holidays are past," Steven said.

"But your grandfather never did." Lyndsey smiled. "He was extremely generous."

"He was a good man," Dane said, though his grip tightened a little on Vura's as if to convey his surprise at Randall Murrell's generosity. "And I know he'd be glad you stopped by. Thank you." He shook their hands again. "It was very nice to meet you, but I suppose we should make the rounds."

"Of course," Lyndsey said.

"Maybe we can talk later," Steven suggested.

"I'd like that," Vura said, but Dane was already steering her toward a pair of elderly women who chatted near a rubbery-looking ficus.

The rest of the day was a muddle of solemn faces, dark clothes, and mind-blurring details.

"You doing okay?" Dane asked, and slammed

the door of the Viper, effectively shutting the world outside. He had been a great deal of help to her, strong and somber. She should be grateful, Vura thought, but she was too numb.

"I'm all right." She wondered vaguely if it was true.

"You look tired," he said and, putting the car in Drive, rolled out of Trinity Lutheran's parking lot. In the cavernous church basement, sandwiches, punch, and lemon bars had been served.

Such a strange tradition, Vura thought, feeding the survivors.

She glanced out the window. Darkness was settling in. The moon was on the rise, bright as a sunflower as it drifted over smoky-lavender hills.

"I wish I'd had a chance to get to know him better," Dane said.

Vura's mind drifted vaguely. "Who?"

He grinned at her tone. "Who do you think, silly? Your grandfather."

"Why?" She turned fully toward him, trying to focus. "You didn't even like him."

His grin twisted, looking sad and a little wounded. "He didn't like me, Vey. There's a difference."

"That's not true," she said, and knew she was lying. Even after they had learned of her pregnancy, Gamps had been against the idea of marriage.

"He never thought I was good enough for his little princess."

"Princess?" she repeated and raised her brows at the stark ridiculousness of the notion, but Dane shook his head.

"Master builder, then," he corrected. "Whatever. He thought the sun rose and set on you. Wasn't enough of a reason to give us a loan, though. Not when your name was connected to mine."

Vura glanced out the window again. She had never been comfortable with asking for money. But Dane had insisted that ten thousand dollars was all they needed to give them a leg up on their future. "Gamps was a big believer in making it on your own."

"Didn't have anything against giving a small fortune to a bunch of delinquents he never met, though, did he?"

She scowled. "You mean the Eagle Butte kids? How do you know how much he gave them?"

"You think those two Bible thumpers would have come a hundred miles if he'd doled out a couple measly bucks?"

Memories settled in, mellow with age. "Gamps met Gamma Rosie there."

"Your grandparents met in the pen?"

"It's not a penitentiary."

"I'm just kidding," he said and, reaching across the console, took her hand in his. "Trying to lighten the mood." He squeezed her fingers. "You look so sad."

She didn't argue. Miles sped away beneath the Viper's tires. Highway 385 was nearly devoid of traffic, a fact that wouldn't change much until tourist season.

"Your grandma Rosie was a nice old lady, huh?"

Vura exhaled softly, letting her mind retreat to a thousand quiet scenarios. "She made sweet clover soap just like her mother did." She glanced toward the cottonwoods that grew in a cluster beside a nearby field. Their leaves were bright as silver dollars in the moonlight. "Right up to the end." Tears threatened, but she held them back. "She knew I loved the scent, so she . . ."

He squeezed her hand again. "I guess it makes sense that the old man supported the Ranch then, since he met his girl there, but . . ." He shook his head. "Maybe it wasn't the money at all."

"Maybe what wasn't the money?"

He shrugged, ran his thumb across her knuckles. "I could never make my own dad happy. Maybe I just wanted to know *someone* believed in me enough to"—he shrugged, chuckled at his own foibles—"to invest a few bucks. Truth is . . ." He gazed into the distance. "I'm going to miss the old man."

"Gamps?" Dane had called him Captain Scrooge on more than one occasion.

"I'll never have the chance to prove to him that he was wrong about me."

"You don't have to prove anything."

He gave her a wistful smile, a knowing glance from the corner of his eye. "You really don't understand, do you?"

"Understand what?"

"What it's like to play second fiddle."

She shook her head, and he breathed a quiet laugh.

"Look at you, Vey," he said. "The cherished granddaughter. The perfect mother. The successful businesswoman. The adored daughter."

"That's ridiculous."

"I know I was wrong to leave you for the fracking field, but I guess . . ." He sighed, slowed the Viper, and pulled into their drive. The house looked old and sad beneath the endless, star-studded sky. "I didn't know how else to prove I was good enough for you."

"All I ever wanted was to be with you. I don't need you to make a fortune," she said, and wondered if it was true. Maybe she had pushed him too hard. Pushed him away. Guilt slid sneakily into the cracks around her heart.

He turned off the car and twisted toward her. "Maybe I thought that if I could make *him* proud, I'd make *you* proud."

She stared at him. Were his eyes welling up?

"I *am* proud of you," she said.

"Are you?" he asked and, leaning in, squeezed her fingers in his.

"When we were dating . . ." She sighed, thinking back, feeling her stomach clench at the memory of the turmoil he had caused in her. "I thought I was the luckiest girl in the world to be noticed by Dane Lambert."

"How could I not notice the girl who set fire to Lizzie MacKenzie's hair?"

"That was an accident." It really had been. Just an unfortunate incident involving beakers and an open flame in Mr. Peterson's chem class. Purely coincidental that Lizzie had been disparaging of Vura's braids just days before.

He laughed.

"And if I remember correctly, you still took Lizzie to the prom." Albeit with a somewhat truncated hairstyle.

"I don't deserve you," he said. "But that didn't stop me from marrying you, and it's not going to stop me from doing everything I can to make that marriage work."

Emotions flooded her, and he smiled.

"Come on inside, baby. Let me make it up to you."

A dozen practical duties nagged at her, but she let him draw her inside and up the stairs.

Chapter 23

Vura awoke in her husband's embrace. Their lovemaking of the night before had been slow and sweet and strangely reverent.

"Good morning, beautiful," Dane said. He was nestled up behind her, spooning her, arms a gentle band around her heart.

Outside their far-seeing window, a mourning dove cooed in the predawn stillness.

"What are you thinking about?" His words were a gentle caress against the curl of her ear. "And don't say Mrs. Washburn's kitchen."

She smiled and tilted her face toward his. "You think I could think about something like that at a time like this?"

"I *am* a stud."

"Yeah. Meanwhile, I was trying to figure out how to install the Hillers' solar panels for maximum sun exposure."

He tickled her. She squirmed wildly, then fell silent in his arms again.

"Are you happy, baby?" he asked.

"Yes."

"Glad I'm back?"

"You know I am," she said, and turned in his arms.

"Me too." He kissed her. "I wouldn't want to be

anywhere else, or with anyone else." His eyes met hers, held. "And someday I'll be good enough for you. I promise."

"Don't say things like that, Dane. You're wonderful."

"Well . . . I could have been."

"What are you talking about? You can be anything you want to be."

He smiled, but the expression was tinged with sadness. "Not without an education, Vey."

"An education . . ."

"You know I always wanted to be an attorney."

She opened her mouth, but he placed a finger on her lips, effectively shushing her.

"But I'm a father now. So the family comes first."

"Dane . . ."

"I'm not complaining," he said. "Lily's great, and it's not as if it was your fault. Not like you were trying to trick me into marrying you or something."

She blinked at him and eased back a little. "Is that what you think?"

"Of course not! I mean, I was a catch." He grinned and kissed her nose. "But it doesn't matter anymore."

"Dane . . ." she began but he shook his head, disgusted with himself.

"I've done it again, haven't I? Made you feel guilty. I'm sorry, Vey. You didn't do anything wrong. I mean, yeah, a little birth control might have been in order, but you were so damn sexy. I couldn't control myself. Still can't where| you're concerned, so I'll just bite the bullet."

"What bullet?"

"Listen, manual labor is great for some people. But for me . . ." He sighed and pulled her closer, but she felt stiff now, cold.

"It was good enough for Gamps. For Dad." She didn't add that it was good enough for her.

"That's just it," he said. "I'll never be able to compete with them."

"It's not a competition."

"Isn't it?" he asked, then shook his head as if driving away any uncharitable thoughts. He found her fingers, entwined them with his own. "Baby, I could make four times more money practicing law than I could"—he breathed a disparaging laugh—"pouring concrete."

"Maybe so, but we'd also have to spend thousands of dollars we don't have on tuition."

"I know. You're right." He gritted his teeth. "I'm just being selfish . . . again."

She scowled. Guilt melded with frustration and a dozen other volatile emotions. "Maybe you never really wanted to be a lawyer. I mean . . ." She fiddled with a fold in the pillowcase. "Maybe that's why you let yourself get caught."

He scowled. After graduation, he'd received a football scholarship to the University of South

Dakota. As it had turned out, however, the administration there took a dim view of the use of marijuana in their newly renovated auditorium.

"You think I'd blow my chance again?"

"I didn't say that."

"I was just a kid then, Vey. A stupid kid. But I've changed. Can't you see that?" he asked, and touched her face. "Having you . . . Lily . . ." He shook his head. "I know what's important now. I could do some good."

"I know you could, Dane, but—"

"Environmental law maybe . . . I know how you love the wild places."

"That'd be great," she said. "And you'd be fantastic at it," she hurried to add. Dane had always been convincing, passionate, likeable, and bold. Besides his prowess on the football field, he'd been captain of the debate team. "But I just don't see how we could afford it."

"Well, we couldn't, baby." His tone was effusive, his face bright with hope. "Not before. But things have changed."

"What are you talking about? What things?"

He chuckled softly. "No wonder your grandfather was so crazy about you."

She shook her head, baffled.

"You honestly never considered your inheritance?"

"What inheritance?"

He laughed.

"Dane . . ." She scowled at him. "I have no idea what Gamps had or who he left it to."

"Well, I don't think he gave his entire fortune to those Eagle Butte con artists, do you?"

"Fortune! What fortune?"

Exasperation seemed to lie just below the surface, but he remained patient. "Randy Murrell was a pretty smart cookie, Vey. You think he didn't invest in grain futures or gold or something?"

"Gold?"

"Then there's his farm. The land alone's got to be worth five hundred thousand."

"How do you know that?"

"I'm just saying, the man wasn't exactly a pauper."

"Even if that's true, the money will go to Dad or his sister or—"

He laughed. She felt the muscles across her shoulders, so recently relaxed, tighten.

"Baby, I love you, but you're just being naïve. Auntie Lou is like . . . a hundred years old. What's she going to do with three quarters of a million dollars?"

Was he just pulling these figures out of the air? The numbers baffled her. Tugging the sheet to her chest, she sat upright. "That's not the point, Dane. The point is, the money's not ours."

"Not ours, baby. *Yours!* But, hey . . ." He braced himself on an elbow to catch her gaze. "I under-stand if you don't want to share."

Frustration melded with tenderness. "It's not a matter of sharing. I would if I could, but the money's not mine. I've got nothing to share. Nothing but a tumbledown house, a struggling business, and a little girl who . . ." For reasons unknown, the thought of Lily made her want to cry suddenly. "Who would like to spend more time with her daddy. I was hoping that would be enough for you, too."

"And it is!" He sat up quickly, letting the sheet pool around his naked lap. False modesty had never been one of Dane's flaws. "Of course it is. But there could be even *more*. This is my chance to make something of myself. Your dad would give you the money if you asked. It'd be a loan. Just a loan." His expression was earnest, his eyes imploring, but was there a shadow of desperation in his voice?

She stared at him as the seconds ticked away. "Is there something you're not telling me, Dane?"

"Not telling you! Like what?"

"Like . . . I don't know. Are you in some kind of trouble?"

"Trouble! Geez, Vey, you make it sound like I'm still some stupid kid when I'm just trying to . . ." He took a deep breath, calming himself. "Don't you see how it could be for us? I could pay your old man back in a minute once I got on with a good firm."

She scowled. Outside, a barn owl crooned secrets to the dawn. "A good firm where?"

"I don't know," he said, and laughed as he swept an expansive hand through the air between them. "Anywhere you want to go, baby. L.A., Chicago, New York."

"New York?"

"I'm just saying, the sky's the limit."

"I don't think Milly and her goslings would be very happy in Manhattan."

He laughed. "We could stay in South Dakota if you wanted to. Maybe work for a nonprofit. Or pro bono for one of the reservations."

"But if you worked for free, how would we pay Dad back?"

"I can't win with . . ." He blew out his breath and laughed a little. "The point is, I'd do whatever made you happy."

She stared at him, catching a glimpse of the chinks in his logic, and he drew back a little, watching her.

"But maybe I'm not important enough to bother your father about."

A dozen sharp rejoinders came to mind, but she bit them back. He had a right to dream, too. "How much would you need?" Just asking the question made her stomach ache and her frugal nature, honed by a hundred hungry ancestors, revolt.

"Well . . ." He exhaled. "Law school's not cheap."

"How much?"

"A couple hundred thousand maybe."

The number left her breathless.

"But I wouldn't need it all at once," he rushed to add. "Maybe, though, if we paid a hefty sum up-front, they'd give us a discount . . . save us some money in the long run." His eyes searched hers. "And isn't that what we're talking about, baby?" He ran his hand down her bare arm. Goose bumps shivered in the wake of the caress. "The long run?"

She stared at him, trying to figure out a way to explain that she couldn't, just *couldn't* ask for that money, but outside, an engine rumbled into the yard, distracting her.

"Or maybe we're not," Dane said and, drawing his hand away, straightened.

She pulled her gaze from the window, found him scowling at her. "What are you talking about?"

"Maybe your little fling with the chief was more than I realized."

A half-dozen uncertainties struck her at once, reminding her how tumultuous life with Dane could be. He had a way of throwing her off balance, of keeping her just a little off center. "I didn't have a fling with anyone."

"Really?" His eyes bored into hers. "So there haven't been any fantasies? No longing glances? No breathless, touchy-feely moments?"

"I . . ." Guilt flooded in like hot lava, heating her cheeks. She was innocent . . . except for that dream. That so-vivid dream. And that one touch of their hands, more intimate than a kiss.

"I'm right, aren't I?" he asked, and lurched from the bed. "You're here making love to me, and all the time you've got the hots for *him*."

"No! I just . . . I don't . . ." She stopped herself, closed her eyes. Felt the shame drop on her like a hammer. "I'm sorry." The words were barely a whisper. "Nothing happened. Just a . . ."

"Just a what, Vey? Just a kiss? Just some groping? Just a roll in the hay?"

"No! Nothing like that."

"Nothing?" He paced a few strides, naked and entirely unabashed. "No fantasies about"—he gritted his teeth—"skinny-dipping in the moon-light?"

She winced as the words struck her like an arrow.

"You slut!"

She jerked as if struck and he glared at her, but finally he scrubbed his hands over his face and shook his head.

"I'm sorry." His shoulders slumped. He stepped up to the bed. "That wasn't fair. It's just that . . . the thought of you with someone else . . . I'm just so . . ." He curled his hands into fists, then let them fall by his sides. "But it's no fair taking my guilt out on you."

"Guilt?" Premonition soured her gut. "What do you have to feel guilty about?"

"For leaving you alone. For abandoning you when you needed me. I thought I was doing the right thing, but now I realize you—" He paused, blinked. "You don't think I cheated on *you*, do you?"

"No," she said, but the truth was a little less certain. "No, of course not."

"Because I never would, baby. Never. Even though . . ." His jaw bunched. "Even knowing you allowed another man to touch you." He shook his head as if unable to continue. "But it's my fault. I never should have left you alone. Your grandfather was right." Regret shone painfully in his eyes. "I don't deserve you. I never will."

"Don't say that."

"You know it's true."

"No, I don't."

"Then let me prove myself to you," he said, and knelt suddenly on the bed beside her. "Let's start over, Vey. Start fresh. I don't need the full two hundred thousand. Maybe just half that for starters."

"A hundred thousand . . ." She shook her head.

"You're right to doubt me," he admitted. "You never would have turned to someone else if I hadn't let you down."

Guilt again, as powerful as a sledgehammer. "I'll ask him," she said.

He froze. "What?"

She exhaled heavily, going for broke. "I'll ask Dad for a loan."

"You mean it, baby?"

"Yes." It was hard to force out the word. She had taken such pride in standing on her own two feet, on starting Saw Horse Construction without help from anyone.

"You won't regret it," he promised and hugged her tight against him.

"And I'll . . ." She closed her eyes and pressed her cheek against his shoulder. "I'll tell Tonk he has to move his horses."

He sighed, tightened his grip for a minute, then eased back. "You don't have to do that, baby."

Their gazes met. "I don't want you to have to think about . . . I mean, we didn't even kiss."

He scowled at her.

"We didn't!" So why did it feel like they had? "But it wouldn't be fair for him to be around if it bothers you."

He tilted his head a little, eyes boring into hers. "Are you sure that's the reason?"

"What?"

"You're sure it's not that he's too tempting to resist?"

"Tempting? No. Geez," she said, but the memory of his hand against her skin spread confused heat toward her heart. "He's just . . . irritating."

He stared at her a moment, then laughed, relieved. "He does have that kind of I'm-all-that-and-a-bag-of-chips look to him, doesn't he?"

"Yes." She couldn't quite meet his eyes. "Totally."

"Then I don't see a reason he has to go."

"But what about—"

"I mean . . . he's paying, right?"

"Yeah, but—"

"And he's already bought the posts and stuff for the fences."

"I know." Guilt accosted her from every angle. "I guess I'll have to pay him back for the supplies."

"But money's already tight." He shook his head. "Because of me. Because I wasn't pulling my weight."

"That's not—" she began, but he stopped her.

"You'd never feel right about going back on your word, baby." Sliding his hands down her arms, he drew back slightly and found her eyes with his. "I know you. And I don't want to be the cause of any more trouble. No more guilt."

"All right. I guess." She scowled, confused, but maybe that was what love was all about. Being kept a little off balance. "If you're sure."

He nodded, stroked the hair back behind her ear. "And you'll talk to your dad today, right?"

"Today?"

"Unless you're not sure about things." A shadow clouded his eyes. "About us."

Her stomach twisted. "I'll ask him."

"Thank you, baby. Thank you," he said and, kissing her quickly, turned to retrieve his jeans. In a second, he was pulling them on. "If it would be easier, I could give him my info so he could deposit it right into my account."

"I don't even know if he'll agree to it," she said.

"For his baby girl?" He was already shoving his arms into the sleeves of a button-down shirt. "You know he will."

She shook her head. "It's not like Gamps's funds are going to instantly appear in his bank account. I have to assume these things take time."

"What things?" He fastened up buttons, tucked in the tail.

"Wills and stuff."

"Well, that's just a formality, isn't it?" Reaching for his shoes, he shoved aside a carpenter's level and sat on the room's only chair. The sight of him lacing them up sent a little shiver of loneliness slicing through her.

"What do you mean, a formality?"

"Come on," he said, and rose briskly to his feet. "It's not like your old man doesn't have the cash."

She blinked at him. It was strange how vulnerable she felt now that he was fully dressed and she remained, stark naked and strangely isolated. But she stiffened her back. "He works hard for his money, Dane."

"And you think I don't?"

"I didn't say that." But where was that money?

"Are you changing your mind already?"

"No, but I just feel . . ." She shrugged, lost.

"What do you feel?" he asked.

"Guilty, I guess."

"For asking your old man for a few bucks?" He scoffed, found her eyes. "Or for what you did with the chief out there?"

She winced, and he softened immediately.

"I shouldn't have said that," he admitted, and settled onto the bed beside her, but she could feel his restlessness like a wind against her back. "It's just . . ." He touched her face. "It's just hard knowing you have feelings for someone else when I want so much to work things out with you. To make an incredible life together. That's what you want, too, right, baby?"

She nodded.

"Okay, then. Okay." He kissed her, so softly, so gently, making her feel silly about her doubts. "Then I trust you." He smiled, rose to his feet, hand dropping slowly, reluctantly from her face. "Listen, I hate to leave, but I want to check when summer classes start."

"Now?"

"That's when our new life starts, baby," he said. "Right now."

She nodded, felt his influence like high test whiskey in her tipsy system. "Right," she breathed.

He turned away, but stopped at the door, gaze lingering. "Tell your dad thanks. He won't regret it. And neither will you."

"I know."

"I love you."

"I love you, too," she said, but he was already gone.

Chapter 24

"What do you mean, he needs it done by Monday?" Vura asked, and wondered if her heart had stopped dead in her chest. It was Friday morning. There was no way they were going to finish up their current project without working all weekend and half the night.

Glen shrugged, stout shoulders rising and falling in resignation. "Says he needs it done quicker than he thought."

"Well, he can't have it done quicker than he ..." Vura propped her fists on her hips and ground her teeth. She had known from the start that Rick Derby wasn't an easy man to work for, but Saw Horse Construction had laboriously built a reputation of being a can-do kind of company, and she had no intention of ruining that hard-won reputation now. "Maynard?" she asked, and turned toward her most unpredictable employee. The front of his T-shirt read IT'S GETTING HOT IN HERE . . ." She could only speculate what the back might suggest. He tilted his head and gave her a lopsided grin. Maynard was an energetic prankster, who could, at times, be more trouble than he was worth. On the other hand, he might, if sufficiently motivated, achieve more in an hour than most could accomplish in a day.

"I promised Teri I'd pick out china with her over the weekend," he said.

Vura held her breath, hopeful. "So . . ."

He shrugged, grin widening. "So working overtime in the rain for crappy wages in bad company looks pretty good."

She laughed a little, loving him. "Hip?" she asked, and glanced at the old man. "You have plans?"

"What?" He seemed to jerk from his reverie. "No. What plans would an old duffer like me have?"

Maynard raised his brows at his guilty tone. Vura scowled.

Hip shuffled his steel-toed boots and glowered. "I'll be here," he said.

Glen pulled his gaze from Hip. "I'll do my best."

Vura nodded, grateful to the core. Glen's best was pretty damn good. In fact, a girl couldn't ask for a better trio of go-to guys to have in her corner.

"Thank you," she said, and felt soppy gratitude seep into her system like warm gravy. "You're incredible."

"Well, I don't know 'bout those two," Maynard

said, and tilted his head toward his coworkers. "But I *am* pretty amazing."

She laughed. The sound was strangely watery. She'd been feeling as emotional as a prom queen all week. Certainly it had something to do with her grandfather's death. And the fact that her stomach was queasy, making it difficult to eat, didn't help. But she was good at hiding any girly feelings that might sneak up on her. Living in a construction fishbowl had made it a necessity.

"What's wrong with you?" Hip asked, gnarly brows dipping.

Or not, Vura thought, but she did her best to fudge. "What are you talking about?"

"You're not going to start blubbering or something are you?" the old man asked, and shuffled his feet again as if ready to make a break for it should a single emotion make itself known.

She managed a snort. "Will you work for less if I do?"

Maynard laughed, Glen stared, and Hip opened his mouth to speak, but she answered before he could lose whatever too-close-to-the-truth statements he might have planned. "No, I'm not going to cry. But you might once you realize what needs to be done in the next two days."

"How much?"

She hit them with both barrels, holding nothing back.

The news was met with groans and curses, but

the sounds were music to Vura's ears. She was good at getting things done. At making things happen. It was what she did.

Still, by the time she dragged herself into her truck and rumbled off the work site, she felt as if she'd been beaten with a crowbar and hung up with the drywall.

"Hey," her father said, and raised quizzical brows as she stepped into his kitchen. "What happened to you?"

"Rick Derby."

Quinton snorted and shook his head. "Told you to think twice before you took that job."

"Really?" she said, and dropped onto the high-backed stool she had made in shop class at age thirteen. It was rife with imperfections . . . and her father's most prized piece of furniture. "You're going to play the I-told-you-so game?"

"Yup. Derby has always been a . . ." He paused and glanced toward the living room where Lily played.

"A what, Dad?" Vura asked, and felt her mood.

"You want something to eat or not?"

She chuckled a little. "Whatcha got?"

Opening the refrigerator, he glanced inside to take inventory. "Lasagna. There's some chili left and it looks like"—he reached inside to pull the aluminum foil from a baking dish—"tuna casserole maybe?"

261

"Holy frostbite, Batman," she said, and shoved her legs out in front of her. "Dane was gone for more than a year. You think anybody delivered so much as a frozen pizza?"

He shrugged. "Guess you have to be a helpless male to receive the bounties of—"

"Mama!" Lily galloped into the room, riding the stick horse Tonk had given her a few months before. Bear, big as a moose and twice as hairy, ambled along behind. A pair of fairy wings had been affixed to his massive neck.

Vura gave her father a glance, but he just shook his head.

"Hey, Lily Belle," she said and, setting the stick horse aside, settled her daughter onto her lap. "What'd Bear do wrong this time?"

"Nothin'," she said, not sparing the humiliated beast a glance. "He just felt like being a pixie today."

"A pixie." She glanced at the giant mutt. He looked a little like a mix between a Newfoundland and a nightmare, but not particularly fairy-like. "You sure?"

"Right, Pops?" she asked, and flickered her morning-bright gaze to Quinton.

"If anyone can make him a pixie, you can, Lily Bean. You hungry?"

She scrunched her face in thought and said, "Yup," before plopping to the floor, grabbing her steed, and trotting back out of the room.

He watched her go before turning back to his daughter. "So, what's the verdict?" he asked.

"About?"

"Dinner," he said and glanced into the fridge again.

"Oh. Don't heat up anything for me." She crossed her legs at the ankles, feeling fidgety. She had made a promise. A promise she had not yet found the courage to fulfill.

He straightened, turned. "Who are you, and what have you done with my daughter?"

"Funny," she said.

He grinned a little, settling his hips against the counter behind him.

At seven years of age, she had decided he was the handsomest man in the world. The years since then had done little to alter that opinion.

"There have been other times when I wasn't hungry."

"Name one."

"Remember when I got the flu in sixth grade?"

"And you threw up on . . . what was the kid's name?"

"Lizzie MacKenzie." Maybe she'd had a little more of a vendetta against Lizzie than she had realized. But Dane had been attracted to her girly ways even then.

"Didn't you burn off her hair, too?"

"That was an accident!"

"And the puking wasn't?"

"The point is, there have been other times when I wasn't hungry."

"Only when you were pregnant."

"Man, you are hilarious today," she said, tone dry as she wildly counted off days in her head. It had been nearly a full month since her last period. Hadn't it? But she'd only had sex once in the last . . . millennium, and that was a few days ago. On the other hand, if she had learned anything it was that once was enough.

"I'm thinking of starting a standup routine. Lily Bird," he yelled. "What do you want for supper? Lasagna or tuna casserole?"

"Hot dogs."

He shook his head and reached for a pan.

But no, wait. She was wrong. Her period wasn't due for another four days. She was sure of it.

Relief flooded her and was followed by a quick wash of guilt. Would it be so bad to have another baby? Lily was the light of her universe. And Dane was back. Back and ready to start over.

"You okay?" Quinton asked, and turned on the oven.

She punted. "What are you doing?"

"I found a place that sells ready-to-bake hot dog buns."

She stared at him.

"Lil likes them better than off the shelf."

"Tell me the truth," she said, trying to find the easy rhythm she had shared with her father for as long as she could remember. "If she suddenly took a liking to fresh swordfish, would you be out fishing the high seas?"

"She's my only grandchild."

She grinned. The room settled into silence as he pulled a bag of organic broccoli from the bottom drawer of the refrigerator. When she was a child, more than one determined divorcée had threatened to move in with them if he didn't serve his "adorable daughter" something green every once in a while. Thus the institution of peppermint ice cream . . . served every weekend without fail. But apparently, he took his nutritional duties more seriously since grandfatherhood had struck.

Her mind wandered, shambling down lanes filled with laughter and tears and a hundred lonely ladies. Had he fought off their advances because they could never live up to her mother's memory, as he had said, or had he remained single for her benefit alone? The question made her feel teary again.

She cleared her throat.

He glanced at her from the corner of his eye.

Rising restlessly, she rummaged around in a nearby drawer until she came up with a knife. She had no idea what she planned to do with it.

"Hey, Dad . . ." She paused, not so much to get his attention as to quiet her jumpy stomach.

"Yeah?" he asked, and began chopping broccoli. "Hand me that colander, will you?"

"Colander?" She raised her brows. "When did you start channeling Martha Stewart?"

"When I realized Lily was in peril of dying of malnutrition. Here . . ." He reached out. "Give me that."

She passed him the sieve. "I've got something to ask you."

"Okay," he said, and handed over a stainless steel pot half-filled with water. "You can heat that up without burning the house down, can't you?"

Normally she would have been able to manage a snappy comeback, but her smart-"asterisk" side wasn't feeling very chipper. He sobered a little.

"What's going on?"

"Nothing." Coward, she thought, and closed her eyes. She'd already been avoiding this discussion for days, but it was time to jump in, to prove she would do whatever she could to make her marriage work. "Dane needs . . . Well . . ." She paused, already botching it. "*I* need a favor."

"Oh?" His salt-and-pepper brows dipped a little. Was there censure in his expression, disappointment in his tone?

She pursed her lips. No good could come of reading more into the situation than necessary. "Isn't it awesome that he's back?"

He tilted his head.

Geez! *Awesome?* She sounded like a tween on happy pills.

"How's his job search going?" he asked.

Pulling a banana from the bunch on the counter, she busily peeled and sliced it, dropping the little discs into a bowl. "That's what I wanted to talk to you about."

He nodded thoughtfully and opened the bag of frozen rolls. "Well, my crew's full, Hobgoblin. But I guess I could ask around. See if anyone else is hiring."

"That'd be great. Thanks. But . . ." She cleared her throat again. "Maybe Dane's not really cut out to be a"—she squirmed a little, then gritted her teeth and told herself to get a grip—"a blue-collar laborer."

He wiped his hands on a tea towel given to them by some long-forgotten female and faced her. His expression had changed, just the slightest degree. Hardened a little.

"I mean, he's good at so many things," she said. "And . . ." She shook her head. "He wants to make a better living . . . you know . . . for Lily and me. So I was thinking . . . wouldn't he make a great lawyer?"

His hands went still. The kitchen fell like a stone into silence, but finally he spoke.

"How much does he want, Bravura?"

Chapter 25

By the time Vura reached home, she felt strangely old, oddly worn.

Lily yawned like a sleepy cub as she was lifted from her car seat.

Vura squeezed her tight, drawing from her little-girl resilience for a moment.

Lily stirred sleepily. "What's wrong, Mama?" Weren't children with Asperger's supposed to be oblivious to others' emotions? It was just one reason Vura was certain her daughter had been misdiagnosed.

"Nothing." She eased up her grip a little. "Nothing's wrong, honey," she said, and chastised herself for her neediness as she carted the drowsy child to the house. The screen door stuck for a second, but she managed to pry it open. From the over-cowed living room, an aging sitcom's laugh track guffawed emptily. The sound set Vura's teeth on edge, but she scolded herself for her moodiness.

Every tread groaned as though it carried the weight of the world as she made her way upstairs. Lily groused for a moment about goslings growing up without her, books that would go unread, and teeth that surely didn't need to be brushed *every* night, but finally she scrubbed them desultorily then tugged her nightgown sideways over her head. By the time she was tucked into bed with a decidedly un-snuggly stick horse, her eyes were already dropping shut.

The steps whined again as Vura made her way back downstairs. Dane was settled into the second-hand recliner she'd purchased from Re-Uzit. The TV prattled on.

"Did you lock up the chickens?" Vura asked, and did her level best to be congenial. Or perhaps she really only tried to *sound* affable.

He sat up with a sleepy start. "Oh, hey, I didn't even hear you come in."

"Looks like it's a good thing we're not in a high crime area," she said. He stared at her for a moment, then chuckled as he rose to his feet.

"Yeah, sorry. I guess I'm not much of a watch-dog when I'm wiped out like this." He stretched, knocking over one of the three empty beer cans beside his chair.

"Are the chickens locked up?" she asked again.

"I thought maybe it was still too early."

She didn't bother glancing outside. It had been dark for an hour and a half, but Dane wasn't a farm boy, she reminded herself. Then again, it was impossible to tell how long *he* had been sleeping. "Are you familiar with the phrase, 'go to bed with the chickens'?" she asked, and managed a smile to take off the biting edge of her tone.

"No, but it sounds kinky." He prowled toward

her. The freshman girls had called it the Lambert swagger. His arms felt strong and warm when he wrapped them around her waist. "Tell me more."

"It implies that poultry roost early," she said.

"Ahh, sage advice," he crooned and bumped his hips against hers. "Wanna hit the hay and teach me all about the birds and the bees?"

"I'd love to," she said, and wasn't sure if it was absolutely true. She did know, however, that she would have given her liver to sleep for a week. "But I've still got some things to do."

Things, her bitchy side snidely whispered, that he could have done hours before.

"Okay, well, I'll tell you what . . ." He kissed her neck, then settled his lean hips against the wall behind him, drawing her between his spread legs. "You go take care of the beasts of the field, and I'll fill the tub so you can have a nice long bath when you get in."

"That'd be great," she admitted. "But I've got to get right to bed."

"Well . . ." He waggled his brows at her. "If you insist."

"To *sleep,*" she corrected.

He grinned sheepishly. "You do look tired, baby," he admitted and slipping his hand up her spine, gently kneaded her neck. "But hey, at least I can give you one of my patented rubdowns, right?"

The massage felt great, but the problem with

Dane's back rubs was that they generally avoided her back and concentrated on areas he found more appealing. Areas that did *not* ache from a day of hard labor.

"You know what I'd like even more?" she asked and, bending her neck, eyed him from a crooked angle.

"You name it, I'll rub it."

"Could you lock up the birds?"

He sighed. "Maybe you'd better do that, baby. I don't want to goof anything up."

"It doesn't take a genius to count a few chickens and shut a door, Dane."

He stiffened. "So you're saying that even I could do it?"

"Well, that hasn't really been proven. Last time, half of them were still on the loose when I went out the next morning."

"Oh . . ." He pulled away from her, already bristling. "So now I'm stupid and lazy?"

"No." She pursed her lips. "I'm sorry. I'm just tired," she said, but he had already backed away, eyes narrowed.

"You know what I think?"

She had to forcibly keep from wincing at his tone. "Dane—" she began, but he shook his head and continued.

"I think you don't want your old man to give me that loan. That's why you haven't asked him. You enjoy lording it over me. You like having everyone see how successful you are while your husband . . ." He threw a wild hand at her. "Poor old Dane Lambert can't find a decent job to—"

"I asked him."

He paused, brows still lowered. "Yeah?"

"Yeah." She nodded and moved past him. Fatigue had turned to an ache deep in her bones.

He followed her into the kitchen. Four cups, a half a ham sandwich, and a pan of cooling soup had been left on the counter. She gritted her teeth and toted the dishes to the sink. Above her, countless chickens looked on in disapproval.

"Well, what'd he say?"

Plugging the drain, she ran hot water into the stained stainless steel. "He said he'd think about it."

"What do you mean, he'll think about it? What's to think about?"

She paused to stare at him, fingers dipping in the water. "It's a lot of money, Dane."

He made a scoffing noise.

She swung toward him, anger popping up unexpectedly, but he raised his hands as if in self-defense.

"I'm sorry. I'm sorry, baby. You're right. Of course you're right. I shouldn't have even asked him."

"You didn't ask him. *I* did," she said, and wasn't that what really rankled?

"I know." He shook his head and exhaled heavily. "And I know it rubs you the wrong way, but aren't I worth it?" He grabbed her hands, suddenly animated. "Aren't *we* worth it?"

She pursed her lips and tried to let go of the tension. "Can't we talk about this later? After I finish up with the chores?"

"No, we can't." His tone was belligerent. She beetled her brows at him, ready for battle, but he chuckled. "Because *I'm* going to do the chores for you."

She considered arguing out of spite, but perhaps she should leave childishness for those who didn't have children of their own. "Thank you," she said finally and felt suddenly silly, then grumpy, then guilty. The panorama of emotions was exhausting. "That's nice of you. But listen, I'll take care of the outside stuff if you'll wash the—"

"I'm doing the outdoor chores, too."

"But what if—"

"Doesn't take a genius, remember?" Kissing her softly, he turned away. "Go to sleep," he ordered, glancing over his shoulder. His hair, wheat straw gold, fell charmingly over one brow.

"Okay."

"And dream about what I'm going to do to you when you're not so tired," he said and, winking, left the room.

Bravura awoke and stretched. Beside her, Dane was sprawled out on his stomach. She eased out of bed and wandered toward the window, doing her best not to disturb him.

Outside, the sun had just crested the eastern horizon, but she felt surprisingly rested, wonderfully refreshed. Mist shrouded the world, casting it in a film of mystery.

Pulling on jeans and a sweatshirt, she tapped down her ancient staircase and stepped silently outside. The air felt chill and damp, but there was a secret stillness to the foggy morning that never failed to thrill her. Off to the left, Tonk's tired Jeep stood silent. A meadowlark warbled to the uncertain morning, and from somewhere in the muffling haze, hoof-beats tattooed a loping pattern against hard-packed earth. Vura turned, searching for the source.

For a moment the entire world seemed suspended. Then a horse galloped from the mist. She was as silver as mercury, dark eyes wide, nostrils flaring. Her mane, alabaster white, flowed in the wind like silk, and upon her bare back, a dark warrior rode. His hair, long and black as midnight, streamed behind him. The two flew as one. For a moment they were stamped against the hoary sky and then they were gone, swallowed by the mist and the long-sweeping hills.

Goose bumps shivered up Vura's arms. But she shook herself free of her silly imaginings. It wasn't as if she was some giddy schoolgirl who fantasized about brave warriors and swift steeds.

Laughing silently at herself, she hustled toward the chicken coop, but something burst from the fog ahead of her.

Bravura gasped and the horse, startled by her movement, reared. Stumbling backward, Vura nearly fell, but Tonk was already slipping to the ground, already rushing toward her. Grabbing her arm with one powerful hand, he steadied her.

"You okay?" His voice was graveled with worry.

"Yeah." It took her a moment to gain her balance, longer still to control the waver in her voice. Memories of forbidden dreams stormed in. "Of course. I'm just . . . You scared me."

"I am sorry."

"It's okay," she said, and pulled self-consciously from his grip. "I wasn't thinking about . . ." . . . his hands, gentle as sun-warmed waves . . . bare skin against bare skin . . . his voice as deep as midnight against her ear. "I should have been looking where I was going."

"Where *were* you going?"

She glanced around, vaguely wishing she could remember.

"Bravura?" he coaxed.

She shook her head and laughed at herself. "To feed the chickens."

He raised a dubious brow. "Early risers, are they?"

"I've got to get to work."

"On Saturday."

"I've got a job that needs to be finished before Monday."

"I am sorry about that, too."

"It's good to have work."

He nodded, but his gaze never left hers. "Are you doing okay?"

"I'm fine," she said, and felt uncomfortable with the half truth, her breathlessness, his nearness.

"And Lily, she is well?" His eyes bored into hers, pinning her as if he could read her thoughts. The fantasy of them together, moonlit waves soft as dreams against her skin, slipped slyly through her mind.

His brows notched up another quarter inch.

She cleared her throat and assured herself she was being ridiculous. He could *not* read her mind. "No life-threatening injuries yet today," she said.

"Well, you've made it to dawn," he said, and she laughed.

"Listen . . ." She glanced at Skylark. The mare's eyes were dark and enormously wide. Faint wrinkles were etched above them, giving her an expression of anxious wisdom. "I wanted to apologize for the other day."

"What day is that?"

Vura scowled. Did something in his tone suggest that there were any number of days from which to choose? "I shouldn't have yelled at you for letting Lily ride," she said and, reaching out, stroked her hand down the mare's gray-satin neck.

The silence stretched out.

"So I can put her back up?" he asked finally.

"What?"

He scowled, looking surprisingly tense. "I will understand if you say no."

She blinked at him. "You want to teach Lily to ride?"

"Ai."

"Why?"

He inhaled deeply, and for reasons unknown she couldn't help but remember the day at the rodeo, when his chest had been bare, his hair adorned with feathers. "I think you know," he said.

She scowled, wondering if the man had ever yet given her a simple answer.

"Know what?" she asked.

He paused, scowled, and then looked away, the stoic warrior persona firmly in place. "That she is special."

Her irritation washed away in a rush, leaving a strangely ashy residue in its place.

"Yes, or no?" His voice was low, but now she wondered if there might be a tinge of embarrassment in his eyes. "I will not ask again."

"Okay." She cleared her throat, found her voice. "Yes."

He watched her in silence for one long second, then nodded gravely.

"But you'll be careful, right?"

He held her gaze, expression as solemn as a sacred vow. "Ai."

"Really careful? Really, really careful?"

Humor tugged at the corners of his full, ready-to-laugh lips. "Do I look foolish enough to invite the wrath of a woman such as yourself?"

"I'm not going to answer that," she said, and he chuckled a little as he turned away, taking the magical mare with him.

Stifling a grin, Vura headed toward the chicken coop. From a few yards away, a pheasant crowed to the dawn. She searched for the source, and there, not five feet away, she saw the body.

Chapter 26

A gasp sliced the air behind Tonk. He twisted toward the sound.

"Bravura?"

Her sob cut through the fog like a spear, and suddenly he was running, sprinting toward the chicken coop. In a second she was visible, standing absolutely still, shoulders hunched, hands covering her mouth.

He slowed his pace, mind churning, eyes searching for the cause of her anguish. "Bravura?"

She didn't turn toward him, merely shook her head.

"Hey . . ." He stepped closer. "What—" he began, but in a moment he saw the little body. Its downy wings were flung wide, its neck twisted at an ugly angle.

"No," she breathed, and at that moment it stirred, just a twitch of its tiny body, but she was already moving forward, already lifting the weightless form from the ground. "No," she repeated and turning, raised her gaze to Tonk's.

He felt the strike of her eyes like the blow of an ax. "I am sorry," he said, and wondered how many times he had apologized to this woman. This woman who disliked him.

"She's hurt," she breathed.

Far worse, he thought, but kept the dire musings to himself. "Ai."

Tears shone in her eyes like dewdrops on moon flowers. "Can you save her?"

Holy hell! He almost stumbled backward. What did she think he was, this woman who disliked him? "I do not think so, Bravura."

Anger flared instantly in those wildflower eyes. "Then I will," she said, but he spoke before she could pivot away.

"Does Lily need to witness another death?"

She pursed her lips, lowered her brows. "She's not going to die."

He glanced at the gosling. The long neck drooped limply. The dark eyes were closed. It was impossible to guess if it had already expired.

"Bravura—" he began, but she stopped him with a snarl.

"She's not going to die!"

He nodded and tried to turn away, but it was physically impossible, so he drew a calming breath, exhaled slowly. "I will take care of her if you like."

"Take care of her?" Her eyes scoured his. "What do you mean, take care of her?"

He searched for an answer that was unlikely to cause him bodily harm, but she spoke before he could conjure up such an improbable response.

"You're not going to kill her!" she said, and drew the animal against her chest with maternal zeal, but in that instant the gosling jerked up her head. A long wheezing sigh escaped, and then she relaxed, limp and lifeless in Bravura's cupped hands.

They stared in immobilized tandem.

Silence strained between them.

"I will . . ." He tried to judge her reaction, but she was perfectly still, frozen in place. "I will care for the body if you wish."

She nodded. Bending slowly, she returned the tiny thing to the grass, then backed away a step. "Yes." She cleared her throat, clenched her hands, and nodded. "Thank you."

He watched her.

"That would be . . ." She filled her lungs and cleared her throat. "I'd appreciate that," she said, but didn't raise her gaze to his.

He felt her pain as if it was his own and glanced away. Why in heaven's holy name was he drawn to this woman? It was a mistake. Someone somewhere had made a horrible mistake. He shuffled his feet, exhaled carefully. "It is okay to cry."

"Cry!" she said, and laughed, but the sound wobbled dangerously. "I'm not going to cry. It's only a . . ." A sound escaped her throat, something between a hiccup and a sob. "Only a . . ." she began again, and he could take no more.

Covering the ground between them, he touched her hand. She lifted her face. Her eyes struck him, wide and ravaged, burning on contact, and then she was in his arms, pressing her face to his shoulder.

There was nothing he could do but hold her. Nothing but breathe in her essence, absorb her agony, and let the moment take him.

Her sobs were heart-wrenching, deep and guttural and excruciating. Lifting one hand, he let his fingers drift down her dark-river hair, let himself have that one weakness.

But finally she fell silent and took a wavering inhalation, face still hidden against his chest. "I'm sorry." Her voice was low and raspy. "I just . . ." She raised one hand and swiped at her cheek. "I don't know what's wrong with me."

He squelched the awful urge to tell her "nothing." To assure her that she was perfect. Despite a hundred glaring flaws, she was inexplicably flawless. "There is no need to apologize for grief."

"Grief." She laughed. The sound was horrible, grating against his newfound need for honesty. "It was just . . ." She paused to draw a shuddering breath. "Just a goose."

"It was a life." He stroked her hair again, though he knew he shouldn't. Knew he should draw back. Refrain. "Another life."

She said nothing.

He pulled in a quiet breath and searched for strength. "And you've not yet mourned your grandfather."

For a moment he thought she would argue, would draw away, but she remained as she was, body softening a little in his too grateful arms. "I didn't think . . ." She paused. "I know it's stupid. I mean, he was sick. And old. I know that . . ."

He waited, let her think, let her talk, let her simply be.

"I just didn't think he'd die."

Why did this seem so right? "Perhaps it is the greatest honor of all."

She said nothing.

"When we cannot let go of those we love," he explained and wondered what it would be like to feel such devotion to one's progenitors. His own father had died two years before. He hadn't bothered to attend the funeral.

"He was . . ." She paused again to exhale. "He

was so . . . well, he was kind of a grouch, really."

He couldn't help but smile. "So you two had a good deal in common?"

There was a moment of silence. Then she chuckled, relaxed a smidgeon more, and sighed. "He didn't like geese, either."

"I didn't know you disliked them," he said, and wondered what it would be like if she lost a pet for which she cared.

"They're awful. The adults," she explained and shivered. "Snooty and bossy and mean. Like . . . cats with feathers."

So she didn't like cats, either. Luckily, Princess was confined to the inside of his house where the two would never meet.

"We had the same little toe, too."

"You and cats?"

"Me and Gamps."

"Ah . . ."

"It's weird and . . . hideous."

He lifted his chin a little, letting his gaze sift over the hills behind her. The fog was lifting like a bride's lacy veil. She had chosen a good spot here. A kind spot, nestled in the fragrant earth, haloed by the endless sky.

"Does your father share your deformity?" he asked, and felt her tense again. So there lay the deepest source of her pain, he thought, and assured himself it was not his task to probe that pain. And yet he felt a need to do just that.

"Dad's old, too." Her words were no more than a whisper.

He closed his fingers in her hair, allowing himself just a moment of that mind-bending ecstasy.

"What if I lose him?"

He could feel the warmth of her, the life, as vibrant as the west wind, as powerful as the sun.

"You've sustained hard losses of late, Bravura. But you will be happy again. The world will be right."

She nodded slowly.

"We are given gifts," he said, and forced himself to release her hair. "Some of which we will keep forever. Some for just a short while."

"I have Lily."

"You have Lily," he said, and wished with a heart-wrenching yearning that he could say the same. Stupid. Undeniably stupid. But so painfully true. He loved the child as he loved the mother, and there was nothing he could do to change it.

The world fell into a wistful silence.

"Do you have children, Tonk?"

Overhead, a red-tailed hawk soared on the warming thermals. He watched its gliding path and wondered why a child with whom he had spent barely a half a dozen hours would feel as if she were his own. "None that are blood kin."

"I don't know what that means," she said, and pulled back a little to find his eyes.

284

He felt the withdrawal like a direct strike to the heart but smiled into the pain and shrugged, searching for a cautious balance between practicality and honesty. "I cannot pretend it makes sense, but from the first I have felt that Lily—"

"What the hell's going on?" Dane snarled, and Vura jerked like a broken puppet from his arms.

Chapter 27

"Dane!" Embarrassment washed through Bravura in a flood of shame. But guilt was her overriding emotion.

Her husband stepped toward them, brows beetled. "I asked a question."

"You lied!" The words spurted from her lips like venom.

"What?"

"You said you'd lock them up. But you lied. Again. And look what happened." She waved wildly toward the little body on the grass.

His gaze flickered to the gosling and away. "So you're a whore because of some dead duck?"

She never saw Tonk move, never expected him to, but suddenly Dane was stretched out on the ground, nose bloody, Tonk leaning over him.

It took her a heartbeat to realize what had happened, longer still to lurch forward and grab his arm.

"What are you doing?" she rasped, but Tonkiaishawien's gaze never left Dane's shocked face.

"Take it back," he growled.

"Tonk, geez—" she began, but Dane laughed.

"Seriously?" he said, and croaked another chortle. "I was right?"

She dragged her gaze from Tonk, pinned it on Dane, shook her head.

He staggered to his feet, swiped his knuckles beneath his bloodied nose. "You really *do* have a thing for him. *Him!*" He said the word in blooming disbelief.

"Nothing happened," she promised.

He laughed out loud. "Well, that's what I assumed until I realized you were such a little—"

"She is your wife." The words were growled like a curse through Tonk's clenched teeth. "You will apologize now."

Dane narrowed his eyes, considering. "Let me get this straight. It's not just that you want to bang her? So you're what? In love with her?"

No one spoke. No one moved.

Dane threw back his head and laughed. "Oh buddy, you poor, miserable bastard. You're in love with my wife."

Every instinct in Vura made her want to rail and cry, to accuse and rant, but she exhaled softly, clenched her fists and reached cautiously for reason. "He's not . . . He doesn't . . . I found the

gosling. It was dying and I was . . . I was . . ."
Devastated beyond reason. "Upset . . . Tonk was comforting me." She set her teeth gently and attempted to drain the tension from her rigid muscles. It was like trying to push back the sun. "You said you would lock them up, Dane."

His gaze dropped to the gosling. He dabbed the back of his wrist to his nose. "That's really what this is about?"

She nodded, though really she wasn't sure about anything.

He huffed disbelievingly. "Listen, Vey, I'm sorry. I was just so tired after cleaning the kitchen and everything."

Everything? she thought, but didn't let loose the word. Instead, she swallowed, nodded, exhaled softly. "I see." She tried to sound mature, controlled, but her eyes welled with tears, hot and furious. "Well . . ." She shook her head. Dane stepped forward.

"Hey . . . baby . . ." Putting his hands on her arms, he rubbed gently, as one might a fractious mare. "Let's go on inside, okay?"

She didn't look at Tonk, couldn't. Instead, she nodded miserably. Dane put a gentle hand on her back and guided her toward the house, leaving their guest behind them.

Once inside, the silence seethed between them like a witch's brew.

Dane shut the door quietly. Their gazes met.

He grinned, charm seeping back to his face like a mask that had been momentarily displaced. "Geez," he said, and chuckled. "I guess I made a mess of things out there."

She said nothing.

"Listen, baby, I'm sorry. I just . . ." He shook his head. "I saw you with him and I guess . . . I guess I went a little crazy. But you can't really blame me, can you?" he asked and, stepping forward, grabbed her hands. "You're my wife. The thought of losing you . . . I just couldn't bear it."

"Do you care about me, Dane?" she asked. And if so, did he think of her as a cherished wife or more like property . . . a car maybe, but not so new, not so shiny?

"What are you talking about? I'm crazy about you, Vey! You know that."

In the past those words had been enough to send goose bumps careening giddily up her spine. Perhaps they should now. But she felt woefully disenchanted. "Then why couldn't you do what I asked?"

He stared at her quizzically. "You mean the birds?" he asked, and laughed. "I didn't even think you liked them. But listen, honey, if I had known how attached you were to those things, I would have bundled them up in my jacket and carted them up to the bedroom. But honestly . . ." He grinned. "They're just geese." He waved toward the outdoors. "I'll go to the feed store right now and buy you a new one."

She watched him in silence. For a moment his lack of understanding was mind-boggling. She considered trying to explain, but it was impossible to know where to begin. And really, was it worth the effort? "I just . . ." She glanced toward the stairs and hoped with pulsing desperation that her daughter was still asleep. "I don't know what I'm going to tell Lily."

"Lily?" He said the name as if he had forgotten her existence, as if the thought of her hadn't so much as crossed the periphery of his mind.

Anger welled up like a fountain, fueled by disappointment, fired by grief. "Lily," she said. "Your daughter. Remember?"

"Of course I remember, Vey, I just—"

"Do you? Because it seems like you've forgotten everything else. Our plans. Our vows. Our—"

"I've forgotten? *I've* forgotten our vows?" he snarled and jerked toward her. For one wild moment she thought he might strike her, might reach out and slap her face, but then he wheeled away and stormed across the room.

The front door shuddered closed behind him.

Rage quaked inside Vura. She jerked after him, but a small voice snapped her to a halt.

"What's wrong, Mama?"

She stopped, trembling. And her day began in earnest.

● ● ●

"Good job today, guys," Vura said, and dropped the tailgate on her truck. Her fingers were cold. The air felt sharp. It seemed late in the year for snow, but it was still April, so who could say?

"Yeah, and Hip only went nutso once," Maynard said.

He was referring to Johnston's unusual lapses into what seemed like daydreams. Sometimes they would find him staring into space with an expression that looked suspiciously like a smile. A niggle of worry zipped through Vura, but she needn't have been concerned about his tender feelings. Hip could take care of himself. Had been for seventy-odd years.

"Nutso or not, I can still get more done by noon than you can manage before dark."

"But I'm hell on wheels after midnight," Maynard said, and pointed to his shirt. It read, I'M BATMAN.

Hip made a disparaging remark about men who wore tights, and the argument began in earnest.

"How you doing?" Glen asked, kindly drawing her from the interplay.

"What do you mean? I'm fine," she said and, tossing the last of her tools into the bed of her Chevy, slammed the tailgate shut. Pain radiated through her upper body like the peal of a bell, but she gritted a smile.

"You should get that looked at," Glen insisted

and nodded to the forearm she had hidden beneath the sleeve of her waffle-knit shirt. "Them shingles hit you pretty hard." They had, in fact, fallen from the roof with terrifying force. Luckily, she had jumped aside in time to save her head. "You mighta broke something."

"I didn't," she said and, seeing that her tailgate hadn't closed properly, gritted her teeth against the impending pain and slammed it again.

"Don't think she'd be able to use it like she just done if it was busted," Hip said.

"That's nothing but an old wife's tale," Maynard argued and grinned. "Then again, I hear you might have yourself an old wife any day now, huh, Hip?"

They snapped their attention to Maynard like spaniels on a bobwhite.

He grinned, loving the attention. "I guess him and your favorite pinup girl's been spending some late nights together." He raised his ginger brows. "And . . . according to Teri's cousin's favorite aunt . . . a couple early mornings."

"What?" Vura asked, not sure if she was thrilled or appalled . . . until she remembered the woman's hideous red-on-white kitchen. Then she was appalled. "Hip, are you dating Colleen Washburn?"

The old man snorted. "If Maynard's brain was half so big as his mouth, we'd have something to talk about. Hey . . ." he said, and shambled toward his truck. "I'd be happy if there was just some sort of connection between the two."

Glen chuckled, Maynard snorted, and Vura, fiercely grateful for the distraction, slipped into her Chevy and drove away.

Once out of sight, however, she pulled into the McDonald's parking lot and sat. Just sat, letting the day drain away from her. She wasn't going to cry. That would be stupid. Almost as stupid as it was to get hurt. Carefully tugging up her sleeve, she stared at the injury. The shingles had struck her forearm at an oblique angle, leaving a bruise that blushed puce and olive and a spectacular shade of violet. She shook her head. It was probably more practical to take another hit of ibuprofen than to burst into tears, but before she could do so, her phone rang, startling her. She longed to ignore it, to wallow in self-pity, but that was just another luxury she couldn't afford.

She pulled the cell from her pocket, saw the call was from her father, and felt a familiar bite of worry tear at her.

"Is everything all right?" The words spurted from her lips.

There was a momentary pause during which she held her breath.

"With Lily? Yeah, everything's fine." His tone implied that he hadn't considered things could be otherwise . . . also a lovely luxury. "But what's going on with you?"

She glanced at her arm. If she looked closely, she could just discern an intriguing shade of russet. But how had he learned of her injury?

"Glen called," her father said. "Are you okay?"

"Glen called you?" She scowled. Geez, it was as if she were back in high school, being tattled on by her lab partner. Sometimes girls' hair just caught on fire, okay?

"Said you had an accident with some shingles."

"It's nothing."

"Glen doesn't call about nothing, Bravura. You seen a doctor yet?"

She laughed out loud. It sounded a little maniacal to her own ears. "Holy cow, Dad, it's just a scratch. I've gotten worse opening mail," she said, and dropped four Advil into her slightly unsteady palm.

"Then you should be more careful with your letter opener. I want you to go to the emergency room."

"That'll cost—"

"I'll pay for it."

She rested her head against the cushion behind her, letting fatigue course through her like river water. "I'm okay. Really. I just want to see Lily. How's she doing?"

He sighed. She could imagine him settling his hips against the counter they had installed together when she was twelve. "She's already asleep."

"At . . ." She checked the clock on her dash . . . 9:17, on a Saturday night. She'd been lucky he'd been able to babysit in a pinch . . . again. "Oh . . ." Guilt again, familiar but unloved. "I guess it's later than I realized."

"In more ways than one."

"What?"

"Listen, if you're not going to see the doctor, then go home and get some sleep."

She yearned for the comfort of Lily's presence, but her father's house was a half-hour drive while her own humble abode would take her less than fifteen minutes. "I guess I'll do that."

"I'll bring her out first thing in the morning."

"You don't need to. I can come pick her up."

"I'll bring her. Just get some rest," he ordered and hung up.

She stared at the cell in her hand. This was for the best, she told herself. She was tired. Exhausted, really. And who wouldn't be? It had been an awful day, starting poorly and not ending much better. She stared at the ceiling of her truck, replaying the scene with the gosling, with Tonk, with Dane. She should go home and hash things out with her husband, she thought, and physically winced at the idea. But Quinton Murrell hadn't raised her to be a coward.

Lifting her phone again, she dialed Dane's number.

Voice mail came on in a moment.

"Yeah, y' got Dane. I'm busy right now." A guitar riff filled the air. "But leave a number. I'll buzz y' right back." The guitar again. "Or not."

The message was eerily reminiscent of high school. As if the years since had never happened. As if they had never grown up, conceived a child, gotten married. Clicking the End button, Vura pursed her lips and stared at the dash. The digital clock stared back. Dad was right, she should go home. Get some sleep.

But guilt was battery-acid bitter. And Tonk's house was even closer than her own.

Chapter 28

Tonkiaishawien sat back and studied the canvas. Acrylics weren't his most successful medium. His gifts lay more in clay, in the rich, centering texture of earth where he could bury his hands, could immerse his soul. But the image on canvas was taking shape. The brushstrokes had a bold life to them, the pallet was pleasing. In short, it wasn't horrible.

He snorted at the thought. Great. That's just what he had been striving for all these years . . . not horrible. Lifting his brush, he prepared to try to find that perfect balance between playfulness and confidence in his subject's laughing-water eyes, but the doorbell interrupted his work.

He winced. Sometimes he was a flirt. He knew that. In the past he had been more than happy to reap the benefits that might accompany any well-accepted flirtations, but lately . . . He scowled. Perhaps he could pretend he wasn't home, hide inside like a shy hermit.

Mutt cocked his head, raised his one good ear.

Across the room, Princess growled a warning at such outrageous behavior.

The doorbell rang again. Tonk groaned in silence, realizing the truth; he was two days late on the rent . . . again. The fact that he now had ample funds generated by the success of the images he had crafted of Sydney Wellesley's famous mustang—a success that surprised *him* more than anyone—he still had trouble paying his bills on time. Mariam Pretty on Top, his AA sponsor and self-proclaimed therapist, thought his dysfunction might stem from the fact that he still believed he deserved to fail. Cousin Riley thought it more likely that he was simply a dumb ass.

Rising to his feet, Tonk wiped his hands on the rag left nearby and turned down his stereo. Kids these days fiddled with iPods and MP3s, but they didn't know what they were missing when they eschewed the liquid warmth of a metal needle on vinyl.

Skirting a painted war drum commissioned by a lady in Connecticut who was *certain* she had Native roots, though they had yet to be unearthed, he grabbed his undelivered check from the kitchen counter and made his way to the door. Mutt padded along behind.

"I'm sorry—" he began and stopped cold at the sight of Bravura Lambert. For a second his heart bumped madly, and then it seemed to stop, to lie dormant in the stillness of his chest like a cold lump of clay that refused to be finessed. But he tightened his hand on the door handle and remembered to breathe.

She skipped her gaze to the check in his hand and grinned a little, a sassy saloon girl slash of humor on that freckled girl-next-door face. "You paying me now?" she asked.

He stared at her, mind oddly blank, body dumb as a post.

She motioned toward the check, then slipped a thumb in the hammer hook of her overalls. She was outrageously cute, hideously gorgeous, impossibly real. "To stay out of your life, maybe?"

He scowled and wondered dismally where the hell his glib tongue had run off to. Holy crap, he'd be happy to speak at all. But she was too close, too genuine and honest and earthy. Yet behind her living-water eyes she looked worn out, scrubbed bare.

"I thought you were someone else." They were the only words he could manage for a moment. He cleared his throat. "Honey Halverson."

Mutt edged forward to nudge her hand with his

motley nose. "Hey, good-looking," she said, and scratched him behind his tattered ear before lifting her gaze back to Tonk's. "Do you have to pay all the women in your life?"

"She's my landlady."

"Of course she is," she said.

He stared at her.

"I . . ." She glanced at the toes of her work boots, scratched the dog again. "Sorry. I was just kidding." She looked left, exhaled softly, and shuffled her feet. "Could I come in, maybe?"

Panic washed through him like a wild tide. "Here?"

She raised her brows and watched him as if he was nuts. Which, come to think of it, had a fair probability of being the case. "Well, yeah, if you've got a minute."

A thousand excuses galloped through his mind. The best one was the lateness of the hour. But it had not yet reached ten o'clock, and the idea that he couldn't manage to stay up later than a kindergartener might make him seem like something of a pansy. He stepped back reluctantly, and she moved inside with that bold sashay that was hers alone.

He closed the door. They stared at each other. She tapped a finger on the pant leg of her overalls. They stared some more. She glanced around. "Is that . . ." She raised her brows, left dimple making a brief appearance. "Is that disco music?"

"What?" The question ripped him from his Bravura-induced trance. Making a quick about-face, he goose-stepped to his stereo and clicked it into silence.

" 'Y.M.C.A.'?" she asked, and made a C shape with her arms above her head.

He should have been playing his Native Spirit mix tape. Or Celtic Nights or Pipes in the Wind, but the truth was, he loved disco. And there was no accounting for love. "Did you want something, Bravura?" he asked. "Or did you just come by to . . ." He stopped, breath catching in his throat. Her impromptu Village People dance had displaced a sleeve enough to allow a glimpse of her left arm. "What happened?"

"What? Oh!" She flushed a little. "It's just a . . . I had a little accident. It's nothing."

Rage roared through him, almost blinding in its intensity. But he clenched his fists, bottled his anger, and practiced the hell out of step eleven. "How many other accidents has he caused?"

"What?"

He inhaled deeply, one cautious, cleansing breath, then exhaled just as carefully, but the rage was still there, white-hot, though contained now, shaped. "If you need help . . ." He paused for a second. "Monetary or—"

"Wait!" She took a quick step back, shook her head and laughed out loud, but the sound lacked the raucous, all-in quality that had called to him from the moment he'd first heard it. "You think Dane did this?"

He said nothing.

"My husband would never hurt . . ." She paused for just an instant, perhaps remembering the crude way he had spoken to her earlier in the day. "He'd never hurt me. Not physically."

He watched the words form on her lips, heard the sincerity in her tone, but weren't there women's shelters around the globe filled with just that sort of heartfelt earnestness?

"Who, then?" he asked.

She stared at him a second longer. One dark brow moved into a slant.

"If you actually think I'd let someone use me as a punching bag, you're more deluded than I thought, Tonkiaishawien." She said the words with just enough sass to make him believe. A modicum of tension slipped from his shoulders.

"Why are you here, Bravura?"

She sobered, shuffled her feet. The sass slipped a notch toward uncertainty. "I, ummm . . ." She glanced toward the window as if longing to be elsewhere. "I came to apologize."

He held his breath, certain he had heard her wrong.

"We treated you poorly this morning."

Yet he had been the only one to throw a punch.

"Dane isn't usually the jealous sort."

And wasn't that a strange truth? If she were his,

he would be exactly that. Jealous of every moment they were apart, of every person who shared her life. And holy crap on a cracker, who needed that kind of crazy? "What type is he . . . usually?" he asked.

She nodded as if in concession to unspoken truths. "These past few years have been hard on him."

"And for you?"

"What?"

"How have they been for you?"

"Well, I . . ." She looked surprised, as if she had never quite considered it. "I have Lily."

"And he does not?"

A rogue flare of anger sparked in her eyes, but she blew out her breath and shook her head once. "I just came by to say I'm sorry that he accused you of . . ." For a moment she didn't seem quite capable of forcing out the words. "Of being in love with me. I know you were just being kind."

He managed a nod and one step toward the door, though he wasn't sure how. "I accept your apology," he said. "But it is late and I have an early day tomorrow."

She pursed plump-berry lips. "He had no right to accuse you of anything."

"I am glad that you realize this," he said, and put his hand on the doorknob.

"I know that you're not . . ." She breathed out, a long, smooth exhalation that made her chest rise and fall beneath her faded-plaid shirt. The skin above the collar was as smooth and creamy as kaolin. ". . . that you're not in love with me."

"Good." He turned the knob.

"Well, I guess . . ." She searched for words. As she did so, her gaze strayed slightly and fell with a jolt on Princess's take-your-best-shot expression. "Is that a . . ." She paused as if not wanting to make some awful blunder. "Is that a cat?"

"Ai." He didn't glance toward the animal. "I believe it is."

"What's its . . . his . . . name?"

"Princess."

Her lips formed a little O of surprise. Perhaps it was because the cat looked a little more like some scientific experiment gone horribly wrong than like any type of royalty. "What happened to its . . . her . . . tail?"

"I do not know." But his best guess was that in one of her former lives she had engaged in a dispute with a grizzly. Sometimes in the quiet of the night, Tonk still worried about that poor bear.

Vura nodded. Despite her aforementioned lack of affection for the species, she didn't seem to be particularly repulsed by the animal's awful features. Or at least she was unafraid, which was more than he could say for most. "How about her ears?" The left one was missing a fair-sized notch. The right one was simply missing.

Mutt whined. Vura stroked him distractedly.

"Perhaps she did not wish to make the dog feel unattractive."

"So they're friends?"

He let his gaze stray to the cat finally. "Do demons make friends?"

She laughed, stopping his heart. "Look at you, taking in strays, creating beauty . . ." She paused, giving his system time to jolt back to life. "Underneath all your irritating ways, you might be a pretty nice guy, Tonkiaishawien."

"Do not count on it."

Their eyes met in a velvet clash, but she jerked her gaze away and swept it across the room.

Tonk held his breath, dreading, fearing, and knowing, instantaneously, when the horrible truth dawned on her.

Chapter 29

Vura remained exactly where she was, not quite able to move, to think, to draw a normal breath. But she finally, through terrible force of will, managed to blink.

The painting propped on the nearby easel, however, remained the same . . . an Indian maiden so real she all but galloped from the canvas. Dressed in buckskin and beads, she sat astride a painted mare. The leather of her moccasins looked so authentic, it seemed she could feel the rough suede against her fingertips. The glass beads were just a little faded, a little imperfect, as if they had been worn in wind and sun. The horse, though wildly beautiful, was rugged and scarred. A mustang that had survived life on the open plains. An animal so genuine and tangible, it was as if you could smell her earthy aroma, could feel the heat of her breath upon your cheek. But it was not Tonk's incredible skill that shocked Bravura Lambert.

What made her heart pulse to a shuddering halt was the fact that the maiden's face was her own.

She hissed out a careful breath and turned her gaze toward Tonk, but in so doing, her attention snagged on a painted gourd. The face on that piece was barely visible, just a shadow of an image, really. A vague glimpse, and yet there was something about it, something in the tilt of the lips, the hint of a dimple . . . something that she saw every day in the mirror.

"What . . ." The single word was as breathy as a prayer. Stumbling closer, she studied the gourd from another angle, but up close the similarities were only amplified. "I don't . . ." She shook her head. "I thought you didn't . . ." Her brain felt scrambled, oddly muffled. "You don't like me."

He stood very straight, very still, like the wooden Indian who stood guard outside the Wall Drug Store. "I do not know what you speak of, Bravura," he said, voice cool, demeanor dismissive. "But it is late, so I suggest we—"

"What I'm . . ." She waved a stuttering hand toward the painting propped on the easel, then let it flutter toward the gourd. "I'm talking about this . . . this . . ." She glanced toward the disturbing canvas again. "I'm talking about *me,*" she breathed. "My image on your . . . art."

For a moment the room was absolutely still and then he laughed.

"Bravura," he said, and stepped away from the door. "I knew you to be illogical at times, but I did not realize the depths of your vanity."

"The depths of . . . I . . ." She faltered and glanced at the painting again and in that instant it turned into nothing more shocking than an appealing piece of art boasting a proud mustang and a mildly attractive woman. "I'm sorry, I . . ." Embarrassment flooded her, washing through her system, burning her cheeks. She shook her head. "I guess I . . . I must be more tired than I realized," she said, and nodded at the glaring truth of her words. "I just . . ." Turning robotically, she shambled toward the door. It wasn't until she had almost reached it that she caught the chips of unlikely amber in the woman's sky-blue eyes. She stopped, breath held as she stared into her own gaze.

In all the world, nothing stirred.

"Perhaps I should have asked your permission."

Tonk's words were no more than the quiet rumble of distant thunder.

She turned toward him, moving erratically, like an uncertain top about to topple to the floor. "I don't understand."

He watched her, gaze steady. "Then you are not as bright as I believe you to be, Bravura Lambert."

"You don't . . ." She shook her head, trying to think, to understand, to make some sort of sense of the situation. "You don't hate me?"

For a moment she was certain he would deny everything, would tell her she was delusional, would *prove* she was. But he huffed a quiet laugh.

"Tell me, Bravura, do you mistake every man's obsess—*interest* . . ." he corrected himself. A muscle danced in his chiseled jaw. "Do you mistake every man's interest for hatred?"

"Every man's . . ." She laughed, shook her head. "Men *aren't* interested in me."

He looked baffled and frustrated and irritated all at once. She would never know how he managed it, but finally he shook his head. "Did you always think so poorly of yourself, or is that, too, a gift from your husband?"

"I don't think poorly of myself."

He raised one brow, watching her, questioning her.

"I don't," she repeated.

"Tell me then, Bravura Marie, at what do you excel?"

She huffed a laugh, then backed away a step as if she could put space between herself and such a ridiculous question, but he followed her.

"What qualities do you possess that make you most proud?" he asked.

"I didn't come here to brag."

"That's just as well, because I do not think you capable of such a thing."

"I can brag," she countered and wondered why she was so irritated by the idea that he thought otherwise.

"Then do so, Bravura. If he has not stolen your self-worth, tell me of your greatest accomplishments."

"Well . . . I'm a . . ." Uncertainty washed through her. Or maybe it had been there all along, though she remembered times in her adolescence when she had been nothing but certain of her talents. Now, however, self-doubt seemed to be tearing away her footing, sweeping her under like shifting sands. When had that happened? And how had it occurred without her knowledge? She would never be a great beauty, but there had been a time when that hadn't mattered, when she was aware of her value, despite that lack. "I'm a really good . . ." She refrained from shaking her head, though it was as difficult as calculus. "I have excellent . . ." She set her teeth and let her gaze drift to his hands, his beautiful artist's hands. "I have good hands, too," she murmured.

"What?"

She snapped her gaze to his. "My hands." She swallowed. "I've always liked them."

For a second she actually thought he would laugh, would break down and double over, but he kept his expression passive, his perfect body still. "What is it about your hands that you value, Bravura?"

"Well, they . . ." She glanced at them, almost rolled her eyes, then took a wild step toward the door. "This is ridiculous," she said, and reached for the knob, but he grabbed it first. Their fingers brushed. She jerked hers away.

"Tell me of your hands."

She blinked, sure, absolutely certain that one random brush of his fingertips hadn't stolen her ability to think, hadn't rendered her speechless.

"Your hands," he repeated.

She tucked them self-consciously into the pockets of her overalls. "Well, they . . . they're skilled. Not like for cooking and stuff," she hurried to add. "But for . . ." She wobbled her head a little and wished to God she had never come. "For finishing work, that kind of thing . . . they're pretty good. I mean . . . I'm not as good as Dad. But I . . ." She raised her chin, feeling like an idiot. "I can hold my own."

"What else?"

She glowered at him, challenging, but he refused to back down, refused to back away.

"I'm tough," she said and, feeling the truth of the words soothe her, straightened her back. "I can get things done that most women . . . most *people* wouldn't want to do."

He nodded, just the slightest bump of his stubborn chin. "Go on."

She exhaled, feeling steadier. "I like my hair."

The shadow of a smile shone in his eyes. Maybe it was because of the challenge that had infused her tone.

"I'm not vain about it," she hurried to add, defensive despite herself. "But it looks decent . . . even though I don't fuss."

The smile had almost reached his lips, but for reasons unknown she no longer wanted to wipe it from his face.

"Anything else?"

"I'm honest. I try to be honest, and I'm steady. I do what I say I'll do. My men trust me. I can see things other people miss sometimes. Potential," she explained. "In a building. In a person." She nodded. "And I'm a good mother. A pretty good mother."

He nodded as if a great truth had finally been laid bare. "Do not forget again," he said, and opened the door.

She glanced outside.

"Good night, Bravura," he said.

She remained as she was. For reasons entirely

unknown, she felt as if she had been tossed into the deep end of a pool and had forgotten how to swim. So she floated, weightless.

"Tonk, I . . ."

"Good night," he repeated and nodded once as if she were excused, as if she had no choice but to leave.

She nodded back, and in a minute, though she didn't exactly know how, she found herself in her truck, alone and strangely lonely.

She sat in silence, blinking into the darkness. But she was being idiotic. She wasn't alone. Dane had returned, she reminded herself, and starting her Chevy, she headed toward home.

Chapter 30

The spring breeze fluttered tantalizingly against Vura's cheek, soft and elusive as a butterfly. Its velvety caress carried the earthy scents of wildflowers and cook fires. Beneath her, the painted pony stirred, mane brushing softly against her leather-clad thigh.

"*Maska Adsila.*"

Vura glanced to her right, and there, buckskin calf pressed to hers, rode a tantalizing warrior. The eagle feathers in his midnight hair fluttered capriciously against his high-boned cheek, but it was the smile he gave to her alone that made her catch her breath, his eyes that made her dizzy. He leaned toward her, head tilted, lips canted and—

"Hey."

She awoke with a start, found reality with a barely contained gasp.

Dane was sitting on the bed beside her. He chuckled. "Easy," he said. "I didn't interrupt a hot dream or something, did I?"

"No!" The lie came so quickly, so easily, causing instantaneous shame, but she sat up, shushing the truth. The dream *hadn't* been erotic . . . not in the strictest sense of the word. It was deeper than that. More disturbing. "No. Of course not." Clearing her throat, she glanced toward her bedroom window. Light had just begun to seep in from the east, casting a rosy glow over a snowcapped world. "What time is it?" she asked, and scrubbed at her face. But remnants of cook fires and wildflowers remained in her mind, still slightly more real than reality.

"Not too late for some nooky," he said.

She pulled her attention back to his boyish grin. He had been conspicuously absent upon her return home the previous night. The night when she had seen the images of herself in Tonkiaishawien's art. Or had that, too, been a dream?

"Was it about me?" he asked.

"What?" She shook her head, realizing that her gaze had been pulled to the distant hills outside her window again. Life had taken another odd spin.

"The dream." Reaching out, he fiddled with a wayward lock of hair that had coiled against her shoulder. "Was it about me?"

"No. It . . ." She blinked, stopped herself. "Where were you last night?"

He laughed. "So you *were* dreaming."

She pursed her lips. "Where were you?"

"Last night?" He scowled, looking confused. "What do you mean? I was here."

A little shard of crazy sliced in, but she extracted it carefully, caught his eye. "When I got home." She said the words slowly, succinctly, as if he might be a little slow on the uptake. "You weren't here."

"Did you miss me?" His grin slanted up another quarter of an inch.

She remained silent, watching him. Seeing him. Really seeing him. Maybe for the first time.

The shadow of a scowl lowered his brows, but his grin won the bout. "I must have gotten here just a couple minutes after you did, but you were already sawing logs. I didn't want to wake you."

She watched him.

"So I bunked down on the couch."

She opened her mouth to ask why, but he spoke before she could voice the question.

"Now that you're awake, though . . ." He shrugged, then leaned in to kiss the corner of her mouth. "We might as well make use of that dream."

Guilt filtered in. She glanced to the side. In the doorway, a small dollop of snow melted leisurely onto the ugly floorboards. It remained stubbornly outlining the divots left by the shoes he still wore.

Suspicion felt hot and shameful on her soul, but not so sharp, not so painful as before. "So you just woke up?" she asked.

He shrugged. "Looking for work is harder than an actual job," he said, and traced a finger down her arm.

She shifted away. "Any possibilities?" she asked and, drawing her legs from under the covers, winced a little as she scooted past him and tugged a long-sleeved shirt over her bruise. It pulsed a little, but nothing she couldn't bear.

"Not yet," he said, and twisted to watch her pull on her jeans. "Hey."

She turned toward him.

"You okay?"

"Yeah. I'm fine," she said and, nodding, found, as she trotted down the stairs, that it was shockingly true. Even as she stepped outside and set her palm on the hood of his Viper, even as she felt the heat of the recently used engine, she knew that she was right; she was fine . . . despite his lies. Or at least, she would be.

"I'm a mustang," Lily said, and charged into the kitchen on slapping hands and flying knees.

Vura laughed and poured orange juice into a glass cup. She tried to avoid allowing her daughter to drink from plastic. It was ridiculously difficult.

Thirty-six hours had passed since she had visited Tonk, had met his cat, had seen his art.

"Well, the mustang had better eat her Raisin Bran before her Pops arrives."

"Mustangs don't eat Raisin Bran," Lily declared and reared to paw the air with splayed fingers. "Besides, I have to gallop across the range, right now," she said, and dashed into the living room, elbows and knees flying like pistons.

"Oh no, you don't," Vura said, and rushed after her. Lily squealed and pivoted toward the stairs, her mother in hot pursuit.

Seconds later they tumbled onto the couch, laughing and panting.

Vura was still gasping for breath when her cell phone rang.

"Hey, Dad."

"What's wrong? You okay?" Worry was already straining his voice.

She tickled her daughter one more time and straightened. "Of course. Why wouldn't I be?"

"You sound winded."

She smiled at his concern. Ridiculous, really, how good it felt to know he was there. That he cared. "Rounding up wild mustangs is exhausting," she said as her daughter dropped onto the floor with a defiant whinny.

There was a moment of silence, then "Is the steed in question smart as a firecracker but kind of accident-prone?"

"Good guess," she said, and headed back toward the kitchen to continue breakfast preparations. For her, a gourmet meal generally involved toast. "What's up?"

"My temperature."

"What?"

"I think I've got the flu."

"You don't get the flu." She glanced up as her daughter made a quick circuit through the kitchen and back into the living room.

"Tell my immune system that, will you?"

"I'm sorry."

"Not as sorry as Ethan's going to be."

"What'd he do?"

"If he'd told me he was coming down with the bubonic plague, I would have handed him a white flag and sent him home for a week," he said and, turning from the phone, coughed hard enough to hack up a kidney. He sounded listless and raspy when he resumed their conversation. "Maybe Dane can take care of the Lily today, huh?"

Vura scowled, just now realizing the problems her father's illness would cause her. But that wasn't *his* concern. Or at least, it shouldn't be. "Don't worry about it. I'll figure out something."

There was a pause filled with angst and parental guilt. She had come by her self-reproach honestly.

"Hey, listen," he said, making an audible attempt to sound healthy . . . or at least alive. "Maybe I could—"

"No," she said, cutting him off at the verbal pass. "You couldn't. You're going to rest."

"I can rest and take care of Lily."

She laughed at the absurdity of such a ridiculous notion. "No mortal being can rest and take care of Lily."

He couldn't, in good conscience, argue, it seemed, and in a minute they hung up.

Vura slipped the phone back into her pocket and rose as footsteps sounded on the stairs leading from the upper floor.

"So the house is still standing," Dane said, and appeared in the doorway. His hair stood up at odd angles, lacking its usual panache.

She raised her brows.

"The noise," he explained. "I thought maybe someone had detonated a bomb."

"I'm sorry if we woke you," she said, but he shook his head.

"I had to get up anyway." He shuffled closer. Despite his disheveled appearance, he still smelled good. Like . . . She tested the scent. Spiced peaches, maybe. He wore distressed jeans and a black shirt with a yellow rose embroidered above the pockets. A shirt that begged for attention, Gamps would have said. "Got to get to work."

"You got a job?" Surprise speared through her.

316

"Neut Irving just called." He took a sip from the mug she'd left by the sink, made a face, and returned the coffee cautiously to the counter. "I thought you'd be glad."

"I am," she said, and shushed a hundred nasty suspicions; wasn't it odd that the one time her father couldn't care for Lily was the one time Dane would be employed for the day? "But I have to get the Snellings' windows installed and—"

"Why can't your crew do it? Isn't that what we pay them for?"

"Glen's finishing up the Hillers' solar panels. Maynard's bidding a job in Hot Springs, and Hip took Mrs. Washburn to Tampa to get her brother's blessing."

"What?"

"Exactly." There was talk of a June wedding. The idea of the cantankerous lovers/haters canoodling in Mrs. Washburn's blood and alabaster kitchen almost blew the top right off of her head. She pushed the thought aside to spare her sanity. "Anyway, I was thinking maybe you could spend the day with your daughter."

"Isn't it your dad's time with her?"

"He's sick."

"That's too bad." He shook his head once, glanced at the coffee again, and thought better of it. "If I had known that, I would've told Neut 'no go,' but he's in a tight spot and I hate to break my word."

"He just called this morning?"

He nodded. "He's paying cash, but listen . . . I'll call him back if you want me to. Tell him I can't—"

"No. That's not necessary," she said. "I just didn't hear your phone."

He nudged the cup. "Great coffee, by the way," he said, and smiled at the lie. "I put my cell on vibrate last night. Didn't want it going off and waking Lily."

"Oh. Well . . . maybe you could take her with you."

He canted his head. "You really want to expose our little girl to Neut's crew?"

"She's practically been raised with Hip and the boys."

"Yeah, well, I think your dad's scared the bad language right out of them. Anyway, isn't there a drop-in day-care place in Custer or somewhere?"

"Maybe, but . . ." She shrugged, feeling itchy.

"But what?"

Vura glanced through the kitchen door. Lily was grazing on the carpet. Ever since the Redhawks' arrival in their lives, flooring had been prairie grass and frosted Wheaties, crimped oats.

"Listen, Vey . . ." Dane's voice had taken on that we-gotta-talk tone that made her teeth grind and her stomach cramp. "You're doing a great job with her. Everybody knows it. Mother Teresa couldn't be more patient with a kid like Lily." She waited for the "but." "But . . . she's growing up. She's going to need other people. Maybe special schooling, even. I hear there's a great place in Sioux Falls."

"What?"

"It's not that far away. We could see her on weekends or—"

"On weekends!"

Irritation zipped across his sleep-deprived features. He'd gotten in late again the previous night. Drinks with the guys, he'd said. You couldn't put out too many feelers, and he was determined to get a good solid job, make some real money before he went back to school. So he'd had a couple beers with friends and potential employers at the Drop On Inn's little pub. "I thought that's what you wanted. A specialist."

"Well, yeah, maybe once a month. Or a couple times a week. But I'm not sending her away."

"I'm just trying to help," he said, and snatched his keys from the counter. "I gotta go."

"You're not even going to shower?"

"See you tonight," he said, and hurried out the door.

Vura turned back toward the sink. Outside, the engine of his Viper rumbled as if angry with the world. She ran water over the dishes and added detergent. It wasn't until she was slipping a pair of plates into the suds that she noticed he'd forgotten his wallet. Grabbing it, she ran to the door, but he was already turning onto Big Rock Road.

Pulling out her cell, she punched in his number and was rewarded a moment later by the distant sound of his ringtone.

She scowled as she made her way upstairs. On the wooden sawhorse beside the bed, his phone sounded off loudly.

She stared at it, cell still to her ear. But finally, she ended the call. Lifting his phone, she held it like another might a spider. Cautiously, as if it could bite. But she was being ridiculous. So what if it wasn't on vibrate as he had claimed? That didn't mean anything. He had probably just switched it back to normal when he realized Lily was awake. Or maybe . . .

The thing rang in her hand. She jumped as if stung, then, laughing at herself, glanced at the display. She didn't recognize the number.

Something twisted in her stomach. She tightened her grip, fighting a dozen internal battles. Privacy was a big issue with Dane. They had sparred over it on more than one occasion. Coming to a rapid decision, she reached out to set the phone aside, but her last conversation with Tonk rang in her ears.

"I'm honest," she had said. So maybe it was time to demand the same of others. Still, her voice sounded feeble in her own ears.

"Hello?"

There was a pause, then, "Who's this?" The woman's tone was cautious, a little surprised, and strangely chirpy.

Vura tightened her fingers around the rubberized frame. "This is Bravura Lambert." Her throat felt dry. "Can I help you?"

There was a moment of silence, then, "I must have the wrong number," the caller said, and hung up.

Dread crept like poison through Vura's chilled system. She stood immobilized, drowning in uncertainty, in hopelessness, in doubts. But she was tough. Hadn't she told Tonk that, too?

Exhaling shakily, she pressed Send and listened to the little unit ring in her ear. But no one answered. Instead, she got a prepackaged suggestion to leave a message.

Breathing slowly, she ended the call and let her eyes drop closed. But how long could she pretend? What was the saying? There were none so blind as those too gutless to see? Or maybe she was paraphrasing.

Opening her eyes, she steadied her hand and checked Dane's incoming calls. There had been none that morning. None until the "wrong number" from the woman with the chirpy voice.

The guilt had almost burned away by the time she scrolled down the list of callers. Chirpy had mistakenly phoned five times in the past two days.

Apparently she was a slow learner.

A noise boomed in the room. It took her a moment to realize it was the sound of her own laughter. It echoed spookily in the stillness.

"Mama?" Lily's tone was uncertain.

Vura turned with a jerk, smoothing her emotions, stilling the tremble in her hands.

"Are you all right?"

"I will be," she said and, placing the cell back on the sawhorse, lifted her daughter against her heart. "We will be."

Chapter 31

Vura tossed Lily's giddy-up bag into the backseat of her pickup and tried to think. But a dozen emotions swamped her. Fear, anger, sadness, guilt. She couldn't seem to fish a single one out of the mix. It hardly mattered, though. She had time for none of them. The Snellings expected new windows and her father was sick, leaving Lily with her for the day. The good news was, her period had finally arrived. Funny how awful and bloated and weepy the good news was, she thought, and realized there would be no time to wonder if Chirpy had been one of the "friends" from the inn the night before. No time to agonize over the memory of the woman she'd met at the rodeo. The woman with the big hair and odd voice. The woman who had smelled like peaches. The woman whose name . . .

"Tonka!" Lily sang and gave Vura's hand a quick jerk. "Mama, Tonka's here."

Vura closed her eyes for a second. She had almost escaped, but she should have known it wouldn't be so simple. Steadying herself, she fixed a bland expression on her face and turned slowly. "You're here early," she said, though in truth, she could practically set her watch by Tonk's morning arrival.

"What has happened?" he asked.

She forced a laugh. "What are you talking about? Nothing happened."

"Did you already exercise them?" Lily asked. Accusation was bright in her wild urchin eyes. Though Vura had agreed to let her learn to ride, there had not been an excess of opportunities as of yet.

Worry touched Tonk's features as he searched Vura's eyes, but his expression softened when he dropped his gaze to Lily's. "Ai. I rode the Sky Bird while leading Bay."

"So Arrow had to stay home alone?" Censure was sharp in her tone. "Like me?"

Humor flickered in his eyes, but he hid it well. "And I fear he is feeling rather sorry for himself."

"Him too?"

"Ai." He almost smiled now. "But perhaps if you gave him this"—he pulled a carrot from the back pocket of his tattered jeans—"he would quit moping."

"Okay," she agreed grudgingly and grabbing the treat from his hand, dashed into the barn.

Silence washed up in her wake.

Vura forced herself to meet Tonk's gaze. "Listen, I'm sorry, but we have to get going."

"Your father is not coming to fetch her this morning?"

"He has the flu."

Worry troubled his brow again. "Then who will look after her?"

Her stomach twisted, but she forced herself to shrug, easy-breezy. So Lily would stay with a stranger for a few hours. It wasn't the end of the world. "There's a daycare in Custer that takes drop-ins."

"You have left her there before?"

"No."

"But you know someone who has recommended this place."

She cleared her throat and reminded herself that she owed him no explanations. "It's gotten good reviews."

"By whom?"

She clenched her teeth. He wasn't helping. "Listen, I'd love to chat but—"

"She could stay with me."

Her jaw dropped. "I . . . That's really nice of you. But I don't think—"

"I am not a monster."

"What?"

"I am not like my parents."

She pulled a pair of Lily's socks from the pocket of her Carhartts, wondered vaguely how they had gotten there, and shoved them into the giddy-up bag. "What . . ." She glanced at him. "What happened to them?"

He drew a breath through his nostrils as if needing the strength. "My father cared for me . . . in his way." There was the slightest twitch of a muscle in his cheek. "My mother left when I was seven. For L.A., I believe." Only a hint of nostalgia shone in his eyes. Just a shadow of pain. The words were delivered almost dispassionately.

"I'm sorry."

"As was I, although—" He stopped, straightened even more. Vura would not have thought it possible. "She was not a good role model. Still, she taught me much, about weakness, about greed. The Redhawks shared other lessons. You could speak to Hunt. He would vouch for me, for my sobriety."

"It's not that I doubt—"

"I would sooner lose a limb than see her hurt," he said, and softened as his solemn-Indian gaze shifted to the barn door through which they could watch Lily slip wisps of hay into Arrow's stall. She was chattering happily, scurrying busily, former pique forgotten as if it had never been.

"I know you'd be good to her," Vura said, and found that it was true. There were times when Hunter spoke of his brother with amused exasperation, but there was always respect, always trust. And Vura valued Hunt's opinion as much as anyone's, far more than most. "Still," she began, but when he tugged his attention from Lily, his dark-water eyes were suspiciously bright. "Are you . . ." She narrowed her eyes at him. "You're not going to cry, are you?"

His back stiffened like a lance. His lips, full and well defined, pursed at such slander. "I fell from the hayloft at age ten, broke my arm in two places."

Vura watched him, waiting.

"Dislocated my shoulder at age twelve."

She raised one brow. If this morning got any weirder, she was just going to call it quits and go back to bed. "Okay."

"Did not complain."

"All right."

"Had a kidney stone while riding in Browning. Finished the race before I passed out."

"So . . . you're *not* crying?"

He raised his chin. "Do not leave her with me if you don't wish to. The choice is yours," he said, and turned away, but she stepped forward and grabbed his arm.

"Okay."

He pivoted slowly back toward her, saying nothing.

"You can take her for the day."

His expression remained exactly as it was. Then he nodded slowly, as if taking some solemn vow.

"But she's a handful."

He scowled a little as if affronted. "You think a warrior child should be otherwise?"

"No, I guess . . ." Holy crap. "I guess not." She grimaced. "You won't let anything happen to her?"

"Much will happen," he said. "She will learn of the horse, the People, the old ways."

"I meant, you won't let anything *bad* happen."

"I will treat her as my own, with all due care."

She breathed in, catching his gaze.

"Okay. Okay, then." She felt like an idiot. "If it's all right with Lily, it's all right with me."

He nodded, sober as a post. Vura shifted her gaze to her daughter and raised her voice. "Hey, honey . . ."

The girl's tiny hand stilled on Arrow's painted face.

"Come here a minute, will you?"

She trotted over, sneakers already grubby, nose sprinkled with dust. "Arrow will forgive Tonka if he leaves the others at home tomorrow."

"Did she tell you that?"

"He," Lily corrected sternly. "Swift Arrow's a gelding. Geldings are boy horses that can't be daddies." She scowled, fair brow crinkling. "How come they can't be daddies?"

327

"I . . ." Vura began and had no idea where to go from there. "Maybe Tonk can explain that to you later today."

The expressive eyebrows lifted. "How come not now?"

"Well . . ." Vura exhaled softly. "I have to get work, but if you want, you could stay with Tonkiaishawien for the day if you promise to be—"

"I do!"

Vura scowled. "I don't want you to—"

"I won't!"

"I'm going to be gone for a while but you can—"

"Okay."

Vura turned in exasperation to Tonk. "I guess she's yours."

His eyes looked suspiciously bright again, but Lily drew his attention away.

"Will you teach me everything about horses?" Her voice was little more than a hopeful lisp.

He nodded once. "I will do what I can, *Sihu*."

"Can we ride all day?" she asked, and lifted her arms to Tonk.

He reached down with reverent slowness, displaying the same aching care his brother showed in Lily's presence.

"We cannot," he said, "for there is much work to do. Horses are meant to graze, but the fences are not yet ready."

"You can't put them out all day right away," she said, tone solemn and a little preachy, "or they might get sick."

He nodded. "Spring grass can be too rich for them."

"They could col . . ." She scowled, searching for the right word. "Collin."

"Colic," he corrected. "Ai. We must be cautious."

"And we gots to get rid of the barbed wire so they don't cut themselves like Courage did."

"You know much about horses already."

She nodded, three rapid-fire jerks of her chin. "I have the *Encyclopedia of the Horse*. But I bet you could teach me even more."

"I will try."

"Like how to run like the wind," she said, slyness slipping into her eyes.

His own shone with amusement. "You must learn to walk before you run, small warrior."

"How about if you teach me to walk right now?"

He laughed. "We'll let them finish their breakfast first."

"But that could take forever. Horses can eat for twelve hours a day, and there are only twenty-four hours altogether so that just leaves"—she thought hard—"twelve hours to ride, and Mama makes me sleep part of that time."

He chuckled again. "We will ride this day," he said. "If you promise to listen closely and do as I say."

Vura cleared her throat.

They turned toward her in surprised unison as if just remembering her presence.

"And if it is acceptable to your mother, of course," he added.

"Mama?"

"You'll be careful?"

Lily nodded solemnly. Tonk did the same.

"Very, *very* careful?"

The nods again.

"All right, then," she said, and left, knowing, absolutely *knowing* it would be crazy to feel jealous of that intangible something Tonk shared with her daughter. But, she admitted as she rumbled toward the Snellings and their unfinished windows, sanity was overrated.

Chapter 32

"It doesn't hurt," Lily said.

Tonk lifted his gaze from the cut on the child's ankle to fix it on her eyes.

She fidgeted a little. "Much," she added.

He resisted a smile. Her mother, he realized, had not been exaggerating when she'd said the child was a handful. In fact, it had taken both his hands and all his wits to keep Lily entertained and safe throughout the day. And he had done well . . . until her task of finding unwanted barbed wire had caused this little scrape on her leg. His stomach knotted. Certainly it wasn't a serious cut. His biological parents would never have noticed such a small laceration. His adopted mother, however, the woman known on the rez as the Hun, would have kissed it better, though he'd insisted he needed no woman fussin' over him. Didn't need one. Didn't want one. But would be eternally grateful he had had one. He would always remember her eyes, bright as dawn from sunup to sundown. Her booming laugh, her unquenchable love for life. And her hands . . . soft as thistledown when he was hurting, hard as steel when he'd messed up beyond the generally accepted limits of mess-ups.

The memory of her softened the knot in his stomach. Still, Bravura Lambert was neither a monster nor the Hun. What would she think of this situation?

"Perhaps we should take you to the clinic," Tonk said.

Lily scowled, thinking. "It's not a good day for that."

"What?" He met her eyes.

She blinked, solemn as a surgeon. "Dr. Shelby isn't in on Mondays."

The fact that she was aware of her doctor's schedule was a little disconcerting. "So what would your mother do if she was here?"

She pulled a thoughtful face. "Well . . . Mama loves me."

331

He raised his brows and waited for her to continue.

"So I think she'd probably want me to ride horse until I feels better."

He managed to contain his laughter for a full three seconds, but that was as long as he could resist.

She grinned, charming beyond reason. "Please?"

He shook his head. "I've no wish to make your mother angry."

"You're not afraid of her, are you?"

"Do I look like a fool?"

"Only sometimes," she said, and wrinkled her nose.

Impressively perceptive, he thought. "You seem to see your doctor on quite a regular basis."

"That's because I'm accident-proned."

He nodded.

"But Mama says that from now on if it's not spurting blood or falling off, we're just gonna bandage it up and go about our business."

"Really?"

She nodded solemnly and glared at the wound. "And it's not spurtin'."

"True."

"And my leg's not falling off."

He lifted his palms gratefully. "Praise the Great Spirit."

She shrugged, a quick bob of tiny shoulders. "So I think I'm good."

"You are," he agreed. "But we'll wash it up and bandage it anyway," he added and lifted her into his arms.

"Can I ride after that?" she asked, and twined her arms around his neck.

Contentment settled in, edged by gratitude, underscored by wonder. "We shall see."

"No spurtin'," she reminded him.

There was nothing he could do but agree.

Vura had planned to get home sooner, but by the time she pulled up beside Tonk's battered Jeep, the sun had sunk below the cottonwoods.

Creaking out of her own less-than-stellar vehicle, she headed toward the house, but a shriek, high-pitched and desperate, stopped her in her tracks.

She jerked toward the sound.

"Lily!" she gasped and shot toward the barn.

One rapid-fire glance told her the building was empty.

Another shriek had Vura scrambling through the back door to the paddock on the other side. And there she stopped, breath held, goose bumps shivering over her skin, too scared to move, too petrified to speak.

Lily, her only child, her precious five-year-old daughter, sat alone on a sixteen-hand horse. Alone, without benefit of saddle or reins, she galloped in a circle, arms flung wide.

Inside the circle, Tonk held Arrow's lunge line with casual ease. Still, fear clamped Vura's throat in a tight grip, though it was clear now that neither terror nor pain had caused the shrieks she'd heard. It was joy, unfettered and wild as the west wind.

"Mama!" Lily called, catching sight of her mother for the first time. "I'm ridin'."

Vura nodded, swallowed, and held herself perfectly still lest she scare the animal upon which her daughter's life depended. "I see that, baby." The fear had abated somewhat, allowing her to speak. "But it's time to stop now."

The little brows dipped dramatically toward her trouble-brewing eyes. "But we just started, and . . ."

"We will stop now, Lily," Tonk said, gaze never leaving the loping pair. "Arrow is about to drop to a trot. Are you ready?"

Lily shifted her gaze to his and nodded, though treason flickered across her face.

"It will be bumpy."

"I know."

"Tighten your core. Do not let him throw you forward. Move with the horse. He is your wind."

She nodded again. Tonk breathed a word. The pinto slowed to an easy jog, then to a careful halt. Vura stumbled forward and held up her hands. Lily slid into her arms.

"I was ridin'." She breathed the words like a prayer.

"I know you were," Vura said, raising her gaze to Tonk's. "And you did great."

"Tonka says the trot's rough as a corncob but I can sit it. And the lope . . ." Her expression was awestruck, a sober happiness that transcended smiles. "It's like flying without wings."

"You were amazing, honey, but how about you run up to the house now?"

"But I wanna ride more."

"Not right now."

"I wanna."

"Some other time."

"No! Not some other time. Now! I gotta ride now."

"*Sihu.*" Tonk's tone brooked no argument. Vura glanced toward him, surprised by the sternness. His back, she noticed, was as straight as a reed, his expression, no-nonsense. "What did we learn about Native children?"

Lily scowled for a moment, then ducked her head. "They respect their elders."

"And?"

Her mouth twisted sourly. "They apologize when they're wrong."

He raised one brow.

"I'm sorry, Mama," she said, and turned with a huff to make certain they understood her displeasure, then slumped off toward the house.

The barnyard went silent. Arrow dropped his head to graze.

"I understand why you're angry," Tonk began, soothing preemptively. "It seems too fast to you. Too dangerous, but Lily is not like other children, Bravura. You know this in your heart. Lily is—" He shook his head, searching.

Vura waited.

Seconds ticked away.

"Exhausting?" she guessed.

He scowled as if grossly offended, then let his shoulders slump and sighed.

"I have no idea how you do it every day."

She managed to keep a straight face.

"Even my ears are tired."

She did laugh now. "Tell me about the wraps," she said.

"Wraps?"

"Yeah." She motioned toward her legs. Lily's shins and calves had been entirely bound, knees to feet, in four-inch-wide cotton.

"Ahh . . ." He nodded. "Track bandages. They are used to protect the legs of working horses."

She nodded, waiting. He didn't continue.

"But she's not a horse," she reminded him finally. "Working or otherwise."

He nodded, apparently aware. "She wished to learn the proper way to wrap a cannon bone."

"That's why you swathed her up like a mummy."

"Ai," he agreed and nodded slowly. "That . . . and the fact that she was injured."

"Injured!" A thousand garbled worries, momentarily stemmed, rushed in.

"All body parts are still attached," he hurried to add. "She said that was what's important." For a guy who'd ridden a relay race while passing a kidney stone, he sounded oddly panicked, and somehow that soothed her.

"What happened?"

"A scratch. Half an inch, maybe. I cleaned it and called the clinic to make sure she'd had a tetanus shot."

A scratch. She breathed a mental sigh of relief and shuffled toward Arrow. Despite her uncertainty around the behemoth beasts, they drew her, too. "So you wrapped her entire lower legs?"

He shrugged, watching her carefully, like a prairie dog might eye a rattler. "I am fond of my skin."

She raised a brow.

"Which I thought might be flayed from my body if she was injured again."

She laughed a little. "Am I that bad?"

A flash of humor sparked in his river-agate eyes. "Perhaps you are that good."

She knew his words shouldn't make her feel weepy. And it wasn't as if she was going to cry, going to bawl like a baby. But she turned away . . . just in case.

Silence again, long and deep, before he spoke.

"I will leave you to tend your young one."

"Yeah." She cleared her throat. "Okay."

"And I thank you for this day, Bravura. She is . . ." He breathed a thoughtful sigh. "All things good."

She heard him turn away, heard the gelding follow in his footsteps, and pivoted, breath held.

"Tonk?"

He glanced over his shoulder, just a glimpse of his proud profile juxtaposed against the narrow braid nestled in his loose midnight hair.

"Are you busy tomorrow?"

There was a pause, long and thoughtful. "Ai."

"Oh . . ." She nodded, understanding. "Okay."

"But I would appreciate the help of a small flower, if she is not otherwise engaged."

Vura nodded. "Yeah, I think . . ." Her eyes stung. Why would this man see the wonder in Lily? Why? When others who should, did not? "I think I can clear her calendar."

Their gazes met, sparked, held, and for a moment she thought he would return to her. Would touch her and make the world right. But he only nodded once and turned away.

Chapter 33

The front door was nearly silent when Dane pulled it open. But Vura heard it. His footsteps were ghostly quiet against the carpet as he stepped into the darkened living room. But she heard those, too.

And her hand was almost steady as she pulled the lamp's chain.

"Vey!" He jerked as if he'd been shot.

She smiled, amused, despite a thousand nagging worries. It was four o'clock in the morning. She hadn't slept for twenty-two hours and she was about to do the hardest thing she'd ever done in her life.

"Hi."

"Holy—!" He laughed at his jittering nerves. "You scared the living crap out of me."

Living crap . . . that . . . actually . . . might be what he was . . . and yet she felt oddly civil. Strangely content.

"Where have you been?"

He scowled. "Working. I told you this morning I got a job with Neut."

She felt old suddenly. Letting her grandfather's afghan pool onto the couch, she rose to her feet. "You used to try harder, Dane."

He turned as she moved past him, his scowl still

in place. "What are you talking about? It's . . ." He glanced at the clock on the wall. "I just put in a long, hard day."

She stepped into the kitchen, turned on the light, illuminating a thousand ugly chickens. "You used to be able to make your lies believable. You used to do that much."

"You're calling me a liar? Is that what you're doing? I'm working my tail off and you—"

"Mitsouko, isn't it?"

He shook his head. "Geez, Vey, you're not even making sense."

"Just because I don't douse myself in perfume, doesn't mean I can't recognize a fragrance."

Something skittered through his eyes. Fear, maybe. But in a second it was gone. "Well, I wasn't at the work site this whole time. We had a couple of beers after."

She dumped her coffee in the sink, wondered if she'd ever learn to make a decent cup, and turned. "We?"

"The boys and I."

"Which of them prefers a peachy scent?"

He stared at her a second, then laughed. "Tracy was there, too. She musta been wearing something."

"Tracy?"

"Teresa Coldwell. Andy's kid. She's doing some finishing work. Not too bad at it."

She made no comment, just watched him.

How, she wondered, had she been so blind for so long?

"You remember her," he said. "She used to hang around the construction sites with her old man." He grinned, took a step toward her. "Kinda like you, but not so pretty."

"I called Neut."

"What?" His brows dipped.

"I called Neut Irving." She took an apple from a bowl on the counter, a knife from its wooden block. "He said he hasn't seen you in months."

"Well . . ." Anger jumped in his eyes, but he calmed it. "I wasn't working directly under him. It was just one of his crews. He's got about a hundred of them. I'd almost forgotten how backbreaking that—"

"Your girlfriend called today." She cut out a slice of apple.

"Vey . . ." He breathed a laugh. "You're going nuts. I don't—"

"Minnie Mouse voice? Not too bright?" Removing the core, she took a bite. Pink Lady apples were her favorite, but Galas were good too. And Granny Smiths, if they weren't too tart.

"What the devil—"

"I tried to call her back, but she didn't pick up, so maybe she's not entirely brain-dead." She rested her hips against the sink, incised another slice.

He didn't bother to hide the anger now, but he infused it with a strong dose of indignation; he was a master.

"So you were checking up on me? Is that what you were doing? Tracking me like a dog while I'm out there busting my hump trying to make a living for—"

"I saw you had time to come back for your phone while I was gone."

His left eye twitched. "I was hoping to get a call from Emerson. Thought you'd be happy if I got a job with them, but I guess there's no way I'm ever going to be good enough for you."

She stared at him a second, and then she laughed. She couldn't help it, but in a moment she was back in control. "Tell me the truth, Dane. Was it *just* the thought of my inheritance that brought you back? Or was it something else?"

"I don't know what you're talking about. I didn't know the old man was going to kick it."

"Even though I told you he was ill?"

He shrugged. "I guess I forgot."

She could almost believe that. He had forgotten so much, including the fact that she wasn't an idiot. But maybe that was her fault. "Were you fired?" she asked. "Is that why you came back?"

His lips moved. That's how she knew he was about to lie, but she was too tired to listen, to pretend she might care.

"I need you out of my house."

"*Your* house?"

"Yes."

"Just because I had a couple of beers after work?"

A dozen rancid lies and a hundred broken promises raced through her memory, but it wasn't worth the effort. "Yes," she said. "Just because of those beers."

He snorted and sidled toward her. "Okay, listen, baby, yeah, you're right. Penn Oil let me go. But I was planning to come home anyway."

He was exhausting, an emotional marathon. But he didn't give up the lies. You had to admire that. "Was Sherri fired, too?"

He stopped dead in his tracks. "Who?"

"The blond woman . . . you remember her," she said, and took another slice of apple. "Met her at the rodeo. Big hair. Big boobs. Wasn't her name Sherri?"

"Oh, *Sherri*." He nodded, eyes shifting restlessly for a moment as if trying to remember how they could have met. "She's a friend. I am still allowed to have friends, aren't I?"

She smiled. Even her face felt tired. "You can do anything you want, Dane," she said and, setting the apple aside, tightened her grip on the knife. "If you leave right now, we'll let bygones be bygones."

His jaw dropped. Years later, if she chose to remember his expression, she might find it amusing . . . if she'd had a few drinks . . . and a really good day. "Are you threatening me?"

"I was hoping you'd understand."

"Geez, you're getting butch. Think you can take me in a tussle now, do you, Vey?"

"I'm willing to give it a try." She held his gaze, steady as a laser. "How 'bout you?"

He stared, broke eye contact, caught her gaze again. "Geez." He huffed a laugh, half-turned away. "Vey, are you listening to yourself?"

"I am," she said. "I'm listening to both of us. Finally."

He jittered, then stopped the restless movement suddenly. "It's your old man, isn't it?"

She raised her brows, interested.

"He put you up to it. Told you I didn't deserve no loan, so you—"

"He said yes."

He shook his head, bewildered.

"To the loan," she explained. "He left a voice mail on my cell. Said he'd give you the money."

"For real?" He grinned. "Well, let's celebrate, Vey. We'll—"

"I'm the one saying no."

His body stilled again. "You're kidding."

She tilted the knife a little. "I'm not."

He ran his fingers through his hair. Was his hand shaking? "What are you trying to do to me?"

"Set you free. I'm trying to set you free, Dane. Like you always wanted to be."

He shook his head. His eyes were wild. "That's crazy. I married you, didn't I? For better or worse. For richer or poorer. I thought we'd be together forever. I thought—"

"You could have it all," she said, and nodded. "You thought you could have a wife waiting at home and a big-boobed bimbo on the side."

"If you're talking about Sherri, we're just friends."

She gritted her teeth, but resentment took too much energy. "I'm sorry. I shouldn't have called her that. She's probably a very intelligent person."

"Sherri?"

She couldn't help but laugh. "I need you to leave now, Dane."

He shook his head, stepped toward her. "Listen . . . baby . . ." he pleaded, but she shook her head.

"I'm done, Dane. Done listening, done hoping." She shrugged. "Done."

"It's because of that Indian, isn't it?"

She prepared to deny it, but maybe he was right. Maybe in some convoluted way, Tonk did have something to do with her decision. Maybe seeing him with Lily had made her turn a corner of sorts.

"You're screwing him, aren't you?"

"No," she said. "I'm not. But I'm not screwing you, either. Ever again."

"We'll see about that," he snarled and took a step toward her, but she raised the knife.

"Don't do it, Dane."

He stopped, thinking.

"I'll use it if I have to."

"You're bluffing."

"You know me better than that," she said, and because he did, he raised his hands in a parody of surrender and disappeared.

Chapter 34

"Nice job," Quinton said, and ran his fingers over the unvarnished wood that framed her kitchen's new doorway.

Six days had passed. Six days, during which she had needed, quite desperately, to keep busy. Six days, which Lily had spent in Tonkiaishawien's doting care.

"The walls in this place are as crooked as a barrel of fishhooks," she complained.

"Why do you think I didn't offer to help?"

"And here I thought you were faking the flu so you could spend more time with Miss Tuesday."

He raised a quizzical brow.

She raised her mug. "Or whoever's hunting you these days."

He snorted. "Is that coffee as bad as usual?"

"I think it's actually worse," she said, and sighed.

Shaking his head, he dumped the horrible brew down the drain and prepared to start a fresh pot.

Vura relaxed against the counter and watched him. There was a comfort to his movements, a warm easiness to having him around.

"I asked Dane to leave."

The pot clattered into the sink. His gaze struck hers.

She laughed at his expression, shrugged, and strangely, felt tears fill her eyes.

"What? When?"

"Too late, I think. Almost a week ago."

"And you didn't tell me till now?"

"You were sick. I was . . . embarrassed."

"Embarrassed!" He faced her, leaving the coffeepot forgotten in the sink. "About what?"

"About . . ." She shrugged again, feeling old and young and foolish and wise all at once. "Messing up."

"What are you talking about? You've never messed up in your—"

"I made so many mistakes."

"Listen to me!" His expression was fierce, his voice low so as not to wake the child he was pretty sure could walk on water. "Lily's the best thing that ever happened to us. To anyone. Ever!"

She smiled. "I didn't mean Lily. I meant"—she shook her head—"you were right. Gamps was right. I shouldn't have married him."

Worry troubled his brow. "You didn't kick him out because of me, did you?"

"What?"

"It wasn't my disapproval that made you get rid of him, was it? I mean . . ." His expression was tortured. "He's not good enough for you. Never was. Never is going to be. But maybe—"

She laughed, oddly relieved. "So you like him, Dad? You really like him?"

"I'm sorry," he said, and gritted his teeth. "Listen, if you want him back, I can learn to like the little—" He cut off his words. "I can learn to love him if you do."

She was tempted to laugh again, but he looked so tormented, she couldn't allow it.

"It's not your fault. In fact, it's anybody's fault but yours."

"What, then?"

"He didn't want to be here."

"That can't be true. He's not brain-dead. Is he?"

Good God, she loved him. "I'm not completely sure. But I know he wasn't ready for this. For us."

"Then he's an even bigger moron than I—" he began and stopped himself. "Sorry. I mean . . . I'm sure you're wrong."

She gave him a smile for the effort. "You know I'm not."

He looked as if he wanted to argue, but exhaled instead, then turned away and ran frustrated fingers through steel-dust hair. "I thought once he was back, once he got a chance to spend time with you and Lily, he'd realize . . ."

"How amazing she is?"

"Yeah."

"I'm afraid all he learned was to tell more lies."

"What?"

In for a penny, in for a pound. "He was seeing someone else."

He winced. "Are you sure?"

"I think I've always been sure."

For a moment she thought he would finally curse, would find those choice words he had eschewed since Lily's birth, but he just shook his head. "I'm sorry."

She nodded. "You going to finish making that coffee or what?"

He shook his head. "Twenty-four years old and can't even make a decent cup of java." He turned back to the sink. "How's Lily taking it?"

"I'm not sure she noticed."

He glanced over his shoulder at her.

She shrugged. "Maybe it's my fault."

"That your husband's an . . . asterisk?"

She chuckled, but guilt had made an appearance. "Maybe I didn't give him a chance."

"And maybe you gave him a hundred chances and he mucked up every one of them."

"Well, I know he didn't have much of a chance with Lily. Not when Tonk has those horses."

"Tonk." His tone was a little shy, a little hope-ful, a little adoring.

"What about him?"

"He just . . ." He wobbled his head a little. "He seems like an okay guy."

"You have a crush on him or something?"

"Don't you?" he asked, and gave her a sly glance over his left shoulder.

The blush started at the roots of her hair. She ignored it as best she could. "I'm a married woman."

"And Dane's a married man. Didn't slow the dumb bast—" He stopped himself again, seemed to find his balance. "So Tonk and Lil have been spending time together?"

"He loves teaching her stuff."

"Like what?"

"Everything. About horses, art, old languages, cumulus clouds, bison, poetry, cooking—"

"Cooking?"

"Don't look so hopeful. So far all their meals have been over a campfire."

"Seriously?"

"It's the weirdest thing. He wears her out."

"I didn't even know that was possible."

"Right?"

"Is that why she's still sleeping?"

"It's like she's been running marathons."

He pushed the button on the coffeemaker. "Do you mind if I wake her up?"

She glanced at the clock on the wall. Both the chicken's wings were on the eight. "Oh man . . ."

She set her mug aside. "It's later than I thought."

"I'll say. You planning to tear down this wallpaper, or are you just gonna get a couple dozen cats and lean in to the crazy?"

"I'm considering the cats," she said.

He grinned and turned for the stairs, but he was back in a minute. "I guess she's not as tired as we thought. Looks like she snuck out again."

"What? That little stinker. She must be with the horses."

They hurried out together. Inside the tilting barn, Tonk turned toward her. His eyes sparked. Her cheeks warmed. Feeling her father's interest flare like a Roman candle, she struggled for something to do with her hands.

"Good morning, Bravura," Tonk said, and turned toward Quinton with old world deference. "Mr. Murrell."

She cleared her throat. It was impossible to say why she felt like a gawky tweenager. "Hey."

Her father looked on, silver brows yanked toward his hairline.

She gave him a scowl.

"Well . . . I guess I'll go . . . check on the birds," he said, and hurried out.

The barn went silent.

Inside Arrow's stall, something clattered.

Vura rolled her eyes. If Lily could bed down with the big gelding, she surely would. "I'm sorry."

"Far too often," Tonk agreed.

She laughed, awkward as a pig on stilts, and hurried toward the pinto's stall. "You were probably hoping for some time alone with your horses.

"Lily, you know you're not supposed to leave the house without telling . . ." Opening Arrow's stall, she gazed around the interior, but no caramel-headed imp popped up beside the gelding.

"Did you lose her again?" Tonk asked.

Vura turned, exasperated. "Where is she?"

He frowned. "I have not seen her this morning."

"Are you sure?"

"It is difficult to miss a tornado."

A trickle of fear edged along her spine, but she fought it back. "Dad's probably right. She must be with the birds. If it wasn't for the horses, the goslings would be all-consuming."

"She likes to read to them."

"My daughter," Vura said and, shaking her head, headed outside, but her phone rang before she'd taken five steps. Pulling it from her pocket, she scowled at the unknown number and answered distractedly. "Hello?"

"Vura . . ."

She stiffened at the cheery sound of Dane's voice. "This isn't a good time," she said, and continued toward the coop.

"Don't tell me. Lily's missing."

Her steps slowed. "How did you know that?"

"Oh . . ." He laughed. The sound was chilling, high-pitched and frightening. "Maybe I'm smarter than you give me credit for, Vey."

Chapter 35

Tonk watched her from a few feet away. He could hear the conversation clearly. Too clearly. His hands felt cold, his knees week.

"Dane?"

"Yeah, baby?"

She shifted her wild-eyed gaze to Tonk's. The fear reflected there sliced his heart like an arrow. "You haven't . . . you don't know where Lily is, do you?"

He laughed, paused. A slurping sound echoed through the phone. "Now, how would I know that, Vey? You kicked me out, remember?"

Her face was pale beneath the random spray of freckles. "What's going on?"

"That's up to you, baby."

Anger flared in her eyes. "I don't have time for this," she said. "You'll have to call back later."

"Later might be too late." His voice had changed. The jocularity was gone, replaced by hard-edged cruelty.

"What are you saying?" Her knuckles were bone-white as she gripped the phone.

"I think she has my ears."

"Dane . . ." She whispered his name. "What have you done?"

"Don't use that tone on me, Vey." There was a whine to his voice now, a scratchy snivel beneath the raspy drunkenness. "I didn't have a choice."

She stumbled a little, caught herself on the stall behind her. "Where's Lily?"

Quinton hurried back into the barn, caught Vura's frantic expression. "What's going on?"

Vura cut her eyes to his. "It's Dane."

"What?" Quinton asked, but she didn't answer, could barely hold the phone. He took it from her, pressed it to his ear.

"Dane," he growled.

"Quinton!" They could hear him clearly, loud and oddly boisterous again. "So you've got time to talk to me now?"

"Lily's gone."

"No," he said, and chuckled. "She's not."

Quinton tightened his fist on the phone. "What have you done?"

"You forced my hand, Quinny."

"If you hurt her . . ." The words were growled. "If you do anything stupid—"

"Stupid? That's what you think, isn't it? You think I'm stupid. Not good enough for them. Never good enough for your little—"

"Where is he?" Tonk mouthed the words.

"Dane . . ." Quinton's voice was steady now,

low and even and carefully controlled. "Where are you?"

"What? Now you want to hang out? Want to be buds?" He laughed again. "Funny. That's funny . . ." His voice drifted off.

"Dane!" Quinton's voice was sharp. "Just tell me where she is. That's all I want."

"Thinks she'll get rid of me now." He breathed a chuckle. "Keep the money to herself."

"What money?"

There was no response.

"Dane!"

"Well, that's not gonna happen, Quinny. Cuz I'm way ahead of you. You think I didn't know the old man was going to bite it? You and your butch daughter were the only ones who were that stupid. Thought he was Superman or something. Immortal. The crotchety old bastard. Treated me like I was some kind of disease. Some kind of insect not good enough to—"

"Tell me what you've done."

He paused. "Nothing that can't be undone. Not yet anyway. But . . ." Liquid courage glugged noisily. "That won't last forever."

"If you hurt her . . ." His voice quivered. "I'll tear your heart from your chest. I'll make you wish—"

"You wanna keep sputtering threats, or you wanna cut to the chase, old man?"

"Just tell me what you want."

355

"A half a mil."

Vura's knees buckled. Tonk wrapped an arm around her, pulled her up against his side.

"What?" Her father's voice was barely a breath of surprise.

"Do you need me to speak more clearly, Quinton? I said I want five hundred thousand dollars."

"You're out of your mind."

"You think I don't know what your dear old dad was worth?"

"How would you when I don't?"

"He was richer than God."

"Dane, listen, he didn't have that kind of money. And even if he did, I wouldn't have access to—"

"Let me speak to him," Tonk said.

There was a moment's hesitation before Quinton handed over the phone.

"Mr. Lambert . . ." Tonk kept himself very still, extremely controlled. Anger had rarely been his friend. "This is Tonkiaishawien Redhawk."

"Tonka Toy!" Lambert laughed again. The sound was disjointed, disturbingly familiar in its inebriated weightlessness. Tonk had laughed just like that a hundred times in the past. "I should have known you'd be there. Sniffin' around. Always sniffin' around. But she's still my wife. Just like the kid's still mine. Till I decide different."

"You outsmarted us all," Tonk admitted.

Vura put a hand to her throat. It was as pale as milky quartz, entirely drained of color.

"That's right. And it's time to pay the piper."

A tear slipped in silent agony down Bravura's cheek.

"They'll pay," Tonk said. "But it might take some time to get that much money together."

"Then they're going to wish they'd moved faster, cuz, listen, I like kids as much as the next guy but . . ." He chuckled. "Well, not as much as you. Geez, I'd think you'd have something better to do than to play cookout with a five-year-old all day."

So he had seen them. Had been watching them.

"Didn't realize I was keeping such a close eye on you, did you?"

"I did not."

"That's cuz you're a patsy . . . and a pansy." He snorted at his own cleverness. "No offense intended."

"None taken."

"Me, I like my girls a little older. Past puberty anyhow," he said, and laughed. There was the sound of a match swiping against a striking surface, a puff of breath.

Tonk tightened his grip on the phone, felt his hand shake, but kept his voice steady. "We'll get the money together."

"Listen, I'm not a bad guy. I don't care where the cash comes from."

"That's good of you. Where do we deliver the money?"

"Now we're talking," Lambert said, and paused to exhale. Tonk imagined him blowing smoke toward the ceiling. But what ceiling? Where? "And listen, if you get the cops involved, I'm gonna be pissed."

"No cops," he agreed.

Vura whimpered.

"No cops," Tonk said again, "but that's a lot of cash."

"Enough. Enough to pay off those loans and have a little pin money left over."

Tonk's stomach twisted. "That inside straight can be murder," he said, guessing wildly. Casinos, the Dakotas' own little version of hell.

"Gambling?" Vura's voice was almost inaudible. "He took my baby to pay off his poker debt?"

There was a momentary hesitation, then a snort. "Flush," Lambert said. "The bastard had a flush."

Retribution quivered in Tonk's fingertips, but he forced himself to relax, to breathe. "Gotta do something to fill the nights in Williston, I suppose."

"Fracking camps . . . it's like legalized slavery."

"I heard it's bad up there," Tonk said, and let his mind spin in a hundred wild directions.

"You got no idea."

"You deserve a little room service after that."

"Soon as I ditch the kid and get to civilization."

The words were slurred. "Get out of this . . ." His voice dwindled.

"Dane!" Tonk snapped and closed his eyes, fighting for control. "I need to know where to deliver the money."

He chuckled. "I'm not stupid, Tonka. Not going to tell you where till you got the cash in hand. No time to decide you're clever and set up a trap that way."

"You're calling the shots."

A chuckle drifted over the phone. More smoke was blown. "You said it."

"Get her on the phone," Vura begged and curled her fingers, tight as talons, into Tonk's sleeve. "Please. Just for a second."

"We need to talk to her," Tonk said.

"You need to do what I tell you to do!" The words were roared.

"Ai. You're in charge," Tonk soothed. "But a couple seconds of conversation isn't too much to ask, is it? To get the sharks off your back?"

Lambert chuckled, companionable as a puppy, unpredictable as an eel. "You got a point there, buddy. Hang on, I'll see if she's conscious."

"What does that mean?" Vura's voice was no more than a tortured croak. "What does he mean?"

Tonk could only shake his head. Terror, cold as icicles, sliced his heart.

"Lily . . . your boyfriend wants to talk to you." Dane's voice was slurred and distant, but in a moment she was on the phone, voice little more than a whisper.

"Tonka?"

Tonk squeezed his eyes shut, tightened his fingers on the phone and remembered to breathe. "*Chitto Sihu.*"

"Tonka." Her voice was stronger now. "I wanna come home. I wanna come home. I wanna—"

He opened his eyes with a snap. "You are the brave one." A dozen reassurances roared through his mind. Something . . . anything . . . to comfort, to console. But there was no time.

She paused, sucked in her breath.

"Nothing bests *Chitto Sihu*," he whispered.

"But—"

"*Run.*" He said the word in Old Cahdoan. "We will come for you."

"I'm—"

"Time's up!" Lambert snapped. "Don't mess this up, Tonka Toy."

"We will do as you ask. Just don't—" he began but the phone went dead.

"What did you say to her?" Vura's fingers tightened again, frantic against his wrist. "What did you tell her?"

Her eyes scoured his. Terror made it all but impossible to meet her gaze. What if he was wrong? Again. What if he caused another catastrophe? "To run."

"Run?" She shook her head. "Where?"

"How'll she get away?" Quinton asked.

"He's drinking. Tired. He'll pass out soon," he said, and prayed he was right.

"You think she can get away? Without him knowing? Without him hurting—"

"How many times did she leave the house without you knowing? How many times did we find her with Courage even though we tried to lock her out?"

"But even if she escaped, how'll we find her?"

"And what if she can't? We don't have that kind of money." She lifted her broken-doll gaze to her father. "Do we?"

"I haven't even seen the will, but maybe if we sold his land. My company . . ." He shook his head.

Tonk pulled his phone from his pocket, pushed a button, and prayed harder.

"Tonkiaishawien," Hunter rumbled. "I was just about to—"

"Lily's been taken."

"What?" Hunter's voice, already a growl, had sunk to the depths of hell. "Taken where? By who?"

"Dane Lambert."

"Her father?"

Vura moaned.

Tonk lowered the phone, captured her gaze. "You need to be strong, Bravura. You need to be. For Lily."

She straightened a little, nodded, but her face was still deathly pale. Fresh anger ripped through him, threatening to shred his control. She was a fighter, a doer, a woman who tried, who achieved, who accomplished, despite the obstacles. Sitting and waiting would destroy her.

"Gather food. Bottled water."

"Water? What . . ."

"They're somewhere in the Hills. Not in civilization," he said. "We will find them, but we may need supplies."

She drew her hand from his sleeve. The first spark of defiance fired in her eyes, displacing a sliver of fear.

"Bring her clothes. Something she's worn recently."

"To track her?" Quinton asked. "Do you have a hound?"

"Perhaps," he said, and knew Mutt was just that. No more likely to sniff out a trail than he was. But action was essential, hope as necessary as air. And he needed time, to be alone, to think, to lean on someone stronger. "Go now," he said. "I'll join you in a minute."

They hurried away, supporting each other.

He lifted the phone back to his ear. "Hunt," he said, letting the broken child in him speak.

"We'll find her, Tonk. We will."

"The bastard took her. He took her." His voice quavered. "Just like Ruby. Just like—"

"No. Not like Ruby. Tonk! It's entirely different. You know that. That wasn't your fault. Neither is this." His voice rumbled in the phone. "And we will get her back."

Tonk nodded, tried to believe.

"What does he want?"

"Five hundred thousand."

"Where do I deliver it?"

Tonk drew a deep breath. Doubts plagued him like locusts, but he swiped them aside, gathering strength from the brother who stood beside him when he couldn't stand alone. "He would not say."

"I'll have it ready."

"There is no guarantee he'll return her even if he gets the cash."

"What are the choices, brother?" Hunt rumbled.

"We could kill him."

"Tonk . . ."

"He took her." His voice broke. He glanced toward the house from which the child of his heart had been abducted.

"Then we'll take her back."

He straightened, feeling stronger. "Ai. We will—" he began, but the rumble of an engine interrupted his words. He snapped his attention to the yard, where Vura was already slamming the door of her pickup, already fishtailing on the loose gravel.

He rasped a curse.

"Go," Hunter said. "I'll do what I can."

Chapter 36

Vura's heart battered like a jackhammer against her ribs, but she couldn't fail, couldn't falter. Not now. "Good morning," she said, and found that against all odds, her voice still worked, her lungs still functioned.

The girl behind the front desk sported a fake copper name plaque that said Ashley and a slightly more genuine smile. "Welcome to the Drop On Inn. How can we make this your best day ever?"

Vura forced a smile. Her cheeks ached with the effort. She clenched her teeth. Beneath the counter, her fingers tightened and released. "I'm here to see Sherri."

"Who?" The girl's smile didn't slip an iota.

Vura laughed and raised her left hand to fiddle with the business cards confined to a clear plastic holder. The muscles across her back and shoulders were stretched as tight as a snap line. "I'm sorry. Sher's such a character. I guess I thought everyone would know her. I called her cell before I came here, but she didn't answer and we've got an appointment."

"An appointment?"

"For a . . . a mani-pedi."

"At Twila's?"

She managed a nod, though she didn't know how.

"Ohhh, I love that place. Have you ever tried their watermelon facials? They're to die for."

"That's what I've heard," Vura said, and braced her knees lest they buckle like folding sawhorses. "But listen, we're supposed to be there in"—she glanced at the clock behind the desk but couldn't decipher the numbers—"ten minutes."

"You're gonna have to hustle."

"Don't I know it." Her hands were shaking. She shoved her left behind the counter to assist her right. "If that girl doesn't change her ways, she's gonna be late for her own funeral."

Ashley laughed. "Mom says the same thing about me."

"Listen . . ." It was hard to breathe, almost impossible to speak. "I'm sure you've got tons of stuff to do, so if you'll just tell me what room she's in, I'll hike on up and shake her out of bed."

"Ohhhh . . ." Ashley's chipper expression crumpled. "I'm sorry. That's against our policy."

"I know." Vura smiled, lips pulling away from her teeth like a snarl. "But she's going to be so disappointed if we miss—"

"Wait," Ashley said, eyes lighting up as she lifted her gaze toward the hallway. "There she is now."

Vura's breath caught in her throat. She turned.

And there she was, just exiting the exercise

room. Dressed in latex and running shoes, she carried a half-empty water bottle and tittered at her balding companion's latest witticism.

He chuckled, adoration in his eyes.

Bravura steadied her hands, calmed her heart, and approached them. Footsteps rustled eerily against the carpet. It was impossible to know if they were hers.

"Where is he?" Her voice sounded hollow.

Sherri turned, painted brows arched high, smile fading slowly. Beside her, Male Pattern Baldness wiped his face with a hotel towel and glanced from one to the other.

"Excuse me?" Sherri's voice was as Minnie Mouse high as Vura remembered.

"Dane." The name sounded guttural, torn from Vura's throat like cockleburs from wool. "Where is he?"

"I'm sorry." She took a step back, face darkening, boobs jiggling. "I don't think I know you."

"Tell me," Vura's voice was rising. Anger roared through her, surfing on a wave of terror, skidding on a raft of frustration.

"I don't know what you're talking about," Sherri said, and bumped against the wingback chair behind her.

"I'm talking about my husband." Vura tightened her fingers, clenched her teeth. "The man you're screwing. The—"

"You're crazy." Sherri glanced to the side,

giving a tentative smile to her balding hero. "I don't know what she's talking about, Robby."

"I'm talking about Dane Lambert," Vura said, and leaned closer.

Cornered, Sherri lowered her voice and her painted brows. "Listen, lady, it's not my fault if you can't hold on to your man," she said, and turned away.

But Vura caught her by the arm, swung her back.

"Hey!" Robby complained, but Vura failed to notice. Instead, she leaned in to the other woman's face, teeth gritted, blood roaring.

"You can have him if you want him. But you'll tell me where he is," she growled and raised her right hand. The nail gun felt solid and ready against her palm, as comforting as a plush toy. "And you'll tell me now."

"Whoa!" Robby breathed and took one foolish step toward them. Releasing Sherri's arm, Vura pivoted toward him, Walt chest-high. "He took my daughter."

His eyes widened, big as saucers. "Wh . . . what?"

"He took Lily." The words were a snarl from between clenched teeth. "I'm taking her back."

"Oh . . ." He nodded, held up his hands, palms out, placating. "Okay. But listen . . ." His wide eyes skittered to the left. "I think she's getting away."

It took a moment to recognize his words, longer to assimilate their meaning. By then, Sherri was already ripping open the door, already lurching outside.

Adrenaline pulsed like venom through Vura's veins. She spun without thinking, leapt without intending to. Blond hair snagged between her fingers. She ripped. Sherri shrieked, tumbled backward. She tried to scramble away, but Vura was already atop her, one palm pressed to her chest, the other steady as the sun against the cool grip of the nail gun.

Sherri watched it with popping eyes.

"Tell me where he is." Bravura's voice was hard, low, a little raspy.

Sherri's was none of those things. "Help!" The word emerged as a strangled squeak from her glossy lips. "Help me. She's crazy!"

Ashley, still trapped behind the front desk like a hapless bunny, squeaked something in return.

"Tell me!" Vura snarled and pressed the gun to Sherri's neck.

"Bravura." Tonkiaishawien's voice barely registered in her brain. She neither knew nor cared when he had arrived. "Bravura, let us talk about this."

"Tonky!" Sherri rasped. Fat tears had squeezed from between her quick-blinking lids. "Help me."

Vura ignored her plea, ignored everything but the woman sprawled beneath her. "Where did he take her?"

"I don't know . . ." She was crying in earnest now, plump tears that left her makeup magically unsmudged. "I don't know what you're talking about."

"You're lying," Vura snarled and tightened her finger on the trigger.

"I'm not!" She was breathing hard, chest heaving. "I just came along for kicks. He said his old lady . . ." She licked her lips, careful now, as if she'd nearly stepped into a trap from which she would never extricate herself. "He said he was in for a big inheritance. It was only supposed to take a couple of days, then we'd hit the road for Vegas or something."

Vura eased back half an inch, remembering to breathe. "He kidnapped my daughter."

"I didn't . . ." She tried to shake her head, but there was no room between the soft flesh of her jaw and Walt's unrelenting steel. "I didn't know that. I swear."

"What *do* you know?" Vura asked, and adjusted the angle of the tool a little.

"Bravura, do not do this," Tonk warned.

"What do you know?" she asked again.

"He called me last night. Said we was going to be rich, richer than God. But I just thought he had some hot tip. He likes to play the ponies at—"

"You were supposed to pick up the money, weren't you?"

"What? No! I just—"

"Weren't you?" she rasped, and shifting the muzzle a scant millimeter, slammed a nail into the industrial-strength carpet.

Sherri screamed. "Okay. Yeah! But I didn't know he was going to kidnap no kid!"

"Where is he?"

"I don't know." She shrieked the words. "I swear. He didn't tell me."

"Then you're no use to me," Vura said, and tipped the gun back toward Sherri's ear.

"Hotshot's cabin!" The words spurted from her lips.

"What?"

"He's got a friend." She was sweating now, sweating and crying and stuttering. "A . . . a smarmy tagalong creep. Always trying to cop a feel. Trying to get me to go with him to his 'hideaway.' But I ain't that hard up. Even spending half my nights alone in this crappy motel without room service or—"

"I swear I'll nail your mouth shut if you keep babbling," Vura said.

Sherri pursed her lips, fell silent, nodded carefully. "I think he's there," she whispered.

"At his hideaway."

She gave a cautious nod.

"Where is it?"

"I don't know."

"Think hard," Vura suggested.

"I told you, I'm not into those creepy—"

Shifting the tool, Vura slammed a nail alongside Sherri's throat. It scraped away a peel of skin and bled profusely.

Her shriek was almost all air this time, a breathy rasp followed by almost inarticulate babbling. "Beaver Road. He said something about Beaver Road. We thought it was . . ." She was gasping for breath, fingers spread like spiders' legs against the floor beneath them. "Dane and me . . . we laughed about how livin' there was the only way he was ever gonna get any."

Vura shook her head, but Tonk stepped up from behind. "Beaver Road? Up by Crazy Horse Pass?"

"Tonky!" She jerked her gaze to his. Blood, red as rubies, was smeared in her bleached hair. "For Christ's sake! For Christ's sake, get her off me."

"Is that where it is?" he asked. "Up by the pass?"

"How would I know? Do I look like someone who'd rough it in some nasty shack somewhere?"

"I am not sure," he admitted and tilted his head toward her tormenter, "but Bravura is angry, and she has many nails left."

"He said nobody'd get hurt."

"Tell us what you know so no one will," he suggested, voice soft, almost soothing in the pulsing tension.

371

"I'm bleeding," she whined, and lifted a shaking hand halfway to her neck.

"But you are not yet dead," he reminded her.

She swallowed, nodded, perhaps understanding the stakes for the first time. "He said he had a good hiding place. Somewhere nobody'd find. Said he'd have to hike in. Rough it for a few days, but after that we'd be rich. I just wanna . . . I just wanna be rich," she said, and started to sob. "I just wanna—"

"Could be one of those hunting cabins up by White Deer Ridge."

Vura turned woodenly toward Sherri's erstwhile admirer, Robby. "What?"

He blinked owlishly, shifted his gaze from her to Tonk. "Up on White Deer Ridge past Crazy Horse Pass, there are half a dozen cabins strung out over ten thousand acres of government land."

"Does one of them belong to a man called Hotshot?"

"Yeah, I think . . ." He shook his head, already backpedaling. "Maybe."

"Would you know it if you saw it?"

"Listen . . ." He sidled sideways. "I got kids, too, but I don't want to get messed up in this." They were his final words before he sprang away, fumbled for the door, and lurched outside.

"Is it?" Vura asked, and turned her attention back to the woman beneath her.

"Wh . . . What?"

"Is one of those cabins Hotshot's?"

"I don't know."

She shot another nail into the floorboards, almost casually now. Terror had receded, leaving nothing but rage in its chilly wake.

Sherri screamed. "I swear to God I don't know. I swear it. I swear. I . . ."

Tonk curled a hand around Vura's arm. "Let us go."

"Answer me!" Vura ordered, but Tonk tightened his grip.

"She waits." His voice was little more than a murmur, barely audible.

Bravura turned toward him, breath held.

"The flower," he said. "She waits for our arrival."

Vura eased off her prey. "What about her?" she asked, and nodded toward Sherri. She was already scurrying backward, hands and feet scrambling frantically. "What if she calls Dane? Warns—"

"Vura!" Quinton Murrell burst into the lobby. His eyes snapped wide when his gaze fell on Sherri, disheveled, sweaty, still bleeding from the neck. "Holy spit! Honey, what did you do?"

She blinked at him, rose to her feet. "We can't let her warn Dane."

"What? Warn—"

"Don't let her make any calls," she said and,

pushing the nail gun into his hand, rushed into the parking lot.

Inside, Sherri ran her experienced gaze up Quinton Murrell's rugged form. Taking in his confident stance, his capable hands, his salt-and-pepper hair, she pushed herself to her feet. "Hi," she said and, taking one lung-expanding breath, blinked hopefully into his eyes.

Chapter 37

It was the longest drive of Vura's life . . . as if Tonk's Jeep stood still and the world lumbered apathetically past. She gripped the dashboard in one hand, the overhead handle in the other.

"How will we know which cabin is his?"

"I do not know." His tone was low. His tendons looked stretched tight and straining through the dark skin of his wrist.

"What if she was lying? They could be any-where by now."

He shook his head, attention riveted on the road that tangled through the pines toward the robin's-egg sky.

"If he sees us coming, he could take her. Could take her and . . ." Her voice broke. "What—"

"Which way?"

It took her a moment to realize they had come to

a halt. The road split, arching off to the right and left.

"You must know this Hotshot guy." Her voice sounded raspy to her own ears.

"I do not."

"You must! You know everyone! Everyone—"

"I don't!" he snapped and closing his eyes, exhaled carefully. "She will be okay, Bravura."

"What if she's not?" The words came out as nothing more than a whimper, a shadow of hopelessness on a ribbon of terror.

"She's smart and strong and . . ." His voice cracked. "We've just got to think."

She nodded, but fear was a blade in her gut, slicing away any hope of coherency.

"About what Lily said." He scanned the hills ahead. "Maybe she gave us a clue. She'd do that. She would—" His words stopped. He frowned, leaning toward the windshield.

"What?" Vura ripped her gaze from his, scraped the tree-dotted skyline with aching eyes. "What is it?"

"I don't . . ." He narrowed his gaze. "Is that . . ." He blinked, shook his head, and stared again. "Is that smoke?"

"What?" Her lungs ached with anticipation. "Where?"

"There." He pointed, and if his hand shook a little, who could blame him? "Above the bluff there. Is it smoke or are they clouds?"

She stared, straining, then blinked when her eyes stung. "I don't know." Hope, she needed hope, but she knew nothing.

"I think . . ." he began and froze as a third wispy cloud bubbled over the treetops.

"What?"

"She speaks," he breathed and pulling off the road, slammed the Jeep into Park.

"She's . . ." Vura shook her head. "You think she's signaling us?"

His jaw bunched with hope too deep to be voiced.

"But what about Dane? He wouldn't . . . How could she get away from him?"

"How could she find Courage in the dark of the night? How could she bring her home when no other could?"

She nodded, hope surging stronger. "We'll follow the smoke."

They were out of the Jeep in a moment, climbing in a matter of seconds.

They scrambled upward. Their breath came hard, frosty in the unruffled air. Grasping a root, Vura hoisted herself up another few inches.

"Can you still see the smoke?" Her throat ached with the effort to speak.

"Not from here." Exhaustion or angst made his voice raspy. "But the red bluff remains to our right."

She nodded and climbed again, mind spinning.

"She must be alone." She kept her voice low though they were still, by her wild calculations, a quarter of a mile from the source of the smoke. "She must have gotten away." She scurried upward on hands and feet, not noticing the blood already oozing from a dozen scrapes. "Must have snuck out while—" she began again, but suddenly her boot slipped, dislodging a chunk of granite. It teetered, then tumbled nosily downward, gathering stones and debris as it went. She caught herself, steadied her balance.

Their gazes met with a clash. "We must be quiet," he said.

She nodded. They climbed again. The first scent of fire found them, just a ghost of woodsy fragrance cranking Vura's muscles tighter with every inch they ascended. And then, off to their right, a faint feather of smoke lifted through the treetops. They scanned the hillside with frantic eyes; there was nothing but trees and boulders, scruffy underbrush, scraggly roots.

But there! A momentary flash of motion.

Tonk raised a finger to his lips, and though every instinct, every aching maternal need in Vura longed to scream Lily's name, she remained silent. Fortifying her strength, she exhaled softly and pointed to the left. He nodded and motioned in the opposite direction. So they parted, creeping through the brush on hands and knees, dropping to their bellies at any hint of movement. It took a lifetime to reach the tiny campsite. The fire was nearly extinguished. Curls of smoke rose lazily from a trio of charred logs. But there was no other sign of life.

"Lily." Vura rose slowly, able to remain silent no longer. "Lily . . ." Her voice teetered in the teeming stillness. "Please be here."

No one answered. But from the far side of the clearing she heard a noise. She hissed a hopeful breath and spun toward it, but all she saw was Tonk stepping out from behind a bull pine.

"Anything?" she begged, but he shook his head.

"Lily!" Panic, loosed from its fragile bondage, consumed her. "Lily!" she yelled and something moved, a quick swath of purple.

"Mama?"

Vura snapped her gaze to the left. And there, not fifty feet away, a tiny figure rose from behind a boulder.

"Lily!"

"Mama!"

Vura scrambled upward, throat aching with unshed tears. "Baby!" she gasped, but suddenly the child was swung into the air.

It took a lifetime to understand what had happened, an eternity to realize that Dane had arrived, had scooped their daughter up against his chest as if she was no more substantial than a dropped sweater.

"Stay back!" he warned and lifted the gun he held in his right hand.

Vura stumbled to a halt. "Dane." His name was no more than a croaked entreaty.

He shook his head and gritted a smile. "Geez, woman, are you some kind of hound?"

"Dane, what are you doing?"

"I didn't want to do this." He squeezed Lily higher, hugging her hard against his ribs. "But you didn't give me any choice."

"What are you talking about?" Terror gripped her lungs, squeezing her dry. "Let her go, Dane. Just . . ." She dropped to her knees. "Please. Just let her go."

"I wish I could, Vey. Really I do, but . . ."

A twig snapped. He jerked the pistol's muzzle to the right. "Who's there?"

The breath had frozen in Vura's throat. She dared not drag her gaze from her husband, dared not give him any clues.

"That your boyfriend?" Dane's voice was cold, bereft of the charisma with which he so easily charmed the world. "Is that who it is, Vey?"

She shook her head, barely able to manage that much, but he placed the muzzle of the pistol against Lily's side and asked again.

"Is the chief here?"

"Yes." The word was no more than a croak.

He shook his head. "You didn't really think you could outsmart me, did you?"

Lily remained frozen, hanging like a broken puppet from her father's thoughtless grip. But her eyes were alive, alive and alert, and sparking with anger.

"Tell him to step into the open," he ordered.

"You're hurting her."

"I don't want to," he said, and tightened his hold. "But you haven't left me much choice."

"Dane . . ."

"All I was asking was what was owed me. But you had to be selfish." He shrugged. "Now look where we are."

"Please—"

He pressed the gun more firmly into Lily's soiled shirt. "Tell him to step into the open before I do something you're going to—" he began, but in that instant, Lily bucked against him.

His grip loosened for a fraction of a second. Her feet hit the ground. She twisted away, and then she was running, skidding over shale, scrambling over roots.

"Run!" Vura screamed, but Dane was already recovering. Stumbling on uncertain footing, he raised the pistol.

"No!" Vura rasped and lunged toward her daughter, but the distance was too great, the climb too steep.

It was Tonk who leapt, who rose out of nowhere and hit his prey from an oblique angle. They rolled, arms flailing before struggling to their feet.

A shot snapped in the air. Tonk jerked, then grabbed his opponent's arm and slammed it against a nearby boulder. The pistol flew through the air like a comet, arcing wildly.

Dane struck with his left fist. Knuckles met flesh in a sickening *thud*. Tonk fell to his knees as his opponent twisted frantically toward his weapon.

It wasn't until then that Vura launched into action.

Lurching uphill, she scrambled over rocks and cactus. Gasping, struggling, searching wildly. There! She dropped to her knees, snatched up the gun.

"Stop it!" It felt solid and ungodly cold in her grip, but she tightened her hold and trained the deadly muzzle on her husband.

He staggered to a halt not thirty feet away.

Their gazes met. The world slowed, stalled, waited.

Dane smiled. That devastating grin that had once seduced her, mind and body. "You're not going to shoot me, Vey."

"Not if you stay where you are."

He chuckled. "No matter what I do. You're not going to shoot me, baby." He took a step toward her. "I'm your husband."

Her arms shook, her heart hitched in her chest. "Don't come any closer."

"The father of your child."

"Father . . ." She rasped a laugh. "You kidnapped her. Threatened—"

"Not kidnapped," he corrected and shook his head, looking confused, misunderstood. "I just wanted some time with her." He took another step toward her. "Just wanted to get us back together."

"You had a gun . . . had a gun to her . . ." The memory made her voice shake, her hands tremble like wind socks.

"To protect her," he said. "I wouldn't hurt her. You know that. You know me, baby. All I ever wanted was to make you happy. Maybe I made a few mistakes." He gestured behind him. Tonk lay on his side, eyes open, palm pressed to his ribs. "Even now, even knowing you've cheated on me, I didn't want to hurt anybody, but it tears me up to think of you with someone else, cuz I love you." He shook his head, brow creasing charmingly. "Come on, sweetheart, you can't blame a guy for protecting what's his. No one could."

"You were holding her for ransom!" Wasn't he? Wasn't that what this was about? Confusion swamped her, washed in on a wave of fatigue, of mind-bending terror. "Your own daughter. Your own—"

"Ransom! You've got it all wrong, baby." He held up an imploring hand, took another step. "I just needed a little cash so I could go back to school. So I could start fresh. *We* could start fresh. I just want to make you proud. Remember how it used to be? Before things went crazy?" His shoes were almost soundless against the rocky soil. "It can be that way again. Only better. Because now we have Lily and I realize"—he shook his head, curled the fingers of his right hand against his chest in earnest agony—"I realize that family is everything." He paused, eyes sad. "Even though you let me down. Didn't believe in me. Just like my old man."

She scowled.

"You're the lucky one, baby. Always had your father to lean on. I suppose I was jealous. Wanted to be your everything. Just wanted to prove myself to you. And I was doing great. On a roll. I was up nearly ten grand when . . ." He shook his head. "I just needed a little stake to get back in the game. But those boys play for keeps. Just needed to pay back the loan, maybe get a little stake to get me back in the game." Disappointment flickered over his boyish features, but he smoothed it away and took another step. Six feet of scruffy foliage separated them. "I forgive you, though, honey," he said, and reached for the gun.

"But I can't forgive you," Vura said and, raising the pistol, pulled the trigger.

He hit the earth with a jolt, shock and fear and confusion bright as cactus blossoms on his handsome features.

"Geez! Vey!" Blood seeped from a hole in his left sleeve. He blinked at it. "You shot me."

Rage, hot and cold and hard as steel, gripped her. "And I'm going to shoot you again."

"No!" he scrambled backward, hands and feet skittering. "No! Vey."

"Because you might be right. Maybe people *wouldn't* blame you." She inhaled carefully, exhaled slowly. Nodded. "You're convincing, and charming and evil and slippery. They might think you deserve another chance. Might think you should spend time with your daughter." She winced, shook her head, raised the pistol. "And I won't take that chance."

"Are you crazy?"

She smiled. "You always made me think so," she admitted, and shrugging, aimed again.

"Bravura." The voice from behind was as steady as the earth. "We heard you had headed this way."

She didn't turn toward him. "Hey, Hunter."

"Vura!"

She smiled a little at the sound of her sister's voice. "Isn't it time for morning chores, Syd?"

"What are you doing?"

"I was just about to shoot my husband"—she squared her stance. Gamps had been a stickler about having a good solid frame—"again."

"Are you sure that's a good idea, honey?"

"She's crazy! She's crazy!" Dane's voice squawked like a banty hen's. Blood dripped from his elbow into the thirsty earth beneath.

"Yeah." Vura tilted her head a little as if considering. "I'm pretty sure."

"Listen . . . Bravura . . ." Sydney's words were quick, her tone soothing. "I don't think it is." Footsteps eased up behind her. "I don't think it's a very good plan at all."

"Well . . ." She shrugged. "You've never been married, have you?"

"Bravura!" Hunter raised his voice. She shifted her gaze to his. He stood ten feet to her right, midnight eyes deep with concern, chiseled face etched in lines of worry. "Little sister . . . I know you hurt."

"He took . . ." Her voice broke. She cleared her throat. "He took Lily, Hunt."

A muscle jumped in his granite jaw, but he kept his gaze on hers. "Perhaps he deserves to die bloody."

She nodded, agreeing.

"But our Lily needs a mother. Needs her here." He stabbed a finger toward Mother Earth. "Not locked away like an animal in a cage."

A needle-sharp shard of reality sliced through her. She blinked.

"They would put you away, little sister."

She shook her head as though waking from a nightmare. "Well, he's not worth that," she said and, handing the weapon to Hunter, stumbled through the brush toward her daughter.

Chapter 38

"And then he swooned." Though Hunter's expression was as solemn as stone, his eyes were bright with mischief, crinkled at the corners like a playful pup's.

Beside him, Quinton Murrell rubbed his hand over his chest as if his heart ached.

Vura shifted her gaze back to Tonkiaishawien. He was well. He was safe, she reminded herself, and fisted her hands to keep from touching him.

"I did not swoon," he objected and slowly settled his hand over her fist. The bruised knuckles looked dark and torn, but she wouldn't cry. She was tough. Always had been. Always would be. But on the monitor above his hospital bed, digital lights blinked and lines wavered, green and red. She blinked, eyes stinging.

"Swooned," Hunter repeated and lifted the back of his hand to the broad width of his brow. "Like an underfed debutant."

"I reclined with manful grace," Tonk corrected and gently squeezed Vura's fist.

Their gazes met in a soft clash of unspoken promises. Bravura exhaled, turned her hand, and let his strong artist's fingers slip like magic between hers.

"Had to haul him down the mountain like a sack of moldy grain."

"Holy . . ." Quinton breathed and clenching his jaw, let his gaze settle on his daughter. Vura shifted her eyes to his, but she still wouldn't cry. Even surrounded by the unyielding strength of the men she loved more than life itself, she would not cry.

"I believe you would have been more gentle with a bag of wheat," Tonk said, and shifted his shoulders carefully. "What were you carrying me with, meat hooks?"

"I don't know when you became such a prima donna," Hunter said, and snorted.

Tonk grinned.

"He's a hero," Lily said and, trotting into the room on her wooden steed, clambered onto his bed, Styx in tow. The hobby horse struck an errant elbow here, a too-close nose there.

Tonk winced.

"No!"

"Baby!"

"Lily!" they all spoke at once, all rushed forward to snatch her up before she tore open any unhealed wounds, but Tonkiaishawien had already curled his free arm around her like a cocoon.

"No." His eyes struck Vura's, and in their river-water depths was a devotion so deep it seemed to flow from his very soul. "Please. Let her stay. She's good medicine."

"And a warrior," Lily said and, twisting, straddled him. Cupping his face in hands already dirty from who knows what, she caught his gaze and grinned, full to the top with brimming joy. "I love you, Tonka."

It took a moment before he could speak. But he nodded finally, found his voice. "And I you, *Chitto Sihu*," he said. A single tear, diamond bright and bulging with emotion, slipped down his handsomely carved cheek.

Silence thrummed in the room like a war drum.

Hunter cleared his throat. Quinton brushed a thumb beneath his eye and turned manfully toward the window.

"Hey!" Sydney rushed into the room, carrying a pot of flowers as big as the moon. "I brought you some . . ." Her footsteps slowed, her brows raised as she glanced from one tearstained face to the next. "Pansies," she said, and grinned. "But it looks like you got that covered."

There was a moment of silence, then Vura chuckled. Hunter snorted and Lily, filled with so much love it all but burst from her pores like lightning, hugged Tonk's neck until he worried that he might, in fact, swoon like that silly debutant.

Discussion Questions

1. Bravura Lambert believes strongly in the importance of family. Did she tolerate too much in an attempt to keep her marriage intact?

2. Tonkiaishawien Redhawk is a wounded soul whose parents failed him on a fundamental level. What are the chances that such an individual can become an exemplary father?

3. Sydney Wellesley and Bravura Lambert are half sisters, but have vastly different personalities. This brings up the age-old debate of nature versus nurture. How would things be different if they had both been raised by Sydney's father? What if they had lived with Bravura's dad?

4. Tonkiaishawien competes in Indian relay races, one of the most dangerous sports in America. Is he punishing himself for perceived shortcomings, or does he simply enjoy the adrenaline rush associated with that kind of performance?

5. Bravura is still dealing with the guilt of disappointing her father by becoming pregnant as a teenager. Does she accept her husband's flaws in an attempt to prove she made the right choice in marrying him?

6. Quinton Murrell has embraced being a grandfather just as surely as he did fatherhood. Did he give up too much on a personal level to raise the girls he adores?

7. Lily is an extremely inquisitive, seemingly accident-prone child. Knowing this, would you, as her parent, ever be comfortable leaving her in the care of someone like Tonkiaishawien?

8. Tonkiaishawien and Hunter think of themselves as brothers even though they do not share biological parents. Do you believe people with difficult upbringings tend to become emotionally closer than biological siblings?

9. Bravura's mother died when Bravura was very young. If she had lived, how would her presence have changed her daughter's disposition?

10. Tonkiaishawien considers himself a recovering alcoholic and a strong proponent of Alcoholics Anonymous. Do you believe that people who have addictions and consequently embrace the twelve-step program tend to be more self-aware?

11. Dane Lambert has a history of making poor decisions. Is he inherently evil or just weak?

Center Point Large Print
600 Brooks Road / PO Box 1
Thorndike, ME 04986-0001 USA

(207) 568-3717

US & Canada:
1 800 929-9108
www.centerpointlargeprint.com